In Another Country

Editors: Lois Tubergen, Irene Evins
Cover design: Terry Roller
Authors photograph: Vivian Page
Cover photo: Peggy Snodgrass

This is a work of fiction. Some situations are loosely based on actual events. Certain locations exist; Edinburg is the county seat of Hidalgo County. The characters, however, are fictional and not intended to represent any actual persons living or dead.

My thanks go out to the many, too many to mention, people who took an interest in seeing this story told and related their experiences to me. I'd like to especially thank my husband, Joe, who believed in me and encouraged me every step of the way. Thanks to Jan Seale who told me I could do it and showed me how, and my editors who sacrificed their time and talents to labor over the manuscript. Many thanks to Tess Mallory and Jimmy Evins for their sage advice, and Marilyn Trent for allowing me to use her beautiful poem.

In Another Country is available for sale online at amazon.com, borders.com, booksurge. com, and through additional wholesale and retail channels worldwide.

LONE MAN Lone Man Publications
P.O. Box 1288
Wimberley, Texas
78676

PEGGY SNODGRASS

IN ANOTHER COUNTRY

Lone Man Publications
2006

In Another Country

Fierce Eden

With bows as tall as themselves,
the nomad Karankawa
roamed the coastal plains and islands
long before Cabeza de Vaca.

They were giants of six to seven feet,
a mysterious, tattooed race,
but they befriended the Spaniard,
the seed of their extinction.

On islands from Galveston
to the mouth of the Rio Grande,
the Karankawa, rulers of a fierce Eden,
live only in the lore of the land.

Along the shores of Texas
their strong spirit haunts the dunes,
and the waves remember.

Marilyn Trent

SUMMER 1992

A *pulsing beat welled up within her. Connie woke to the anxious feeling;
she had lost count. Four, five, or six, no seven, eight, nine, and now her
lips were forming the numbers, ten, eleven, and finally she called out
loud, "TWELVE!"*

*Connie lay very still and listened to the echo of the clock's chimes until only
the ticking of the great clock on the landing traveled up the stairs. Its familiar
measured beat should have had a calming effect, but the feeling of anxiety
persisted.*

*Years ago they installed a security light on a tall pole in the front yard.
It came on at dusk and went off at dawn. Its eerie green light filtered into the
bedroom. She lay in the dimly lit room and listened.*

*She had become so accustomed to the sound of the clock striking the hour in
the night that she usually didn't hear it anymore. Tonight it intruded as in a
dream.*

*She must have been awake when it began to strike. Something other than
the big old clock had broken her sleep. What? Something. Something she couldn't
remember. She held her breath and listened.*

*The dog began barking out at the back, not necessarily anything to worry
about. Its barks became more urgent, and she heard voices, men's voices at the
kitchen door. She heard, there was no mistake, the door being opened roughly,
with force, and men entering the kitchen. They were laughing and talking to each
other in Spanish.*

To Mother,
A Woman Of Grace And Grit

PRELUDE

I t's a treacherous river, the Rio Grande. The Mexicans called it Rio Bravo, rough or angry river. It flooded regularly before it was harnessed with levees and dams. Down where it ran into the Gulf of Mexico, in flood times, its muddy waters spread out shallow and six miles across in some places creating a flat alluvial plain that has been called, incorrectly, the Rio Grande Valley.

When the floodwater receded, the river often changed its course and moved a little, one way or the other, leaving behind *resacas,* horseshoe lakes, old cut off riverbeds where it used to run.

When it switched course, it left a *banco,* the land between where it was now, and where it had been. It was a place where you could cross the river and never know for sure what country you were in.

The culture of the region has ebbed and flowed much like the river. Even now, there are places along this river where you cannot be too sure whether you are in the United States or Mexico.

Things didn't change much for the people living along the river after the Texas Revolution, and later, annexation to the United States. Their status as citizens of a different country hardly affected their lives at all. Ninety-five per cent of the population was Latin, Spanish speaking, and in the borderland, between the Nueces river and the Rio Grande, they continued to practice their customs and language until the coming of the railroad to south Texas in 1904.

The railroad came late to the Rio Grande Valley. A sand barrier of drifting dunes thirty-five to fifty miles across stretched from Corpus Christi to Laredo. When finally, they were able to lay tracks across the dunes, it changed everything. New towns sprang up along its route and carloads of newcomers from the Mid-west came down eager to develop the land that now, due to the rail connections, was accessible to markets where it had not been before. They were businessmen, developers, and individuals who invested their fortunes in the Valley and brought with them a no-nonsense attitude toward law enforcement.

Just five or six years later in 1910, the Mexican revolution sent an army to the border and a rush of refugees out of that country. Lawlessness that was a result of that revolution, and the clash of cultures made the year of 1915 a virtual war zone for all who lived along the banks of the Rio Grande. This era has come to be called the Bandit War and involved famous names such as Pancho Villa and General John Pershing.

Today, changes in the economy in Mexico due to reforms instituted as a result of the revolution has sent a flood of refugees looking for work into the U.S. and the impact of this migration has caused another shift in the culture.

This is a tale about people living through two such cultural changes along the border in one century, and how their lives were affected.

CHAPTER ONE
On Morningside Road
Summer 1991

The teen-aged boy stood at the open garage door and raised a hand to shade his soft brown, almond shaped eyes before he stepped out of the brilliant sunshine and into the darkness of the large room. Out of the doorway, he gave himself a minute to make the adjustment. He looked across a disorganized assortment of equipment and small tools. Heat from the noonday sun radiated down from the building's tin roof and dust motes danced in shafts of light falling through a window at one end of the metal building. Cobwebs clouded the view of leather and metal items on long ignored shelves. Everything in the room had a soft patina of undisturbed dust and rust, except where the woman usually parked her car. That space was empty, and a dinner plate-sized circle of fresh oil marked where the old green Pontiac usually sat.

In the space allotted for a second car there was a John Deere riding lawnmower. Woodworking lathes, table saws, and tool cabinets lined the walls and dust covered coils of rope, welding helmets, and extension cords with wiry caged light bulbs dangled suspended from nails driven into the walls. He saw a set of jumper cables and a shop-vac. He took note. He'd need the car for the vacuum.

There was an oily musty smell, and his feet left prints as he made his way across the room to the red metal tool cabinets standing against the wall under the window.

The old mechanic had been a woodworker, too. The cabinets had shallow metal drawers, each one still filled with the tools of his trade. The top drawer slid out easily, and the boy stood looking down into a drawer that held a jumbled collection of screwdrivers, pliers, rasps, wire cutters, and other small hand tools grimy with oil and dust. He sorted through the jumble and closed the drawer. He was looking for power tools and found several in the deep bottom drawer. He found a hand held grinder and checked the cord. It was still in good shape, and he placed the heavy tool on the floor at his feet.

When he walked out of the garage, he had the grinder in one hand and a jigsaw in the other. His pockets bulged with screwdrivers and other small tools. He draped an extension cord around his neck, and he was wearing a pair of the old mechanic's leather gloves.

A neighbor's house could be seen across a few cultivated rows of neglected farmland. He kept the garage between himself and the view of anyone watching from that house. He walked at a steady pace and didn't run to his old faded green Ford sedan parked in the field road just a short distance away. He threw the tools into the back seat and backed down to the pavement before pulling away to the east.

CHAPTER TWO
Chapin, Texas, spring 1992

The old hotel spread its wings around a brick paved patio where bougainvillea blazed purple in the full sunshine. It owned the space. Its long limber branches covered the paving bricks, crowded out the oleander and hibiscus, and wound its way up the tall fan palm trees.

Its thorny limbs had been hacked away around the edges so the French doors to the lobby and dining room were accessible, but the fountain had been abandoned. Although the French doors stood open, splashing sounds no longer carried into the large high ceilinged rooms of the old mission style hotel.

The guest rooms were fitted out with carpeting and window unit air-conditioners. The lobby and dining room, however, looked much the same as they had in 1929 when the hotel was new. Dark oak furniture with the original black leather upholstery lined the lobby entry and ceiling fans extended down on long rods to cool the large rooms. The floor's Saltillo tiles were polished to a high shine and old photographs, aged to brown, hung mildewing on white plastered walls. A large Texas flag was suspended on the wall opposite the reception desk in the space where in colder climates a fireplace might have been. One of its curled up corners responded to the rhythm of the slowly turning fan blades.

It was a spring afternoon, and warm in the dining room. Connie Rogers was having trouble concentrating on the Tuesday afternoon game of forty-two. The little blue-eyed woman was one of four ladies seated at the table quietly waiting for a new deal.

Connie watched the woman shuffling the dominoes. Her name was Alice and she was in her late sixties. She was the youngest woman at the table, younger than Connie who was seventy-eight. Alice took a long time. Her hands moved over the ivory tiles with deliberation, taking pains to mix them well.

Alice always overdoes it, Connie thought. What difference does it make anyway? Connie was a bridge player at heart. The shuffling ended, and the women began drawing their hands, standing the dominoes on their sides and aligning them so the others wouldn't be able to see what they had drawn.

The old women were taking their time to count the tricks. Connie studied the younger woman's face as she waited for the bidding to begin and thought she looked bored, too.

She comes here and sits in for her mother, and we all pretend Grace will be coming back when she recovers from her stroke. She won't be coming back.

Connie knew the women in the room were a dwindling number, and the game was just an excuse for them to come together. They met once a week to eat a dessert and count heads.

Grace is old now. She's in her mid-nineties, I would imagine. She hasn't been able to follow the game for several years, anyway. We don't care about that, but this time, she won't be coming back. We all know it.

Connie was drinking iced tea in a tall glass. She took a napkin and wiped away the circle of water the glass had left on the wooden tabletop. She looked about the dining room with its four sets of French doors opening out onto the wildly lush patio. Large windows lined up facing the doors on the opposite wall.

A door at the south end of the room led to the bar. The hotel no longer had a liquor license, and the spittoons were gone now, but the atmosphere in the barroom clearly reflected the masculine activities of an earlier era in the border town.

Four tables of dominoes occupied one end of the room. Other tables were set with white tablecloths for the dinner meal. A young Mexican woman was working over them, putting nosegays of pink hibiscus and oleander on each one. Connie supposed she had gathered them from surviving bushes amid the tangle of bougainvillea outside the French doors.

The conversation at Connie's table skimmed along the surface of their thoughts. Tall Lilah, casually self-confidant, had hardly spoken since they sat down. Her hands were large as a man's, and she set the dominoes on edge with precision. Her heavy hair was white, and unlike Connie's fashionable bob, she wore it just as she had as a girl twisted into a bun in the back, with never an escaping wisp.

The fourth woman at the table was Dottie, who in her youth had been a real beauty. She was one of the lucky ones who aged without wrinkles. In her maturity, she was still a beauty only on a much grander scale now, and she always wore brightly colored muumuus. She carefully selected them to compliment the hair she still kept youthfully blonde.

"Perfect," Connie once commented to Lilah. "It wouldn't be Dottie without that wide-eyed innocence and that corn shuck yellow hair."

Dottie kept the thread of casual comments running. You could always count on Dottie, Connie thought; like nature, Dottie can't tolerate a vacuum.

"How's your mother?" she asked Alice.

"Well," Grace's daughter evaded answering the straightforward question. "Mother's taking things a little slower now." Alice smiled and shook her head. "It's hard for us to see her like this. She was always so active. She did civic and charity work, and as you all know, she was interested in politics."

Lilah had an active interest in politics, too, and the comment had been directed at her. "Lilah, did you know Mother was English? I bet none of you knew that she didn't ever get her American citizenship until they elected her president of the Republican Women's club. She was president, and she had never voted in the United States." Lilah had served a term in that office, too, and her face registered surprise.

"Mother quietly applied for citizenship, and I bet none of you even knew." She glanced around at the astonished faces and smiled. She had been right, no one had known.

"She did it very quietly, she was embarrassed. She never told a soul, but now you know!" She continued, "She came here from Canada, but she was English. She was just a kid when they came to the Valley in 1915, fourteen years old. The family brought everything with them they were going to need to farm here all the way from Canada. They farmed with mules then, and they brought three teams with them. They brought farm implements and furniture."

Alice glanced around the table and saw she held the attention of the three other women. These pioneers, like all veterans, listened politely to each other's war stories. "The boys had to ride with the cattle," she continued. "They weren't allowed to ship stock on the train unattended."

"When the train passed through St. Louis," Alice said, "they got off and bought a car, a model-T Ford. Her father and the women made the rest of the trip following the rails as closely as they could in the car. The boys were still on the train. There wasn't a regular road then, and they had to follow the old cotton-road trail through the King Ranch. Turned out, traveling in the car was harder than riding on the train." They all knew about the infamous road that hugged the coastline and was used during the Civil War to bypass the Union blockade.

"Mama said you could still see the cart tracks as deep ruts in places where the sand dunes had shifted, you know, where it was caliche."

The bidding had begun, but Alice spoke over it and continued her story. "Sometimes they couldn't even find the road. Granny learned to drive while Papa scouted out ahead and looked for it."

Alice's story was taking its toll on the game, and they paused play to listen. "The tracks ran through the King Ranch, and they had it fenced. Mama said they had to stop and open fourteen gates to make it across the ranch. When they got to the Valley, the car was so dirty you couldn't even tell what color it was."

It was black, Connie thought impatiently. They were all black.

"They had been advised to bring a shovel along. Good thing, they put it to constant use as the sand offered very little traction. They had so many flats they were afraid the boys would have to wait for them in the end to catch up."

Alice smiled and shook her head, "It was during the heat of the Mexican Revolution, and the boys had problems of their own. The Mexican *banditos* had burned the bridge at Sebastian, and they didn't make it all the way down on the train. They limped in on foot driving the herd ahead of them."

The women laughed politely and resumed play. The other women at the table had made their trip down later on the train.

When Dottie's husband died, she sold the farm and moved into a condominium in town. She wore part of the proceeds they had worked so hard to acquire in the form of a diamond the size of Idaho. Dottie kept the conversation going and gestured constantly with her small hands. The diamond flashed as they moved over the dominoes. Connie was reminded of Lilah's terse comment about her before.

"Dottie is just like a bird," Lilah had once said. "All that fluttering and color and she goes home and snaps that iron gate shut. She's like a pretty little bird in a cage." The comment had been made without any amusement. "That's good enough for her, I guess," Lilah went on, "but it would kill me to live like that."

"Your mother was very young," Dottie twittered. "Why, she was just a girl."

"That's right," the daughter said. "It was an adventure. The Valley was different then. Their property was covered in brush. It was a frontier, rough and wild, and it was dangerous. When they cleared off the brush they uncovered all sorts of bad stuff. Snakes, rattlers, even cougars," Alice leaned forward and whispered, "and there were the bandits."

"It was during the Mexican Revolution," Lilah commented flatly. She didn't expect Dottie to have known it. "Pancho Villa," she added. Maybe Dottie had heard of him.

Lilah said, "Let's cut the talking and play. The other tables will all go home before we finish."

***

The Mexican girl who had placed the bouquets of oleander and bougainvillea on the dining room tables came back and moved between the tables of domino players with slices of chocolate cake on a tray. Coffee was served, and the women ate to the clatter of plates and conversation.

Connie relaxed at the break from the boring game and let her eyes follow a crack in the wall up to the ceiling high above them. A dark circle marked the place where the crack ended.

Water standing on the flat roofed building is to blame, she thought. Besides, plaster walls are unsuitable for the damp and warm climate in the Valley. Those mid-westerners who built this place didn't know that then. They didn't know much about the Valley. They were just developers, promoters. Well, they're gone now. The hotel is all run down and the new owners are so broke they don't even bother to repair the plaster any more. Nobody comes to Chapin. They all go up to McAllen and stay in the Holiday Inn.

This country's going to hell in a hand basket, she thought. Her mood, not the crack, prompted her criticism. Connie loved the old hotel.

It's getting harder and harder to find women who want to join us for dominoes. We can only manage to get four tables now. The replacements are getting younger and younger, Connie thought. One day we'll all be gone, and the fill-ins will be the players. Who will be last? She looked around the room. Maybe me. I may be one of the youngest of our generation, and I may not even count as a pioneer like the rest. She and Hank had come in 1939.

"What have you done with Grace's house?" Connie asked Alice. "You moved her in with you when she had the stroke didn't you?"

"We had to have it torn down," the daughter said.

"Torn down? You tore it down?" Connie was shocked. "How could you do that?" she blurted out unthinking. "She let you do that?"

"She doesn't know. She isn't well. She doesn't drive any more and we just don't take her out there, and, "her eyes slid across the faces which were all turned to her, "we're running out of excuses. I hope she never has to know. Please don't tell her."

Connie was consumed with anger, and she didn't bother to conceal it in her voice. "The very idea! Couldn't you wait for her to die before you tore her house down!"

"We never would have done it. Never! My father built that house. I grew up in it. After her stroke, mother couldn't stay out there alone and with the property vacant, the vandals moved in on it. It got so bad finally that the sheriff said it was a hazard and suggested we tear it down to solve the problem."

No one said anything. She added lamely, "We had to do it. It was a liability."

All hands suspended above the dominoes. The silence around the table was sharp, and the laser eyes were on her.

"There wasn't much left of it anyway," she managed, her voice trailing away.

The whooshing and clicking of the ceiling fans high above was lost in the hum of voices rising from the other tables. Talk had ended at their table. The women laid the ivory tiles down with snapping noises. Conversations from the other tables rose in pitch at the end of each game when they shuffled, but the women at Connie's table had fallen dumb.

***

They chose the old hotel for their afternoon dominoes out of convenience. They moved from the air conditioned Presbyterian Church temporarily when it was being painted and then never moved back.

They quietly accepted the move as proper. The hotel was old, historic really. And it was familiar. Several of the women had even been guests in the hotel years ago when it was new.

Developers had built it originally as a lodge to house prospective buyers. They had bought large Spanish grants of unimproved ranchlands and divided them up into farms. They built roads and lined them with palm trees, oleander, and bougainvillea. The prospects were brought in by the trainload from the mid-west and dazzled with daily excursions to newly planted groves of citrus trees. They were promised fertile delta land and an abundance of water. Cheap labor abounded south of the border, they were told, eager for work.

In the dining room where today the women were playing dominoes, the prospects had eaten meals featuring exotic Mexican dishes. Afterward they strolled under the stars on the patio to the tune of strumming guitars and tinkling waters from the fountain.

They were photographed as they posed with wagons of grapefruit and oranges. Smiling and optimistic, their young faces still smiled down from black frames on the lobby walls where Connie and Lilah were passing on their way to their cars. Connie supposed Lilah was there with her husband in one of the group pictures. Perhaps one of the men in the photograph of two grinning men leaning against a trailer tailgate with a full load of grapefruit was Lilah's husband, Dick.

Lilah caught Connie's sleeve as they moved out, "Connie, we're missing you at bridge. Why don't you play with us any more?"

"Oh, well, Lilah, I'll be back. I've only missed a couple of times, that's all."

"I haven't seen you there in months. I know how you love to play bridge."

"Well, it would be easier for me if we played in the daytime," she said, turning to go. Others were passing around them on their way out, and Lilah drew Connie to the side.

"We have to play at night or we'd lose the golfers. The men won't play in the afternoon. Is it coming home alone at night you're afraid of?" Lilah asked.

Lilah's tall frame was imposing as she looked down at the smaller woman, and Connie answered with a wave and a nervous laugh, "Of course not!" Somehow she didn't want to seem diminished in those sharp blue eyes. "There's a head light out on my car, and I just haven't gotten it replaced."

Lilah tilted her head and gave Connie that look that says, "Well, if that's what you say, but we know the truth, don't we?"

"I'll pick you up. Would you like that? We don't live too far apart and we could come together. We miss you Connie. You love to play bridge, and we need you."

"I'll have it fixed. Really, I've been meaning to." Connie was reluctant to accept the offer. The two had known each other for years and had little in common. It was different now. As their circle grew smaller they were becoming an unlikely twosome.

"I'll pick you up!" Lilah said as they moved out of the musty darkness of the lobby into the brilliance of the spring afternoon.

Connie watched her friend slide into the seat of her sleek black Cadillac, and before she could drive away, Connie reached out and tapped on the window. "Lilah," she said, "why do you think they let the vandals destroy Grace's house?"

"What do you think they could have done about it?"

"I mean the sheriff. Why did he let them get away with it? Destroying property is breaking the law."

"And what do you think he could have done?"

"Well, what has he done in the past? We never had to worry about that before. What did he do before that he couldn't do now?" Connie asked.

"Connie, come on, you know what they used to do. They can't do it any more."

"But Lilah, do you mean to tell me the sheriff can just stand back and do nothing? Does he have that option?"

"Yes, Connie. He does."

"But, Lilah, it's his job! It's the sheriff's job to protect our property isn't it? If we can't expect the sheriff to do it, then who?"

"Well, Connie, I guess we'll just have to do it ourselves," she said, and the window slid up without a sound. Connie watched the black car pull away before she found her Pontiac, old and green, and opened the door.

***

Connie stiffened with impatience at her short wait to turn off the main highway onto Morningside road. She always had to wait at this intersection, but today it was different. There was a new note in her life now; high pitched and discordant, like a whistle in the background and ever present.

I'm seventy-eight years old. I'm not getting any younger.

She watched the cars rushing to slide through on yellow.

Where are all these people going? And where did they all come from anyway?

She turned and began the short three mile drive north to her house.

What's bothering me? Is it Grace? She was old.

Connie's mind was busy. She drove unconsciously up the familiar narrow two-lane road. She passed without seeing the poor little houses that had slowly moved out onto the acreage that had at one time been citrus groves and vegetable fields. She didn't notice the now too familiar graffiti that covered the walls of the business on the corner of the paved farm road she crossed every time she went to town.

Connie's mind ran over the afternoon's events. Grace just got old, she thought. We all do.

She just got old, and now she's lost everything, her health and her independence; they don't let her drive any more. Now she's lost her home.

Connie's hands gripped the steering wheel tightly. Grace was old, she repeated.

I've known Grace a long time. As long as I can remember she's been a respected community leader and now she's dependent on her family.

Connie felt the whistle rise in pitch.

Grace depended on her family, and they allowed the vandals to tear her house down. It just goes to show you, you can't depend on someone else to take care of the things that are important to you. Maybe Lilah's right. I guess we'll just have to do it ourselves. Maybe we should.

But Grace had a stroke, what could she do? What could anyone do if they had to go to the hospital and leave their place vulnerable for months, or even a few days?

What could I do?

It's a shame though. It doesn't seem fair. Grace was always strong and self-reliant. She raised a family and managed to do it without electricity or refrigeration. She raised chickens and killed them herself.

Connie remembered that. She could see in her mind's eye, clear as yesterday, the chickens flopping around in her own yard with their necks wrung in the morning so the family could have the fried chicken of a traditional Sunday dinner.

We're modern now. I buy my chickens at the super market.

Connie laughed out loud and continued on home with her spirits temporarily lifted. When she turned the old green Pontiac into the drive, Puppy was there as always to greet her. Long legged and skinny, the black dog had a narrow muzzle and big sail-like ears that stood straight up and were each one nearly as large as her head. Brown markings told of some long ago relative that must have been a Doberman, but somewhere the meanness had been bred out. The brown around Puppy's mouth made her seem to be forever smiling. Puppy's tail, unlike the stub of a Doberman's, was black and long as a whip, and she used it with enthusiasm to express her joy at the sight of Connie. My guard dog, Connie thought, and smiled affectionately.

To Puppy's consternation, Connie let the car idle in the drive while she sat a few minutes looking up at her white two-story house. Two large Rio Grande ash trees shaded the driveway. The Saint Augustine grass of the lawn was coarse and green and swept up to the house without the compliment of sidewalks. It was a farmhouse. Connie's thirty acres had at one time been part of a much larger farm.

Well, Hank! We killed ourselves paying for this place. Remember how we celebrated when we retired the mortgage!

The whistle was doing its work, and Connie couldn't quite recapture the feeling of their joy.

Things are different now Hank.

The sense of alarm she had been feeling persisted, and she complained aloud, "This country's going to hell in a hand basket!"

Connie pulled the car slowly to the back and into the garage. When the place was a farm, there was a barn in the space where the garage was now. Connie's husband had it torn down and replaced with a large metal building that served as a garage and had spaces for two cars and a woodworking shop at one end. Connie sold her husband's car when he died, and that left an open space; now, she parked her lawnmower there. The tools, however, were still gathering dust and rusting in the workspace at their end of the building.

Connie walked to the house with Puppy leaping and barking her welcome home. She stooped and cupped her hand around the dog's muzzle and looked into her soft brown eyes, eyes that were showing white at the rim from anxiety to be off and running again and not quite sure what the examination was all about.

"Puppy, can I count on you to guard my house if I ever have to go to the hospital for a few days, maybe longer?" The dog listened innocently, her ears folded back and her tail quiet at last.

"Well," Connie said without much confidence, "I know you'll do the best you can."

CHAPTER THREE

L ilah turned off Morningside onto the side road that led to her house. The sun was low, and the black Cadillac moved through shafts of alternating brilliant light and stripes of shadow cast by the tall palm trees that lined the road.

As their farm prospered they had made improvements to the house, and now, it was known as an area landmark. Long and low, its tile roof concealed the many renovations it had undergone in the years Lilah and her husband had lived and raised their family in it.

She pulled the Cadillac into the garage, pushed the button, and watched the door slide down. Allen is back, she reminded herself. She had been alone so long sometimes she forgot.

"Hello! I'm home," she called out as she softly closed the door behind her and made her way into the bedroom.

She sat on the bed to take off her shoes, and she could hear Allen doing something in his old room. It was good to have someone else in the house. She had thought he had come home on a visit, but it was drawing out and now she thought perhaps he had come back to stay. Allen had not returned home after college. He had found a job in banking and then marriage.

Lilah supposed he had done well. He had done well enough to be put in charge of the bank's dealings with the Federal Resolution Trust Corp. A responsible position and a job that kept him so busy that she guessed it was the cause of his marriage failing. Then it all seemed to come apart for him. The bank sold out to a large northeastern bank, and Allen was retired. Retired! He was only forty-seven years old!

The marriage was over and so was his job at the bank. Now he was home and she was hoping it was for good. She was concerned about him, though. He seemed to be lacking in something that Lilah called enthusiasm for life.

The evening was coming on, and the room was growing dark. She turned on a light in the closet, placed her shoes neatly in paper in the cardboard box they had come in, and slipped on her house shoes.

Lilah went down the hall to Allen's bedroom. He was sitting in the growing darkness before the glow of a television screen.

A man shouldn't be watching television in the daytime. There are so many things that need to be done around here, and he lounges in front of the TV like a little boy.

"Allen, did you have a good day?" she asked.

"Yeah," he answered, without looking back at her. "Hi, Mom."

Lilah stood leaning against the doorframe for a few minutes. She could see black numbers moving across the bottom of the screen in a band.

"I have fresh asparagus. Would you like it in a salad or in vinaigrette sauce?"

His full attention was on the screen, and he was slow to answer. She left him to his work and went to the refrigerator, took out a head of lettuce, and got out the cutting board.

He appeared at the kitchen door, "Mom, don't fix me anything. I ran into an old friend today. Do you remember Frank Palma? He's picking me up tonight so I won't be here for supper."

"He's picking you up?" She turned and gave him her full attention. "If you're going to stay awhile, Allen, you need to think about buying a car."

"Mom, I haven't decided what I want to do yet. I don't mind driving the pickup." He cocked his head and smiled, "It's a prestige car around here, anyway." When she didn't seem to get the joke, he added, "I may decide to fly back to Dallas."

"Allen, I could sure use some help. You ought to give some thought to sticking around and giving me a hand here on the farm."

"Mom, we've been through this a million times. I'm not cut out to be a farmer. It's not my style. I'm a banker."

He walked over to the refrigerator and took out a beer. She winced when she heard the snap and the fizz when he opened it.

She couldn't resist a, "You'll ruin your supper!"

Although her back was turned, she could tell by the crisp scrape of the chair as he pulled it out to sit that the comment hadn't gone down well.

"Allen, you're a young man." She put down her knife and turned toward him again. "You aren't even fifty years old. You have the best part of your life ahead of you. You can't just sit around drinking beer and watching television all day!"

"Mom, really! I haven't been watching television. It's a computer. I'm working on the computer, not watching television, and you know it!"

"Well, yes I know." She started to turn away and then, "Your life has been interrupted. It's been interrupted in the same way that World War II did ours. The war changed things for us, but we kept on going. You have to do that too."

"What does that mean!" The young man's face reddened, and his voice betrayed his exasperation with her. "Just because I don't want to be a farmer doesn't mean my life is over."

She pressed on, "I just thought it might be a business opportunity for you. Your father and I started with not very much and built a business here. With your education and business experience, there's no telling what you could do with it."

"Mom! I don't know anything about this business."

"What are you talking about? You were raised on this farm. And anyway, you're not too old to learn."

I learned to run this farm all by myself, she thought. And her mind slipped over the hardships of the war when his father had been fighting in Italy. We were so young then. I was only thirty years old and had two little girls.

"When I learned to run this farm I was too young to have that much responsibility," she said, "and now I'm too old. But you're not."

"You were not too young, and I'm not too old. You wanted to do it, and I don't."

"You'll inherit this farm one day. What will you do with it then?"

A long awkward pause followed, finally he said, "Mother, you just don't get the picture. I'm retired. Period. Don't you think it's time you did too?"

"Allen, you don't get the picture. I'm never going to retire. Period!"

He gave her a big smile, crossed the room, and put his arm around her waist, "Same old Mom!" he said. "Hey, I have some irons in the fire!"

She turned her back and picked up her knife.

"Mom, look," he said defensively, "I don't want to be tied down to this farm right now."

"Tied down? Who wants to tie you down? This is a business, like any other."

"This is not a business like any other. Running a three thousand acre farm is big business. It's a life consuming, full time pain in the ass."

"Watch your mouth!" she snapped. "We had a wonderful life here, and so did you!"

He didn't answer and the sentence hung between them like an indictment.

"Oh, what's the use?" he said it under his breath and left the room, but she heard it and her back stiffened.

She turned the water on and went back to work with the knife. Her hands moved quickly over the asparagus, stripping away the scales. She laid the spears out on the board and began trimming the stalks. The knife chopped down and up and down, whack, whack!

I don't want to be tied down?

Whack!

What's the matter with young people today? Can't they understand that running your own business has responsibilities, but the pay off is independence? The bank sold him out. Here he'd be boss. Can't he see that?

Whack!

I guess we're to blame.

Lilah held the green shoots in the running tap water giving careful attention to the complex layered heads.

We endured hardships he can't even imagine. After the war we wanted things to be different, better. When Allen came along I guess we spoiled him.

She smiled, remembering. *The girls called him our little pet, and I guess they had it right.*

Dick built up this business and intended to leave it to his only son. He wanted him to go to Texas A&M, and I guess he pushed it too hard.

She remembered the confrontation between her well-meaning husband and his rebelling son. She especially remembered the insulting remark Allen had finally made to end the spat, "I'm not going away to college to learn how to shovel cow shit!"

He went off to Southern Methodist and learned how to wear a suit. She smiled. *He was the first. No one in our family ever went to SMU.*

A car honked in the drive, and Allen came back into the room. "Bye, Mom," he said and quickly left through the kitchen door. She heard the slam of the car door and the crunch of gravel as a car began backing down the drive.

Lilah put down her knife and made her way through the dark rooms to the living room windows that looked out across the lawn.

A coach lamp on a pole lit the driveway, and she watched a tan Mercedes with gold trim make the road and slowly move out of sight.

That Frank somebody must have done well for himself, she thought. He must be a banker, too.

Allen never cooled his heels getting out of here.

The light glistened off the dark green leaves of the mesquite trees that studded the lawn.

He only came back here for Christmas.

The cars passing had stilled the cicadas, and the brown insects clung to the gnarled bark of the mesquite trees and piped up again.

He never kept up with any of his old high school friends. Now he says he doesn't want to be tied down to this farm. Well, I do. I'll run it just as I always have.

The cicadas droned on, and she could hear them clearly in the silence of the house now that Allen was gone. It was a familiar hum, but for the first time hearing it defined how alone she was in the big house.

She turned her back to the window and looked into the gloom of the darkened rooms, across the living and dining rooms, to the patch of light that was the kitchen. It seemed far away.

I have lived in this house almost all my life. I've been here alone since Dick died, for ten years, she thought.

It's my home. It doesn't frighten me to be here alone.

She walked back to the kitchen, put on a pan of water, and waited for it to boil.

The blue eyes scanned her kitchen. Lilah squared her shoulders.

If Allen goes back to Dallas, my life will go on just as always. I know when I die he doesn't intend to keep this farm. And the girls? He and his sisters will sell it, and I guess the girls will buy diamonds the size of Dottie's. If he knew it, it would just break Dick's heart!

Lilah glanced skyward and made Dick a promise.

I'll never sell! I'll run this farm as long as I can. I'll live in this house, and I'll never move to the fort like Dottie.

She carried her plate to the table and sat alone to eat.

This is a business; there are other people besides me who depend on this operation for their livelihood.

Rolando helped me through Dick's illness, and he's been here for me ever since. Even if Allen stays, Rolando will still manage the farm.

The kitchen window opened toward the back, and Lilah could see the patch of light cast from the maid's quarter's window.

And Ramona, what would happen to her?

I'm still healthy. I'll come and go as I always have, and if I want to play bridge in the evenings, that's what I'll do.

And no bars, I will not be a prisoner in my own home. I will live as fully and freely as I wish. I will live until I die! And when I do, it'll be in this house while I'm doing whatever it is I want to do.

CHAPTER FOUR
December 1992

They'd been sitting in the dark a long time now and it was quiet in the car. They sat in the front seat, the two of them, and nobody was talking.

The stub they'd been passing back and forth briefly cast a red glow upon very different faces. They were both still boys in their teens, but while one's face was dark and square, with an Indian's nose and high cheekbones, the other boy had a sallow, light complexion. His face was a perfect oval. His nose was narrow, and his eyes were almond shaped and light brown. His hair was brown, not black like his companion, hence his nickname, *el Güero*, which means the blond, or Whitey.

The day had been hot and muggy. The land where the Rio Grande River meets the Gulf of Mexico also borders the Mexican desert to the south. Although it was mid-December, the temperature had risen into the low nineties. Now, the blue norther that had been predicted loomed across the horizon as a bank of thunderheads and was only visible in the night sky when sharp flashes of lightning exposed it, marking its advance toward them.

The low rumbling of thunder had progressed ominously to booming reports, and the boy sitting behind the wheel kept his almond eyes fixed on the storm as it pressed in upon them. The familiar rows of tall fan palm trees that lined the road on both sides were lit by flashes of lightning and appeared strangely white and still in silhouette against what was sure to be a violent storm.

They had arrived early, too early. The long tense wait was aggravated by the sharp smell of ozone. The almond-eyed one waited quietly, and rarely looked at his companion, even when he passed the roach to him in the darkness.

It was not until the first gust of wind hit the car that he spoke.

"Get out."

"It's too early!" The dark boy was taken off guard.

"Get out."

"No Man! Hey, look at the lights! They're still on. They're not even gonna' turn 'em off. Not 'til eleven."

"Get out." The voice was low and steady, but this time the head turned, and the almond eyes were narrowed, and the short dark boy found the door handle.

He stepped out into the ditch and watched the car disappear into the darkness, leaving him alone in the storm. The paved road before him was a narrow two-lane stretch of poured concrete. Even in the darkness between flashes it glistened white, and it would be easy for him to find his way along it.

The gusting wind was kicking up dust, and he raised his arm to protect his eyes and began to move up the road. A few hundred yards ahead he could see the lights of a filling station on the corner. He walked toward it following a path that ran along side the pavement.

The storm had driven everyone inside, and the fuel pumps stood isolated on their island in the dust-dimmed light. He moved into the light, but stayed close to the building and peered into the window.

It was a mom and pop operation. It had begun as a little convenience store with gas pumps out front, and as the town grew north along the paved country road, it had expanded. With the addition of a bar-b-que barrel out behind, it had became a take-out restaurant, and finally with the purchase of a license to sell beer, and a collection of chairs out back, it had become a sort of men's club of the neighborhood.

On a Saturday night there would usually have been men sitting under lights strung along between the trees in the patio out back of the store. They were attracted to the place by the smell of cabrito slowly cooking over a mesquite wood fire, and the powerful allure of music coming from the radio the owner had strategically placed in the window.

Dusty garlands of plastic poinsettias were draped across the plate glass window at the front of the store in celebration of the season. The impending storm had cleared the store, and he saw only the owner, Garcia, standing behind the cash register.

Garcia stood with his back to the window watching a small television set that had been hoisted above the shelves behind the counter.

The boy outside checked what he could see of the room, but Garcia was alone, so he moved to the side of the building and leaned up against it for protection from the wind. He looked out across the deserted patio and wondered why Garcia didn't turn the lights off. They were attached to the bare wires between limbs of the big mesquite tree and were sent thrashing about dangerously, casting sinister shadows across the adobe brick pavers of the patio floor.

He pulled his collar up and hugged himself in the rapidly dropping temperature as the first spatter of raindrops fell. They had come too early, he knew it all along but he was no fool. When Carlos, *el jefe*, sent them out, he had kept his mouth shut, and now he waited. He waited for what seemed to him to be a long, long time before the lights finally went out at eleven. But he was alert when he heard the car slow to make the turn. And he was sure the fair one, 'El Güero', would be there waiting in the shadows of the house on the corner across the street.

The headlight beams swept across the house as the car turned and Güero was there. He was walking toward the slowly moving vehicle. His hands were extended before him gripping a pistol, and he had already begun to fire when the driver, trapped, saw Güero's car astraddle the road blocking the way.

From the shadows of the store the dark boy heard the shattering of glass and the dull thunk of lead on metal, and he heard the startled cries of the passengers they had ambushed in the car. He moved forward out of the safety of the building as the door on the passenger side swung open. He raised his gun, but Güero had already made his way to the car and was spraying the inside of it with bullets. The passenger on his side crouched and tried to slide his way out onto the road, keeping close to the floorboards for protection, but a bullet had found its mark and his body lay partially in the road. He looked up at the dark boy and raised his hand in an appeal for mercy.

The pale one was already coming around to finish him off. But he stopped, stepped back and turned the cold narrow eyes on his frozen companion, motioning with his gun. Seconds passed, Güero motioned again, and this time the dark boy held his breath and fired a bullet into the helpless young man in the road.

CHAPTER FIVE

The room was clearing too slowly for Ignacio, *quítate,* he grumbled under his breath. Get out of here. One of his classmates, much to his irritation, lingered to question the instructor. They stood near the door before the large plate glass windows. The windows had been painted black, but time was doing its work on them and light peeked in through pinhole scratches.

The gym's oak flooring and full-length mirrors hid any hint of the business that had been here before, but Ignacio knew it well. He had come here often when it was a drug store. He grew up in this town when all the stores on the south side of the highway were Anglo, but Ignacio had come with his mother to have prescriptions filled, and once she had bought him a milkshake at the fountain.

Ignacio remembered the pharmacist. He had given him a piece of hard candy when they paid. He knew the spot where the now absent row of shinny chrome stools with red fake leather cushions had been. He had spun himself around on one of them at the fountain and watched it all in the long ago mirror, the other one, the one that was framed with short order menus and coke ads with pretty blond pin-up girls. He had examined his young face in the mirror as he slowly sipped his milk shake.

The pin-up girls were gone now, and he was no longer a boy. Partitions had been installed to separate out an office and a small dressing room with lockers. Ignacio never used a locker overnight. He always rolled his *gi,* the white cotton pajamas, neatly into a tight bundle, navy style, and carried them away with him when he left.

Ignacio sat on a bench and waited for the men to finish their conversation and leave. Finally in exasperation he stood, and barefooted, but in his street clothes, he went through the pattern of kicks he had been working to perfect.

He was an eager student. At fifty-seven, he was the oldest man in the class. Ignacio was short, five foot nine, and weighed only a hundred and sixty pounds. He moved through the kicks and punches with a cat-like precision and power that brought a smile to the instructor's lips.

"Such a tiger!" he often said, and mentioned him to prospective students. "You're not too old to take up Karate," or, "you're not too small," he would say. "You should see Ignacio Salinas. He's a lesson. All you need is to be motivated. Motivation and some hard work are all you need."

The thing that motivated Ignacio was fear. He'd gone to the police for help in evicting renters from one of his section eight rent houses.

The renters vacated and burned the house to the ground as they left. Ignacio reported it to the police. They questioned them and then dropped the case. The ex-renters were not happy to have been reported to the police and they evened the score one night. They beat Ignacio up. This time he didn't go to the police.

"Those police, they don't help," he'd say. "They can't do nothing. They just make it worse." He bought a pistol. He was motivated. He took up karate.

He sat on the bench, put on his shoes, and waited. Finally the men finished their conversation and the student left. The instructor went into the office and at last Ignacio was alone.

Karate, open hand, *mano abierto,* he said to himself as he slid a revolver out of his roll and into the beltline of his pants. My hand is open, he postured to the mirror, see, and he assumed a pose thrusting his open hand forward, palm up.

Ignacio stepped out of the gym onto Chapin's main street. The sun had moved lower in the late afternoon sky and his bicycle now lay in the full sunshine. He stooped to place his tightly rolled bundle into the basket before unlocking the chain that held it firmly to the post. He walked the bicycle out into the street and pedaled slowly away down a street that still had some traffic, but the parking slots were mostly empty just as the stores they had at one time serviced.

Many of the stores were abandoned, but not all. Wade's Hardware was hanging on several years past profit. Glen Wade kept it going by hiring a man to do small engine repairs in the rear, and he added to his inventory a sizeable stock of belts and small engine parts.

His clientele mostly went down to McAllen to the big Ace Hardware store, but they brought their generators and lawnmowers here to be repaired.

He had a table over by his office where he kept a coffee pot. Originally it had been for himself and his employees. The place had become popular as it evolved into a sort of honor coffee bar and gentlemen's club for the farmers and other old-timers. They had gathered an interesting collection of chairs and placed them in a circle. Glen didn't buy them; they just sort of started showing up.

It all began when the barbershop closed. Glen bought the old barber's chair and placed it in the back by the coffee pot. That's when the chairs started appearing.

It was just an assortment of rocking chairs and a wicker peacock chair at first. The *piece de résistance* though, was the barber's chair. It was throne-like in its size and decoration. The big chair had its original red leather upholstery and its ornate chrome fittings suggested some royal ancestry.

Several men came so regularly you could almost always find them there around ten o'clock of a weekday morning. If anything was happening in town, and you wanted to know it, this was the place to come. It outranked the defunct weekly newspaper for speed and accuracy.

The filling station that had also served as the bus station was still in business; only the gas pumps had been removed. Where you could have bought a bus ticket, you now could buy a hand crafted, tin suit of armor or a brightly colored flowerpot. They also displayed wiry welded lawn furniture. It was slow to move and had mostly turned a rusty red color that would have left its mark on your backside if you tried it out.

Highway 83 followed the river south to Brownsville, and the Valley towns strung out along its route like pearls. Main Street crossed 83 and so did Ignacio. He pedaled past the largest building on this street. It had at one time been a grocery store. Alejandro Hinojosa and Bro in large black letters had been emblazoned on its brightly painted blue front. Ignacio had never seen *señor* Alejandro in the store, but Bro had been there every day.

They were both gone now, but the store, still painted a brilliant blue, was as busy as ever. It was the entertainment center for the town. Brightly colored posters advertising the latest releases on video kept the parking slots in the street in front of this store filled. Right next door an enterprising fellow had opened a TV and VCR repair shop where you could have your equipment repaired, or you could buy a new or used video recorder.

Ignacio stood and expertly pedaled on past the *Salon de Bellaza,* but coasted past the tortilla factory and Mexican food restaurant. He allowed himself the indulgence of the powerful smell of the tortillas being pressed out on the complex machinery inside. His Claudia patted them out by hand. He would receive his reward when he reached his own kitchen.

Sam Houston Elementary School had become a book depository. It looked abandoned. Its windows had been covered with plywood and the yard behind the chain link fence had grown up in careless weeds and sprouts from the mesquite beans which had been carried in by birds. The district had built new elementary schools, but not here on Main Street. Its forlorn look reminded passersby of the changing times.

The Catholic Church had become a cathedral in size and membership. Ignacio pedaled past it without even gazing up at its mosaic the size of an outdoor theatre screen featuring Jesus with a thorny crown and his scarlet heart ablaze.

A casual observer may have thought Ignacio was riding a woman's bicycle. He had salvaged the daisy festooned basket attached to the handlebars from his daughter's old bicycle. It was a perfect fit for his *gi* roll and Ignacio hadn't noticed that it looked strange at all. He knew it was a man's bicycle. He had bought it new for his son's tenth birthday; the boy was now thirty-eight years old. Ignacio had refurbished it for himself with a hand brushed coat of Rustoleum green paint.

As he pedaled on out of town the black asphalt of the street narrowed to a poured concrete surface. It took more concentration to navigate here where there was no shoulder. The traffic was becoming a problem on the narrow roadway since the new high school had been built on out north, past the turn off to his house.

Ignacio rode expertly around road signs and other obstacles without much difficulty on a beaten path he took daily. He waved at familiar faces along the way and generally enjoyed himself as he pedaled home. Some days he had time to pause and talk to neighbors and usually stopped to buy a Coke at Garcia's, the store on the corner where he turned off onto his street.

Garcia's had a small inventory of canned goods, bread and milk, candy, and it had gas pumps. The owner's wife sold breakfast tacos there in the mornings, and on the weekends they had barbeque you could take away.

Behind the store, a mesquite tree had flourished to a grand size and its canopy shaded a patio. The owner placed chairs on the adobe bricks beneath it. It became a gathering place for men in the evenings, and Ignacio checked to see if there was anyone there he knew.

No one was sitting under the tree, but he stopped and bought a Coke and stood leaning against the frame of the back door. The owner lived in a house behind the store and across the little patio space with the mesquite tree. The odd conglomeration of chairs under the tree were not so ambitious as those in the hardware store. They consisted of a webbed aluminum chair, two old kitchen chairs that had been long ago painted white but now showed scabby scars where the paint had been knocked away through years of abuse and weather, and four new glossy white plastic chairs.

Ignacio took the Coke and cut away to the cross road that led to his house, riding expertly with one hand. The men had shown Ignacio the spot where two boys had been murdered, and he guided his bike around it in respect.

The neighborhood knew, everyone did, a rival gang had shot the boys, but the sheriff didn't seem to be able to discover exactly which one of the gang members had been the shooter. A couple of the gang members were sent to juvenile boot camp. Other than that, the crime went unpunished, and the problem persisted.

A colonia was growing just past the store and spawning a new gang. The resulting turf war caused the ambush on the corner. The development had been named Loma Linda, pretty hill, although there was no hill and it wasn't pretty either.

Ignacio slowed to check its progress. The slum was outside the city boundaries, thus free of city regulations. The Anglo population in the neighborhood were concerned that the transient, and mostly illegal people who populated the ramshackle buildings didn't seem to be regulated at all.

Their legal status wasn't the complaint from the Hispanic neighbors. The squalid conditions that bred the gangs, and the crime they generated went unreported for fear of retribution. Garcia understood, though, why his business flourished. The men were paid in cash money, his drawer bulged with small bills that were crumpled and smelled of sweat. He kept his mouth shut when the neighbors complained.

29

Ignacio looked across rows of houses in all stages of completion. They were 'hand-made' houses, small and built by the homeowner's themselves. Cars lined the narrow streets, and brightly colored children's plastic play gyms littered the tiny yards along with discarded appliances, white plastic lawn chairs, and piles of trash. There was no garbage collection on this county road other than a private company that would collect it for a monthly charge. It was beyond the means of the residents of Loma Linda; none of the residents subscribed.

Many vacant houses had plywood covering the windows, a sure sign that the owners had moved on. Others were skeleton shapes of walls, unfinished and never to be finished. Weeds grew up and there was no one to cut them down. Chain link fences marked the houses that were occupied.

Ignacio could see all this. He could see the outhouses. He knew they were strictly against the county sanitary regulations. No water without a connection to the sewer line, they were told. But they got around it, and Ignacio knew where to look to see the garden hose that passed from a house to the kitchen window of another. It was obvious to him.

They can't see it for nothing, he said to himself. Maybe they're blind! But he knew it was more likely to be the *mordida,* the payoff. The developers, he knew them so well, had the county judge in their hip pocket. It was no secret.

But for him, Ignacio knew they could see 20-20. They held him to a high standard when qualifying his little rentals, in a poor neighborhood of Alamo, for section eight housing.

He pedaled on the last quarter mile, until, with his house in sight, Ignacio saw the black shape in the road that he knew was Puppy. The dog had seen him early, and as always was waiting in the street for him. Puppy was alert, her flag-ears standing straight up and the long tail slowly moving from left to right. As he drew nearer the black dog sprang into action. She circled the bicycle and raced him up the drive all the way to the house, barking and running out ahead to announce their arrival, before cutting back around to the house across the street where she lived.

CHAPTER SIX

At fifty-four, no one would have called Carl young anymore, but the man he was watching could have spotted him fifteen years, at least. Carl hung back as the old Mexican man, Tony, stood at the kitchen door and surveyed the small room. He was totally absorbed and ignored Carl, who like a shadow, followed him about silently.

Tony examined the twin cabinets that flanked the window with the shirred calico curtain. Once painted white, they were yellowed now from years of cooking with butane. The knobs on the cabinets were cheap glass, dingy with age. Someone had painted the cabinets without removing the pulls and each one had a ragged ring of paint at its base.

He walked over to the sink and although the old man was slightly built, the floor creaked under his weight. He looked down at the worn linoleum and shook his head. A dramatic motion meant to communicate to Carl that he had noted its age and poor condition.

A clean braided rag rug lay on the floor in front of the sink. He stepped over on it, placed his hand on the taps, and shook his head again. They were old and corroded.

"Lead pipes," he said under his breath, but loud enough that Carl could hear. He stepped back away from the sink and took a look at the window frame. The caulking around the glass was dry and flaking away. He put a gnarled old finger up to it, popped a large piece into the sink, and then picked it up and placed it in his pants pocket. He brushed the tips of his fingers over the paint pointing out that it was checked and dry. He shook his head again.

A door across the room led out to a little service porch. He stood looking at the door. It had a glass pane at the top half in about the same condition as the window over the sink. He opened the door and looked out at the little screened porch. His hand still on the knob, he didn't even go out there. From where he stood he could see the screens were rusty and fragile. A hot water heater stood in the corner with pipes running from it to the ceiling. He could see it was old.

"Junk," he said, and he shook his head again.

He stepped back and closed the door. His eyes followed a long wrinkle in the wallpaper to the ceiling. He didn't smile, but he liked what he saw. You didn't see bead board ceilings much anymore, and he wondered if the other rooms had board ceilings, too. He walked back through to check. Good, he thought, and kept it to himself.

Carl dogged him about the house. He saw the old man shake his head, but he never saw him smile.

The old man made a note of the oak hardwood floors in pretty good condition considering the age of the house.

Someone has taken care of these floors. Good.

He noticed the large six-paned windows in every room. Although the caulking was flaking away on them all, and the paint was checked, he was pleased with what he saw, but he shook his head and moved on.

The interior doors were paneled, checked paint, not bad though. The light fixtures were just bare bulbs, nothing there. The wiring was old but it was copper. Salvageable.

The white bathtub sat up high on clawed feet. It had been cared for, no stains. He ran his hand along its curve. The porcelain felt cool to his touch. It was a prize. He would keep it himself. He could use the lavatory, too, and the butane heater was an antique. The bathroom was his. It would be too much to hope that the plumbing was copper. He knew it was lead, hadda be.

The little old light fixture over the sink had a metal chain that dangled down in front of the mirror. He pulled the chain and the light came on. He pulled it again and the light went off.

"OK," he turned to Carl, "just curious," he said, grinning broadly.

A clean cotton chenille bath mat still lay on the floor by the tub. "Pink," he said irreverently. He looked down at it and wondered if the floor was hardwood under the linoleum. He slipped the edge of his shoe under the pink mat and flipped it over. He stared down at the worn linoleum and sighed audibly before righting it again. He was pretty sure he would find hardwood below.

The old lady's bed still stood where she had slept all those years. His eyes swept the room and settled on the vanity. He could see it was in good shape. He didn't smile. He walked over and opened the top drawer of the matching bureau. It slid out smoothly. A woman's personal belongings were neatly folded inside and the musty scent of roses filled the room. He wondered if they were hers. *Biedermeier.*

His eyes slid over to the large man standing in the doorway, and quickly passed on by. The stupid clod, he had no idea. Good. The old fox didn't smile.

"How long she been dead?" he asked.

They had been walking through the house for some time now without exchanging words, and the question caught Carl off guard.

"Dead? She isn't dead. She's in Heritage Manor. She won't be coming home. She's there to stay."

"You got her power of attorney?"

"Of course, I take care of all her business now."

"If we come to some kind of agreement, it has to be legal, just like any house sale. I want you to understand that."

The old man turned abruptly and walked out of the room and out of the house. He stopped out at the front, turned, and looked back. He saw the gingerbread decoration on the porch, and he noted that like all houses of that age it did not have a cement slab.

It'll be easy to clean up here. Good.

Latticework fretting skirted the base of the house.

Good.

"You expect me to clean up the site?" he asked, without even turning to look at Carl. And he didn't wait for an answer. Abruptly, he began walking around the house checking the foundation, with Carl tagging along a few steps behind.

The old Mexican's walk around the house was just a ploy. He didn't need to check out the foundation. He was sizing Carl up, and watching Carl trotting along behind him, he thought he was ready to make an offer.

They had made their way all around the house, and the old man stopped at the front and lit a cigarette.

"These old places ain't worth much."

He drew on the cigarette and let the smoke go down slow and gave Carl time to think.

"The salvage don't bring much. What you're getting is a clean site." He paused, preparing Carl for the punch.

"A clean site, that's what you want, ain't it?" He continued without giving Carl a chance to answer. "Hauling all this old lumber off, well, it's a lotta work, and you gotta break it down. Take a truck and three or four men at least two days, maybe three."

Carl still hadn't said a word. Tony continued, "We'll have to bring a front-loader out here," he turned and surveyed the site, "and I guess we'll need a plane." He sighed, "That's another couple of men."

"Ain't much salvage in an old place like this. Not worth much." The old man's eyes slid up to see how Carl was taking it. "I guess I could give you a hunderd."

Shocked, Carl stammered, "There's a lot of lumber in this house, and the old lumber is weathered hard. It's hard, some say it's better than the soft, green, new wood." Carl's expression was earnest; he continued feebly, "I need at least five hundred."

"The wood's hard," the old man chuckled, "you're right about that! It's hard and it's brittle. You can't cut it or even drive a nail in it easily. It can only be used in special ways. Some carpenters won't even fool with it even though it's really hard." Then he added, "Or because it is."

"I'd take three hundred and fifty," Carl ventured.

The old man heard the falter. "Naw," he said. "The salvage and the clean up, a hunderd is all I can give you." Then he dramatically dropped the cigarette on the ground and pressed it with his shoe.

He glanced up at an anxious-faced Carl, and as if an afterthought he said, "What you gonna do with the old furniture?" He paused and this time looked him directly in the face, "Since I'd be coming out here anyway, I could give you another fifty for it. Save you paying someone to haul it off."

Carl was still struggling with the low offer.

"You could get your place all cleaned up at once and make yourself a hunderd and fifty bucks to boot."

The old man was wise and experienced. He'd been doing this all his adult life. He'd seen a lot of 'Carls' and he knew when he had struck oil. He stopped drilling.

"Well, gimme a call if you decide you want me to help you out with this job," then he turned as if to go.

Carl found his voice, "If I let you have it for that price, can I count on you to leave the place ready for my trailer?"

"That's my job," Tony grinned. "It's what I do," he said.

"Then you got you a deal," Carl said.

The old man extended his hand, "Deal!" They shook on it, and it was a deal.

He didn't smile until he was in his truck, and then he smiled, and he smiled all the way home.

***

The Mexican turned the two ton truck into the shallow bar ditch. The frame groaned as the old slick tires eased down and then up again, one at a time, and the tall sideboards slapped and rattled. The jarring set the ball fringe that outlined the windshield to bobbing, and Jesus on a cord did a bungee dive, up, down, and up again.

His two companions held on and giggled like girls. Chuy's boys were young, but they knew their business. They had come to work. They walked around the house, and within ten minutes they had the radio on to a Spanish station turned up full volume and were hard at it.

They removed the roof in large slabs. The truck was pulled up next to the house and they slid the slabs right down into it. They began to strip the house of its exterior clapboard, removing the planks with the nails still in them. The boys bent the nails over and stacked the planks in piles of like pieces.

The interior sheet rock would be taken to the dump. They pulled it down and stacked it to the side. The old man had already removed the furniture and the bathroom fixtures. By three o'clock in the afternoon they were taking up the hardwood flooring and stacking it up in its own pile in the front of the house beside the neatly sorted windows and doors.

They worked until dark when the old truck made its first trip back over the border, loaded to the limit. A band of little lights bordered the running boards and ran in a ripple, twinkling merrily, as they crossed over the bridge at Hidalgo into the Mexican night.

In the thin, early morning light, they came back and began loading the first of three trips to the landfill. By afternoon they had the lot cleared, ready for the blade that would finish the job.

It took them two days. That was as long as it took, and Mrs. Hobbs' house was gone. It may as well have never existed. In only two days.

A sleek, new, mobile home stands alone on the ground. The paint has a hard enamel finish. The wheels are covered with aluminum skirting. Carl has had a concrete apron poured for it and a redwood deck attached.

The deck runs the full length of the trailer. It has an aluminum awning and a new set of deck chairs. The plumbing is new, and it isn't lead. The bathroom fixtures are new. They are fiberglass, and the light over the sink is fluorescent.

Now when Carl stands back and admires his trailer, he is a happy man.

***

Pink begonias grew in pots at intervals along the railing of the deck. The early summer morning was cool and a soft breeze ruffled their leaves. Carl sat there in the mornings bolt upright in the rocking chair with a hand on each khaki clad knee. He preferred the upright rocker to the soft cushiony deck chairs his wife had bought. A redwood table stood at his side where his glass of iced tea sweated in a ring of moisture.

He sat with each hand positioned carefully. They looked exactly alike from this perspective although two fingers of his right hand were missing. The middle finger had been severed above the second joint and the ring finger was gone below it. But he could see it. Carl could see the mutilation of his right hand without even looking. Its presence was with him always. He could see it in his sleep. It had become as much a part of him as his very soul. It was who he was now.

It's a hell of a thing! It's a hell of a thing, ran through his unconscious mind like a pesky song. "If it doesn't kill you," he had heard, "it'll make you stronger."

Carl raised the right hand and took the glass. He held it up and rotated it with ease, and took pleasure in how he had overcome the handicap. The hand was strong. He was strong. He was a tall man, with broad shoulders.

Fifty-four years old and I can still see as good as ever.

Hawk Eye, old Hawk Eye, his wife often called him and he took it as a compliment.

Abruptly, Carl stood and moved to the deck's railing. He looked across a small section of cultivated ground to the two-story farmhouse where the old widow lived. Carl had seen the Mexican riding his bicycle up past her house to the back, and he watched him drop it into the grass.

He had to keep a close eye on the Mexican. He especially paid attention when the Mexican was in and around the old lady's yard.

She had hired Tony, that old crook, to do her remodeling job. Tony was the Mexican's uncle and the two of them were all over the place while they put in the new downstairs bathroom.

Carl smiled at her innocence. *She needs, she says, a bathroom downstairs so she can live on the first floor if she becomes incapacitated.*

Carl had kept careful note of the whole operation and watched in wonder as she gave the Mexicans free reign of her house. Sometimes she wasn't even at home when they were working there.

He'd heard her complain of missing things from her garage where she still kept her husband's workshop. "The Mexican's a carpenter, and you say your husband's table saw is missing? And you don't know what could have happened to it? Oh, brother!"

Carl couldn't understand why she didn't do something permanent with the tools. The old man had a complete woodworking shop out there when he died. "One day you'll wake up, and the garage will be empty." He told her.

What could she be thinking? He's been dead several years now. Does she think he'll be coming back and need them?

Someone should tell her daughter what's going on. That colonia is moving in on us. It's growing so fast, it gets closer every day. You can't be too careful nowadays. We've got to stick together.

So Carl tried to be watchful for himself and the old lady, too. He saw the dog with the flag-ears jump up on the small man as he dropped the green bicycle into the grass.

Just look at that! Some watchdog! That stupid mongrel is ugly enough to scare anyone away, but she needs a real watchdog living alone over there. Too bad the Fox Terrier is so small. He's the barker. He bites too. But she keeps him in the house.

He watched the Mexican petting the dog as it trotted along beside him.

You'd think it was the Mexican's dog the way it acts. It doesn't even bark when he's in the yard.

The Mexican wasn't going to the door. Carl watched as he walked into the garage.

Sure enough! This beats all!

It was dark in the garage and Carl strained to see what he was doing in there. He leaned forward until his head and shoulders were in the full sun. He was so absorbed that he didn't even notice the heat. His short-cropped gray hair glistened in the morning sunshine, and he didn't raise a hand to shield his eyes.

In only a few minutes the Mexican came riding out on her big green lawnmower. Carl's eyes widened when he saw it, and finally the hand came up to shade them.

He knew it was a John Deere, top of the line. He had seen her on it in the months since he had come down to help his aging aunt. She did the mowing of her large St. Augustine lawn herself.

Carl's focus narrowed until all he could see was a Mexican riding the lawnmower.

He watched the Mexican ride it down the driveway and turn onto Morningside road. Astonished, Carl watched him as he rode to his own driveway and turned in.

Carl's hand traveled down his face. He ran his fingers across his lips and over his chin. Then he put both hands on the rail to brace himself while he considered what he should do about it. He wondered if Connie had given the Mexican permission to go into her garage. He wondered if she even knew he'd been there.

Carl was a good man. He was a good neighbor. He was concerned about Connie. He sat back down in his rocker and the mower was on his mind. Did she know he had taken the tractor? She's an isolated old woman, he told himself, and very naïve, recklessly so. She doesn't realize that these days you have to be careful about allowing just anyone to hang around your house and yard.

He thought about the Mexican riding the mower away, and he shook his head and marveled at Connie's innocence. Some day that thieving Mexican will steal that lawnmower, he predicted, if he hasn't already.

***

Connie let the old Pontiac roll slowly forward so she could get a close look at the trailer. Mary's little gingerbread cottage was gone and in its place squatted a temporary, prefabricated, eyesore.

Mary would just die if she isn't dead already! I don't guess I'd know. He probably wouldn't even bother to call and tell me. I expect one day I'll have to read it in the obituaries.

That cracker-box trailer has wheels under its plastic skirt. That snow-diggin' Yankee is no more than just another itinerant. He's no better than the Mexican trash that's moving in on us up the road.

"This country's going to hell in a hand basket!"

Connie drove as always, leaning forward and gripping the wheel with both hands. Two fingers of the right one extended to hold a cigarette. She always smoked when she drove the car, and Mark, the little terrier, rode on the floor on the passenger side to avoid the smoke. The car dropped into a lower gear as she coasted past the trailer, and Mark jumped up onto the seat to see why.

"Mark, just look at that trailer."

The tiny head with the big eyes had been focused out of the window but turned to look at Connie when she spoke.

Connie hadn't seen Carl sitting on the deck, and when he stood to wave to her, she looked down at Mark and said in a loud whisper, "Just look at him! He waves that hand like it was a badge. He never passes up a chance to flash it!

"He wants everyone to think he lost those fingers in the Korean War. I'd bet money he probably just stuck his hand into a machine when he wasn't paying attention to what he was doing.

"Some war hero!" she said with contempt. "Just look at that burr haircut. He always wears those brown khakis. It looks like he's still in uniform. I'll bet he has a hat like MacArthur's and wears it around inside that trailer."

Connie waved back, and told Mark, "He's shameless! Poor Mary, there's a lesson here. You can't count on someone else, even family. He came down here to take care of Mary, and what did he do? He put her in a nursing home, tore her house down, and now he sits out there like he owns the place. The king of the realm."

Connie put her foot back on the accelerator, and the lurch forward sent the terrier scrambling for balance, and he ended up rolling into his place on the floorboard.

"Honestly!" she went on, ignoring the desperation of the dog, "Just look at that hand! He always shows it off. He makes everyone shake hands. After they've seen it, he wants them to feel it, too. Everybody has to touch it!"

Mark's eyes were closed. He wasn't listening any more, but she continued, "His personal sacrifices are to be admired all the more because he's handicapped." Connie turned south on Alamo Road. "He invites pity. He wallows in it. He uses it." She drove on into Chapin and didn't think about Carl any more that day.

When Carl sat back down in his rocker he was thinking about Connie. He'd been in a bad mood since he had seen the Mexican with the lawnmower.

Carl didn't even wonder why he found this to be so irritating. He didn't think about it. He thought about the lawnmower, and he thought about the nosy Mexican, and his mood didn't improve all day.

***

Now Carl made it his business to pay attention, so he watched the Mexican very carefully. Every time anyone stops by to see her, he observed, the Mexican comes around. Even when it's family, or even when she gets a delivery, he shows up when they leave. Every time.

Carl could plainly see when a car pulled up in Connie's drive. He could see the Mexican, and knew he always came around when they left.

That Mexican has made it his business to know what she's doing all the time. He knows when she's at home and he watches to see when she's gone. She lets him go into her garage, and he knows everything she has in there.

The situation worried Carl.

It just isn't a good idea. If her family isn't concerned, they should be! Maybe they don't realize what's going on at her house. Maybe someone needs to tell them.

It was just a short walk west to Connie's, so Carl began to go over often to check on her. He tried to come every day. When family came to visit her, he never failed to show up. I'm not a Mexican, I'm a friend, he told himself. They need to know she has a friend close by who cares enough to look out for her.

"I know you worry about Connie living alone out here," he reassured them. "The Mexicans are moving in on us, and they'll steal you blind. Just remember, I'm next door, and I'm watching out for her." It was a warning as well as a reassurance.

Carl was an early riser. By ten o'clock he had his chores taken care of and would go out onto the deck with a second cup of coffee and the morning paper. He saw when the black dog came running up to the back door and Connie step out with the fox terrier. He saw the woman and the two dogs walk into the garage, and he picked up his paper. He dropped it again when instead of the car backing down the drive; he saw them come out again.

She didn't take the car, he observed. That dilapidated old Pontiac probably wouldn't start; nothing holds it together but the dirt! He chuckled to himself at his joke, and took a sip of coffee.

She stayed in the back yard.

Well, she didn't go in and call a wrecker. He laughed again, and looked across to the Mexican's house. *And she didn't call the Mexican.*

He put his paper and cup down. She seemed to be out there a long time. He looked carefully, but could not see what she was doing.

She's just standing around in the yard. Why would she do that?

Just to be neighborly, and to see if he could help her with whatever it was that kept her out there so long, he walked over.

Connie was dragging the garden hose around giving her shrubs a dousing. She had watered the fiddle leafed fig, and the grapefruit tree, and now she was watering the bougainvillea, when Carl walked up.

He stood beside her as she held the hose. Together, they watched as the water puddled around the base of the large and sprawling bush. Purple blossoms covered its long limber branches. They draped over the grass and he held one back so she could see the water finding its mark.

"Connie, I've noticed lately you have been getting that Mexican to mow your lawn. Why don't you let me do it?"

"I used to mow it myself," she said. "That's why Hank bought me the John Deere. I used to think it was fun, and I loved cutting the grass." Her voice was thoughtful, and her eyes swept the large yard. "We would come out in the late afternoons, and I would run around the yard on the mower. Hank prepared the way, you know, picked up things, raked and all that. We loved to work together. I'll always get a lift out of the smell of new cut grass.

"Hank's gone now," she put her hand on her side, "and my back is so bad, I just can't do it anymore. Now I get Ignacio to mow it." No remorse, just a statement of fact.

Carl sympathized, "You have to pay him to do it, don't you?"

Her eyes snapped over to him, and she responded, "Well, of course!"

"Then, why don't you let me do it? You wouldn't have to pay me anything."

"Why Carl! I have a big yard. I couldn't let you do that. Why would you want to?"

"Look, it would be good for both of us. You have the riding lawnmower. I could do my yard when I do yours and it would help us both. It's a win-win."

Connie smiled at him, and behind the smile she was considering his angle. With barely a pause, a pause so slight that he didn't notice, she agreed to his proposition.

So Carl took on the job of mowing Connie's big yard, and he didn't charge her anything. It was a win-win.

***

"I hate the weekends," Connie complained to her daughter, Susan. "There's nothing on TV except Spanish and politics." The cable television had not yet made its way out into the countryside. At least, it hadn't made it down Connie's road, as the population in her neighborhood would not have qualified as cable customers.

"I don't think you're really bored," Susan said. "Where's Carl? I've never been here when he didn't show up."

"Oh, he'll be here. He's driving me crazy!" Her voice bristled with irritation.

"Now, Mama, he's just being thoughtful. He's concerned about you."

They sat at the game table, and Connie put her hands on it, leaned back, cocked her head, and raised her eyebrows in amusement.

"You don't think Carl is concerned about you?" Susan asked. "He's so considerate." She was smiling now, too. "He's watching out for you; he has told me so, many times." Susan's tone had taken on a sarcastic note.

Susan mimicked, "Not to worry, we neighbors are looking out for each other."

Connie laughed, "Carl is looking out for someone, that's for sure."

"Mother! I'm surprised at you. Carl is always doing nice things for you. Have you no appreciation?"

"I'd appreciate it if he would leave me alone," she said. "He's always nosing around here, weaseling in on my business."

Susan was serious now, "Mother, I think you may be a little unfair. He's only trying to help you."

"Do you think I want to be obligated to someone like him?" Connie was serious, now, too. "I don't need, and I don't want any help from him. I can take care of myself. He's always concerned that I pay Ignacio for things he does for me. Ignacio and I help each other. When Carl does something for me, it always costs me more than if I paid Ignacio."

Her voice took on a hard tone, "He's nosy and meddlesome, and he wants something. When you've been around as long as I have, you learn to value your independence. Sink, or swim, my fate's in my own hands, and that's the way I want it. I want to pay my own way. I don't want to be beholden to anyone, especially Carl."

A copy of *The Progressive Farmer* magazine served as a coaster for her dewy glass of iced tea, Connie still thought of herself as a businesswoman although she had not been able to find a renter for her acreage in some time. Ignacio was an entrepreneur, and she lived in a house that required a lot of maintenance. She enjoyed bargaining with him over the constant small jobs she needed help with.

"Carl's protective posturing is a slap in the face," she said. "He's a hypocrite. All that fawning and stroking is paper thin."

"Mother, Carl doesn't seem to know how you feel about him."

"Listen, Carl is like a bulldozer. He doesn't listen to anything I say." She paused a moment and added. "It all just slides over his back like water off a duck."

A shadow passed over them and they looked up to see Carl stepping on to the patio. "Well, speak of the devil," Connie said, as she rose to answer his knock at the door.

CHAPTER SEVEN
México, 1980

The fourteen-year-old girl sat primly, her square little feet were pressed into new patent leather shoes. A gift from *tía* Estella, they were tucked up neatly together under her seat.

"Buy her some shoes," her mother's sister had said when she sent the money for the bus ticket and a small amount extra for the shoes and a taco on the way.

"She can't ride the bus barefooted."

Ramona had her arms wound tightly about a box of clothing she gripped firmly in her lap. The brown cardboard box was soft and worn about the corners, but she had it securely tied with a string, and had very carefully printed her name and address on the top, Ramona Alamia, Ébano de San Luis Potosi, just in case.

The air inside the bus was humid and heavy. Ramona released one hand briefly to run it across her face, brushing away beads of moisture. She didn't even notice the pervasive odor of people in close warm quarters, a small discomfort and easily ignored. Ramona was filled with excitement at the prospect of spending the day traveling to the north. She was glad to be on the bus. The ride down to Tampico that she had always dreaded before seemed different today. It was different. This was a special day.

Ramona fanned herself with her free hand and didn't complain. I must notice everything and press it to memory, perhaps forever. Not mother. It is a last goodbye. I will not remember how she didn't look as I gathered my things and placed them in my box.

The stuffy and crowded bus was of the Vencedor line, which served the rural communities of southeastern Mexico. It was a commuter line, so to speak. Its busses bounced along the countryside and carried the working poor into their jobs or into the market places where they could sell their goods. It was not an express bus. It stopped to pick up passengers on a regular schedule, and it stopped to pick them up on random corners where they waited, packages in hand and children in tow. A cigar box filled with coins clinked at the driver's feet; as a consequence, the bus often left the regular route to deposit riders at their doors. They had never done so for Ramona, and she sat perspiring in her best dress.

The bus circled its route through a crowded section of Ébano, not a small city, and made many stops, so many that the driver didn't bother to close the doors. It jolted over the unpaved roads and through the neighborhoods where water puddled and ran in the gutters and was tracked in along with the dust.

The driver's radio was turned up for the entertainment of the passengers. The station was playing music of the country. A woman's voice filled the bus with a plaintive song about a handsome and fickle Romeo to the accompaniment of an accordion. And for their protection, a medal of St. Christopher dangled from the rear view mirror, dancing in unison with the ball fringe, which bordered the windshield.

I will not think of Mother. Where was she when I stood waiting for the bus? I do not know. I have nothing to remember of it. It was a kindness, a favor. She could have seen me from the window. No. I think she was down at the back and may not have even thought about the time.

Or, it was a favor.

It was a favor. I have no memory.

But Ramona remembered. She remembered how on other mornings she had stood in the doorway and held onto the frame as her mother brushed and pulled her dark hair back away from her face.

"¡Ese danos!" It hurts, she had always complained.

"Hush, little *Cachetas,*" her mother would whisper softly in her ear and continue pulling the hair into the *trenza,* or plump braid, that would reach her waist.

Today her mother wasn't there. This she remembered.

A handsome young man of about the same age as the driver was standing at the front and enjoying the air that passed through the open door. For balance he had wedged himself against the dash, exchanging small talk with the driver. Ramona thought he must be going only a short distance, or perhaps the package he had with him was too bulky to struggle with down the crowded aisle. He gripped the pole and stepped down with his box to admit new arrivals with a cheerful greeting and gave the women a hand up with exaggerated gentility.

NO SE PERMITE ANIMALES, hand lettered, and posted at the

front of the bus caused Ramona to grin broadly. She had taken a good look at the young man's package. Holes were punched in it everywhere and it was not only moving, but an occasional scratching noise could be heard coming from it.

The rule was generally ignored because it was not enforced. Her eyes moved back to the row behind and across from her. Openly, blatantly, sat a man, his knees separated, and between them he had three chickens, alive, and trussed by the feet. He sat relaxed, with his hands loosely folded over the binding cord. His eyes were closed. She guessed by his casual demeanor that he had done this many times before. He was probably a regular on this bus.

The passengers had vegetables. They had ball cheese and eggs, and they had chickens. The driver knew they had chickens, but he was compassionate. He knew their mission; but the jingle of coins in the box blurred his vision, and he didn't see the boxed and tethered fowl.

The big tires groaned as the bus passed up onto the pavement and turned out onto the wide boulevard that ran from the central park with the Cathedral and plaza, to the huge petroleum complex at its other extremity.

It was early. The church was quiet. Its big wooden doors were closed and the bell was still. Only the pigeons attended, roosting within the bell tower, not yet accosting the plaza goers. The plaza, too, was deserted. The city had not yet come to life.

Ébano de San Luis Potosi, lay below the Tropic of Cancer. The days were hot and humid. Because it was still early, there was little traffic. A large bronze bust of President Cardenas sat on a splendid pedestal at the beginning of the esplanade. Cardenas was revered as the president who nationalized the oil industry and drove the foreign industrialists from Mexico confiscating their holdings. In Ébano it was Royal Dutch Shell and the British, El Águila.

The oil industry had built Ébano. Its demise was a major factor in the poverty that she and her fellow passengers suffered. Not a single person on the bus appreciated the irony, least of all Ramona, and she admired the statue as they moved by it.

In their odyssey through the neighborhoods, the bus had passed many houses built by the oil companies for their employees, entire blocks of them. Or houses built of the lumber brought in by the oil companies to build houses for their workers, and then reused in newer, old houses. This was not native lumber. The wide milling of the clapboards made them easily distinguishable from the native, especially in an area of soft wood trees where the custom was masonry construction. They had become such an integral part of the city that they went unnoticed by the native population.

The boulevard was wide. Its white concrete surface glistened in the dazzling morning sunlight. A median ran its full course, planted alternately in cocoa palms and profusely flowering oleander.

Flamboyán trees were in full bloom. They grew behind the rows of shops and small businesses. They towered thirty feet high with their stunning large clusters of fierce orange blossoms.

The broad street ran uphill all the way to the refinery. The beautiful drive was difficult for the struggling bus, and it made it with gears grinding. Ramona hoped she was seeing it for the last time.

The boulevard ended just past the refinery gates. The road that would take them into the neighboring state of Vera Cruz, and then into Tampico, split away to the northeast and they followed it. This road was not broad and beautiful, and the glistening concrete gave way to asphalt. Here spans of smooth perfection alternated with eroding repairs of potholes and other potholes long neglected or just ignored. Shops and houses along this part of the road were poor, and the way was congested with people and traffic.

Dust and noise carried through the open windows as the bus lunged forward over the rough pavement. She gripped the rail at the back of the seat ahead and braced with her feet.

Finally, as they reached the high road, traveling became easier. They picked up speed. *Por fin.* They still stopped for passengers, but now the stops were miles apart. This was ranching country, some of the best ranch land in Mexico. Ramona looked out across a rolling landscape of green grass, rimmed by mante trees. Occasionally a saddled horse, or a donkey could be seen standing tied to a gatepost at a little house only yards from the highway. The big houses of the ranch owners were far off the road and only an occasional glimpse of their comfortable lifestyle could be seen from the bus.

The ride down into Tampico took about an hour, and Ramona knew it by heart. As she sat looking out of the window, her thoughts were not on the landscape. She didn't even notice as the ranch land became marshy, and the mante trees changed to mangrove.

Tampico was a port city on the Gulf of Mexico, and she perked up when they began to pass into the salt flats. She knew they would soon cross the Pánico River and shortly thereafter arrive at the bus station.

She was ready. She let her eyes travel over the other passengers preparing to disembark, and she smiled to herself, smugly.

I am different. I have a future.

Ramona stepped down from the bus and walked into the terminal. Her companions scattered among the milling crowd and headed for the exits. She surveyed the large room filled with busy, moving people and felt an electric sensation in her stomach.

I am a woman now. I am on my own.

Tampico is a large city, they had warned. Watch out for pickpockets and thieves. She gripped her box tightly and carried it not by the string, but hugging it before her. She stood among the moving people and searched the busy terminal for the ticket window. She would need a ticket to Reynosa, the large city on the Mexican border with the United States.

She was looking for the Oriente Line. When she saw it, she bought her ticket, one way, third class. Her bus left in an hour. She had a long ride ahead; she would be on the bus six hours. Still, she would arrive in Reynosa before dark.

It was not an express bus, but there would be no animals, and busses of the Oriente Line, even in third class, were air-conditioned and comfortable.

Ramona sought out a seat near the Oriente gate and placed her box on the floor between her feet. Her eyes scanned the crowd, but returned constantly to the large clock on the wall at the high end of the terminal.

Busses were coming and going and people were moving in and out of the seats around her. She wasn't disturbed when a middle-aged man took the seat beside her and placed his arm on the armrest between them. He produced a cheap gold-colored bracelet and laid it out along his wrist and drew it forward so the bangles righted themselves as it traveled along his bare arm. He was unshaven and his broad smile revealed a chipped front tooth.

"I could let you have this for only veinte pesos", he said. "It is my sister's, but she will sell it, cheap. !*Muy barato!*"

Pickpockets and thieves. His hand was on her arm as she reached for her box to leave.

"Wait," he said. "I could make you a better price." But he didn't follow when she moved quickly away and into the public toilets.

Ramona wasn't strong. She was small for her age and she had been ill. Her illness had prompted the aunt's generosity. She leaned against the wall and felt the cool dampness of the plaster as she waited for him to lose interest and go away. The cramps of her illness were gone now, but the bracelet had prompted a memory and suddenly she felt very tired.

Ramona's *abuelita* Maria was growing blind. But she still raised her hand to screw life into the bulb that hung suspended by a long wire in the main room of her house. The raw light cast long and moving shadows across the space, and Ramona had seen the glint of light upon the bracelet that her aunt Estella had worn. It was not a cheap bracelet. It wasn't gold colored metal like the one the man had tried to sell her. It was genuine gold and the light flicked across it as the hand with its long slender fingers, tipped in red, had jabbed toward her sister Cecelia, Ramona's mother.

The finger pointed accusingly. Ramona remembered the red fingernails, but mostly she remembered the bracelet. It was a luxury denied to her own mother. Her mother had no bracelet, and she had never seen her mother's fingernails painted red.

Unlike Ramona's own mother, Estella had married well and now lived in McAllen, across the border from Reynosa, in the United States. As their mother was growing old, Estella came and when she did, she brought money. She came and she always seemed to be in a bad temper, aimed at her sister and usually in criticism of her sister's new husband. He was abusive of her, and she closed her eyes to his abuse of her daughters. This time Ramona was the focus of his obscene attentions. Ramona remembered watching from the doorway and she remembered the bracelet. Her memory of the bracelet reminded her of the angry words between them as well.

No one else bothered her when she finally felt confident enough to move back out to where she could see the posting for her bus to Reynosa, and she boarded with a feeling of relief. When the bus finally pulled out of the station, her spirits soared.

At last! I'm on my way, at last!

She watched the landscape whirling past and tried not to think of the temporary discomfort she had felt at her memory. She thought only of her amazing good fortune. Her sisters, two of them, had gone to Reynosa when they were fifteen. She would be a year luckier. I am luckier! She thought, but she knew she was the same. It had just come earlier for her. It was at their insistence that the aunt had sent for her, not out of any love. The tall, thin, black haired woman had never given Ramona any attention. Certainly good luck had no hand in it. It was the bad luck, rather, of the stepfather that had driven the girls to the safety of early marriages and better prospects on the border.

The new road across the coastal plain had been completed. The route would take them north to Soto la Marina where they would stop for food and refueling, and then west to San Fernando, and north again to Reynosa. The seat was large and comfortable and the bus wound its way past a flat landscape where she saw cultivated fields of onions and corn.

In the distance to the west, on the horizon, she could occasionally see a purple ridge of mountains, but this bus would not be going through Cuidad Victoria and the mountains.

They passed through a tropical basin where large flocks of small green parrots jabbered away in the groves of palm trees. The rural villages had cactus hedges and thatched roofed houses. Some even poorer and many much smaller than Ébano, and her heart lifted. She saw girls of her own age going nowhere and she smiled to herself, smugly.

Ébano is behind me.

***

"Little Cachetas." Estella said, as she stood to hug her niece. Cachetas was an affectionate nickname given to Ramona. It meant 'cheeks', and alluded to her high cheek boned Indian facial characteristics.

Under her breath and to herself, Estella whispered, so this is the little one who caused all the uproar. She looked at the young girl standing before her and marveled, how is it that this one who got all the Indian blood could be the one to cause the trouble?

Ramona, under the protection of her generous aunt, with the support of her older sisters, and carrying all her worldly goods in a small cardboard box began her new life.

***

Ramona's aunt Estella arranged work for her as a maid in McAllen. She was given a bed in her aunt's house for the weeknights, sharing a room with a cousin of her own age; a high school student with whom she had little in common. Ramona worked in McAllen, but she lived in Reynosa with her sister Inez and came there every Friday evening to spend the weekend. She went back to McAllen to work on Monday morning.

Some things didn't change. Ramona hoped she had taken her last ride on the Vencedor, and perhaps she had, however busses were still a fact of life for her. Her Vencedor was now an American line, the Valley Transit. The American line was different, there were no animals, but the people it carried were pretty much the same, Mexicans on their way to work.

Just as the Vencedor, the Valley Transit was not an express line. It made many stops. Ramona usually waited at a very busy one located in the parking lot of a strip mall, the last stop the bus made before crossing the border. It was a straight shot of five miles south to the river and Reynosa, not a bad ride, and she made it every Friday evening at 6:30 P.M.

Just as before, Ramona knew many of the people on the bus. They were mostly women, much like her, and they waited together, boarded and rode to Reynosa together, every Friday evening. They carried packages as before, but now they carried articles they had bought, not things for sale. This time they had been to work and then to market, to buy, and they were carrying their goods home, to Reynosa.

Conversation on the bus was sparse. It was the end of a workday, the end of a workweek. The women sat quietly, their packages and their purses held tightly in their laps. They guarded their purses carefully. They were paid in cash.

Ramona saw the young man when he got on the bus. He was one of the few men on the bus and last to board. He walked up the aisle, looking from side to side for an empty seat. Their eyes met as he passed by and took a seat behind her and across the aisle.

It was a casual incident and was dismissed from her mind immediately. It would have been forgotten forever except Monday morning in the bus station in Reynosa, she saw him again. She had seen him twice now, and couldn't remember ever having seen him before in the two years she had been commuting on this bus, but there he was again.

He got off the bus at the stop where he had boarded Friday evening and made his way across the parking lot to the C. R. Anthony's department store in the strip mall.

Ramona watched him walk across the pavement among the smattering of parked cars at the large grocery store; it was eight o'clock in the morning and early for shoppers. He walked around the corner of the building and disappeared from view.

He didn't ride the bus regularly, but in the next few weeks he was there often enough for her to recognize him, and she found herself looking for him each time she made the short ride across the border.

One morning, returning from Reynosa, she had taken her place in line to buy her ticket to McAllen when she saw him in the next line. He turned and looked back at the line she was standing in. He looked back again, this time at her directly, and she averted her eyes quickly, nervously avoiding his attention.

She stiffened with alarm when he changed lines and came to stand behind her, and she clutched her purse tightly. She had been warned about strangers in bus terminals. By now he wasn't really a stranger, was he? She fixed her eyes on the person ahead and did not look at him as they stood in the slowly moving line, but his presence behind her was the only thing on her mind.

People crowded in as it neared eight o'clock, and they pressed toward the ticket booth rushing to be ticketed and boarded. As the line tightened up, he brushed against her. Her body tingled with electricity when she felt him touch her long hair, still wound tightly in the plump braid. He quickly muttered an apology, his voice low and soft in her ear.

The line moved on, and she bought her ticket and hurried on to the bus. The incident gave her shameful pleasure and she felt humiliated. She thought his contact with her shoulder and his whisper in her ear had been too close, too intimate. It had been improper. She wasn't sure if his touching had been intentional or if it was a chance accident that she had misunderstood.

She didn't misunderstand, however, what she had been feeling, and she turned to examine the reflection of her face in the window. The round face set with large, dark, eyes looked back, and it was prettier than she had thought.

She didn't know if he got on her bus. She sat with her eyes carefully fixed in her lap. The rush of emotion had left her dizzy and flushed.

***

Aunt Estella had arranged for her to work for a lady who had two teenagers. The woman was thrust into the working world herself when her husband acknowledged his lover and walked out to marry her.

Señora Tisdale had been her own housekeeper until her recent divorce. She was a kind and generous lady of whom her departing husband said, "I married her for love and instead I got efficiency."

This remark, made as an explanation to shocked friends, although unkind and harsh, had the ring of truth. The *señora* did not deserve the cruelty of the man's cutting words; she had been a loving wife, and was now heartbroken and humiliated by his betrayal, but he was correct. She was efficient. She was efficient, and she was competent and excelled at anything she put her hand to. Ramona found herself to be working for a benevolent and very strict taskmaster who was also an exceptional teacher.

Ramona's life had been spent in a house that had electricity, but no indoor plumbing. She had never used a vacuum cleaner or any other appliance such as a washer and dryer before. She had a lot to learn. She was bright and motivated and the *Señora* Tisdale was patient, but persistent, and in the two years she worked there Ramona had learned a lot.

Ramona laundered the clothes and she learned that the *señora* wanted the house to be spotlessly clean. In addition, she wanted it to be kept with everything precisely arranged.

The clothes inside the closets were to hang perfectly spaced, the shoes as well. The shoes, which were not in towering stacks of boxes on the shelf, were to be carefully placed in pairs. When she opened the closet doors, the *señora* wanted to see order.

The dishes inside the kitchen cabinets were to be arranged to look just right when the *señora* opened the doors.

The work became routine. The nature of her work was that it did not involve the active participation of her mind any longer. Ramona was free to think about anything she chose while she worked. Sadly, she didn't have much of a life beyond the family. The mechanics of her work and the trips across the bridge had become monotonously uneventful. As a consequence, she found herself thinking about the incident in the bus station, and she thought about it most of that week.

She tried, but she could no longer conjure up the image of his face. In her mind's eye she could see him walking up the aisle of the bus. She remembered a slender man in his middle to late twenties; he wore the coat of his suit unbuttoned. It hung open as he passed along grasping the seat backs alternately as he looked for a seat. She saw it swing away from him, and she remembered that he was wearing a silk tie, and his white shirt was starched and neat.

She felt his breath on her neck and in her hair. She experienced again the sensation of his body brushing against hers and his mumbled apology, "Sorry," he said, "please forgive me."

She saw him as a clean and gentle man, wearing a business suit, and smelling of cologne.

She had been working at scrubbing the shower stall, and she stepped aside and found her reflection in the full-length mirror. She examined her body critically. She wondered if a man like that could be interested in her. Her short, classic Indian body was not and never would be the slender American ideal.

She was young, and her heavy dark hair, still caught up in the trenza, had loosened and formed soft curls about her round olive face. Her cheeks were flushed from the activity, and her large dark eyes sparkled with the notion that, perhaps, just maybe, she may have attracted a man such as the slender man in the business suit.

Now Ramona's mind kept as busy as her body and the time flew. The incident had been incredibly interesting, and she couldn't leave it alone. She examined both sides of it. If it wasn't an accident, it was sinful, the sort of thing she had been warned to guard against in bus terminals. If it was sinful, still, she found it to be distressingly exciting.

She pictured him again, clean and well dressed, but just a businessman in a suit that had stumbled against her in a crowd. That's all there was to it, but now the work was easier, and the boredom of it evaporated.

With the *señora* away at work during the day and the children in high school, Ramona was allowed to play the radio while she worked. The songs on the radio were all sad longing love songs. The pain was delicious and she enjoyed it all week.

As the week drew to a close, Ramona began to think of the bus trip back to Reynosa. She thought about it a lot; she sobered up, and began to scold herself. You fool! This is a fairy story you have made up to entertain yourself.

A novella.

Her thinking cleared. She knew that any man you meet in a bus terminal could be dangerous. If she ever met him again she knew how to respond properly, and this time she would.

I am different, I am better, I have a future. This time she added, *and I am not a fool.*

She was not a fool, but she was young and lonely.

***

After work, the *señora* drove Ramona to the house of her aunt Estella. It was only a few blocks from the aunt's house to the bus stop. As she walked to the bus stop, she considered the possibility that he would be there. She had to come to grips with the fact that he was a stranger, a stranger in a bus station who could be dangerous.

She decided to look for him and if she saw him first she would take pains to be sure he didn't see her, if she saw him first.

If he saw her first, well, that couldn't be helped, but she wouldn't allow him to stand behind her in line again. If some way he managed to do it, she wouldn't let him exploit her like he did last week. However, if somehow he managed to touch her that way again, she'd put both hands on his chest and push him away, and tell him to leave her alone.

She replayed the incident in her mind and embroidered upon it considerably. If he did it to her again, she'd hurt him where he would remember it!

Her mind was occupied with the various ways she'd hurt him, but her body was reliving the pleasure it had given her. The confusion was alarming because she wasn't a fool, and she longed for a repeat of the scene. If it happened again, she would be blissfully happy.

Her longing for him grew as she walked toward the bus stop. The pain of her desire was powerful, and fearful too, and it was real. He was a stranger in a business suit. She didn't know anything about him. She was confused and afraid, and she longed for the danger.

She arrived at the place, the women were there, but she didn't see the man. She scanned the busy parking lot. Men and women came and went from the grocery store and the C. R. Anthony's department store.

They were carrying groceries to their cars, or standing in pairs talking. She searched their faces looking for him.

When the bus came, she hung back and anxiously searched the parking lot for him. Finally, reluctantly, she took her place with the women as they filed on as usual, and he didn't get on the bus.

The threat and the thrill had energized her for a week, and its absence left her drained and empty. She felt hollow and lonelier than she had ever been before.

***

The bus station in Reynosa was within walking distance of her sister's house. Ramona made it every Friday in the fading light of evening. She sank into gloom and began to feel a growing dissatisfaction with everything.

Maybe I'm not so special after all.

She worked harder than she ever had, she was paid more than she could have hoped to earn in Ébano, but she spent it all, and for what? She had no life beyond work.

Her sisters were happy for her, and they wished her well, but she could detect in them a lack of faith that she had a chance to escape the grinding poverty of their own lives.

Her oldest sister, Conception, had married a boy from Ébano when she was fifteen. He was eighteen and on his way to Reynosa to take a job in construction. She went with him, and when she could, she sent for her sister Inez.

Inez married at fifteen as well, a boy she met in Reynosa, an auto mechanic. She had a bed for Ramona, and Ramona was going to Inez's house.

Now, Ramona was a year past the magic age, and she vowed not to sacrifice herself to a man such as the ones married to her sisters, and her mother.

Perhaps I shall never marry. It was the hollowness speaking.

She walked along in the dusk. Her mood sagged on down, and she saw poverty everywhere she looked, and it was not much different from the poverty in Ébano.

Friday evenings are busy in Reynosa, and although she was feeling lonely, she was not alone on the street. The sidewalk where she walked ran along a busy thoroughfare. Some of the cars had turned their lights on. Several restaurants and bars were situated along the route, and their neon signs began flickering on, glowing dimly against the amber sky.

As in Ébano, boys and men sold *cosas* along the street. Here it was green cactus in plastic bags, *nopales,* in Ébano it had been ball cheese. They accosted drivers in cars forced to slow down in the traffic. Women with children clinging to their skirts, and others in their arms had their hands out, begging. She tried not to look at the women, women who were not much older than she was, and a chill passed over her.

The bus station in Reynosa was located in a poor neighborhood. It was, however, a step above the one where Inez lived. Ramona walked down the busy street as long as she could.

Eventually, she turned away south. Walking became more difficult; this street was not paved, although it, too, was busy. The traffic had worn ruts in the street that filled with water when it rained and fogged dust into the houses when it didn't.

Day light faded fast now, and lights came on in the houses along the way. She smelled cooking. These houses, like her sisters', were not air-conditioned, and she could hear children's voices, and adult conversations, and sometimes radios, through the open windows as she passed.

Her sister lived in a residential neighborhood, but it was not exclusively homes. Family businesses flourished. Mechanics labored in shade tree garages, and women operated bedroom beauty shops. Grocery stores dotted the corner lots where some enterprising person serviced the emergency needs of the neighbors, usually one room with a window, where they passed the money and items through. The one she was passing had a single, bare light bulb to illuminate the colorful hand painted sign bearing its name.

She was tired and the smells of cooking caused pangs of hunger, so she picked up the pace. It was dark when she walked up to Inez' house. Inez was in the end of the room that served as a kitchen, cooking supper. The brightly lit room smelled of tortillas and the cozy family setting lifted her spirits. Conception sat at the table feeding the baby in the highchair, and they greeted her warmly as she stepped into the room.

Ramona wasn't surprised to see Conception; she was here often in the evenings. Her husband had found better work, he now tended bar in the *Zona Rosa,* and as he worked this time of the day and into the late night, Conception spent most of her evenings here. Conception lived in another neighborhood, and she had a car. The oldest of the three, Conception did not have any children.

Inez was not so fortunate, she was only nineteen, but she had two children and was great with another, soon to arrive. Inez' husband came home late in the evenings, the bar he frequented was not in the *Zona Rosa*, and he was not likely to visit the work place of his brother-in-law, even if it had been elsewhere, but he kept hours much the same as the bartender, and so the sisters were free to spend the evenings together.

Conception lived in a larger house in a better neighborhood. Ramona would have much preferred to stay with her, but her arrangement with Inez was necessary. Inez needed her to help, and she needed the money Ramona paid her for room and board.

Ramona helped with the children, and she slept with the older of them as well. Soon, in less than a month she would be sleeping with two of them, as the baby bed would have a new occupant.

It was late when Conception went home. When they all were in bed, and Inez' husband, Hernando, was not among them, his absence frightened Inez, but it did not worry Ramona. She worried when he was here. She dreaded the sound of the screen door when he opened it to enter the house. He didn't even sneak in. He opened it with a jerk and a slam.

She lay in her bed and held her breath and waited, fearing the worst. It was always the same. Inez whined and nagged and Hernando reacted with anger and abuse. Ramona hated it when he abused her sister, so much like her mother's husband.

She despised the ugly man with the dirty fingernails. She wished he would go away and not come back at all, at least not until Inez could have the baby.

In the quiet of the night, waiting for Hernando, Ramona had the time and the privacy to think about the man again. She was coming to terms with the myth she had spun.

I am a fool.

She had thought about it so much all week that she couldn't remember what had actually happened. Her feelings about it were confused as well, her longing desire and her guilt were hard to reconcile in her young and inexperienced mind.

It was just a dream, *a sueno,* she admitted.

I am nobody. This man wasn't interested in me.

The loss of the dream was still very painful, and she mourned its loss. She vowed to never again feel such disappointment. She would protect herself.

And that night, waiting for Fernando, she made a promise.

I'll never marry, but if I do, it will be to a man like the one in the bus station, a businessman, with a business suit, and clean fingernails, and a clean, white, starched shirt

CHAPTER EIGHT
Morningside Road, 1992

Ramona laid the sheet on the bare mattress and as she partially unfolded it, taking a corner in each hand, she said, "I dreamed of the cat again last night."

She raised her hands above her head, and when they came down the sheet billowed out, filled with air. When it settled, the centerfold came down precisely in the middle of the bed. The two women began smoothing it with their open hands.

"Was it bad?" Lilah asked, and she lifted the corner of the mattress to make a fold, pulling the fabric tight, and tucking it under.

"It was the same as always," Ramona replied, her face somber.

"The cat always comes to me when I've had a bad day." She sighed, her mind was already moving on. "Saturday was a bad day."

"The funeral was in Reynosa?"

"Yes, it was in Reynosa. It was Saturday in Reynosa. It was hot, dusty and Saturday in Reynosa, it was very sad."

"She was an old woman," Lilah said. Her voice was flat. It was a statement of fact. She too was old.

Ramona placed a pillow under her chin and held it pinned there as she drew on the pillowcase.

"She was old, but the cancer took her slowly. In the end Delores had to miss a lot of work. She was sick, too."

Lilah looked at the younger woman with concern. Her face's smooth, dark, Indian features concealed her distress, but Lilah knew her well. Ramona had worked for her more than ten years now. She had been living in the servant's quarters beside the garage since Dick had died, and Lilah saw her every day.

"I saw you looking for the cat," Lilah said. "She isn't coming back, you know. Like Delores' mother, she, too, was old, and nature takes its course."

"She sleeps at the foot of my bed."

Lilah tossed her head. "Pshaw!" Her hand waved in dismissal. "Only in your dreams!"

"This time she came up and stood on my chest. Her nose touched my face." Ramona spoke in a low voice, almost a whisper. "She never did that before. It was a kiss for a really bad day."

"It was a nightmare. Forget it."

"*Señora* Lilah, it wasn't a nightmare. It's a comfort for me when she sleeps at my feet."

The bed was made and turned down for the night. Lilah put a consoling hand on Ramona's arm. "You'll be okay, and Delores will be better off now that her mother is dead and out of pain."

"The funeral procession took us out the Monterrey highway."

"It's a shame you had to go that way. It's a very busy road, especially on Saturday."

"Yes, it is, and no one respects the dead anymore. The cars, they sped past us, and the drivers, they cursed us. They shook their fists at the inconvenience."

"The nerve." Lilah turned her back and seated herself at the television set. "What's the world coming to?" she said as she turned it on.

Ramona left the room and returned with a plastic basket of clothes to be folded.

"Deaths always come in three's." She put the basket on the bed.

"Only an old wives tale," Lilah said over her shoulder, her attention directed to the program she wanted to watch.

Ramona wouldn't be distracted. "There have been two already."

"A superstition. Don't do this to yourself. Perk up! You are just depressed. It's natural to be sad after a funeral. Delores is your friend. You knew her mother."

"The procession was long and moving slowly. A man in a new car pulled around us, and as he passed my car, he hit a man."

She had Lilah's attention now, and she turned to look at Ramona.

"He killed him!"

"Did you see it?"

"I saw it for almost an hour."

She had started to separate out the towels. "I saw the walker before I saw the car. He was young, not a boy, a young man. He was an athlete.

He wore the clothes of a soccer player." She folded a towel in the middle and then into thirds.

"The driver didn't see the man?"

"No! He was looking at us. He was gesturing with his hand and shouting his disrespect for Delores and her mother, and all of us."

"You held him up and probably made him late for the soccer matches!"

"Don't make a joke of it, *Señora* Lilah! I saw the man's face. He saw the car, and he knew he had no chance. I can see it still. Perhaps I shall always see it."

There were two stacks of towels now, neatly, uniformly folded.

"Don't do that to yourself." Lilah's interest had become concern.

"He flew up into the air and hit the windshield with such force that it sent him bouncing back out in front of the car. A large crowd gathered. They penned us in. We couldn't get away, and the emergency attendants couldn't get through to help him. But it didn't matter. We knew he was dead. There was a lot of blood."

"What did you do?"

"There was nothing we could do. Someone came and put a handkerchief over his face, and then we waited. It was very hot and dusty. We had been crying. Now we were crying again."

"Did you go to the cemetery?"

"No, those ahead went on. We were too late. I was with Mary, and when we could get away, she took me to my sister's."

Lilah turned back to her television set, and Ramona left the room carrying the basket full of folded clothing to be put away. But she wouldn't let it go. She returned and stood at the door.

"Deaths always come in threes."

Lilah turned and gave her a stern look, "Don't do this."

"Before, the gray one had a saucer of milk when I had my morning coffee. We had coffee together every morning. I think she was Chinese. She folded her feet back neatly tucked under as she lay in the patch of light that fell on the floor before the window."

Lilah lost her patience, "She was French, you know she was French. She came from Belgium. You know that."

Ramona turned away. *She was Chinese. She was a calm and patient hunter. Not French.*

"*Señora* Lilah, cats have nine lives, *verdad*? That is what they say."

"Ramona, forget it. She's gone. She's gone and she isn't coming back. Don't be so superstitious."

She sleeps at the foot of my bed.

CHAPTER NINE

The mobile home was old. Its paint, no longer glossy, had faded to a powdery pale tint of the original color. It squatted on dusty old tires, blocked, and bare of skirts. This trailer, unlike Carl's, had no covered deck. Instead the metal door with its tiny window stood starkly naked of any covering to protect it from the weather. Four concrete blocks had been shoved up under the door, so the man stepped up to tap on the glass and then stepped down again to wait for a response. He heard sounds of young men mumbling and moving about, but he waited several minutes before any one appeared at the door.

"Oye! Carlos," he said when his cousin, a man in his mid-forties, at last stood above him at the open doorway. The short, dark, and very muscular Carlos was tucking a stiffly starched white dress shirt into his black Levis. It was late afternoon, and the low western sun beat directly into the open doorway. It picked up the gold conchos on his black belt and the gold metal tips on the long narrow toes of his black boots. His shirt was open to the waist and the highly faceted golden eagle pendant he wore on a long chain caught the light and glinted softly yellow.

Carlos didn't speak to his cousin, Amado, the man in the yard. He focused his attention on the tan colored Mercedes sedan that had pulled up savagely onto the narrow strip of what had been the previous owners modest lawn. From where he stood he could only see the driver who was leaning out of the open window and smiling up at him.

"So what's goin' on here?" the driver said, with wide-eyed innocence, indicating the three old cars also nosed in on the grass, "You havin' a party?" and he turned laughing to his companions in the back seat.

"Hey, Frank!" Carlos's mouth broke into a wide grin, flashing white teeth against the brown of his face. "Same 'ole, same 'ole!" he said, holding the door back and looking down at Frank Palma, a man he had once served with a subpoena and now that Carlos was no longer a deputy, had become a valuable business contact. Carlos stepped down and walked over to the car, his face still broken into a broad grin.

"It ain't even dark yet, your boys gettin' a early start?" Frank said. The trailer was still the object of their snickering laughter.

"Hell, no!" Carlos joked, bending down to get a look at who was in the back seat of the car. "These boys just don't know when to go home. It's more like they're gettin' a late stop!"

The men responded with loud guffaws. It was no secret what was going on in the trailer. Carlos, '*El Jefe*', was a Mexican Fagan and he seduced the boys with cocaine and sin.

Carlos acknowledged the dark men in the back seat with only a nod. He recognized the hired *pistoleros*, and so he ignored them and kept the banter up, focusing their attention away from himself and on the trailer.

"This old trailer's real popular with the boys," he drawled, "and, well," the eyebrows went up, and the dark eyes twinkled, he shrugged dramatically, "I guess it's just my magnetic personality."

Another round of course laughter.

"Well, they're young!" the driver quipped.

"Yeah, well, anyway," Carlos put his hand on top of the car and leaned close, "They was young!" he paused for the effect, and then added, "Them boys that keep hangin' around here, they grow up pretty fast. As a matter of fact, they was lookin' a lot like old men when I walked out of there!"

The driver abruptly stopped smiling, "Carlos, I got a easy pick up on five kilos of coke. You interested?"

"What, now?"

"Sure, we need to go now, or tonight, while we got it spotted."

Carlos looked back at the trailer and smiled.

"Naw," he grinned, "I don't think '*Las Ratas*' are goin' anywhere tonight."

The driver was deadly serious. He looked at Carlos intently and didn't laugh.

"We got it spotted now. Tomorrow, who knows?"

Carlos knew Frank hadn't brought the strong arms along because it was going to be a push over.

"You expecting any trouble?" he asked.

"Hell, no! The Gringo made the buy last night. He's soft and green." Frank shook his head, "He's dumber'n shit," then he added, "but it ain't no boy's job."

"Where's he got it?"

"What do you think? It's at his house. No problem."

"At his house" meant breaking and entering. For a job like this Carlos liked to send the boys. If everything didn't go off just right, being juveniles, they just got their wrists slapped, or at the very worst they were sent away to boot camp.

When he didn't get an answer right away, Frank pressed, "Come on, get in and go with us now. Later on tonight, we'll go on down there and do a little business, make it worth your time."

Carlos took a good hard look at the men in the back, and with only a moments hesitation, walked around and took a seat in the front. The car backed out and pulled away leaving his cousin Amado standing on the beat-down grass, amid the old cars, without so much as a wave goodbye.

CHAPTER TEN

Streetlights reflected off the sleek black Cadillac as Lilah guided it out of Chapin. She had been distracted all evening. The large, confident hands shuffled and dealt the cards subconsciously. She had to be reminded to bid when it was her turn. When she didn't win as usual, she didn't even notice. The conversation flew over her head. Now, on her way home she thought being alone wasn't the worst thing that could happen to you. If Allen was there, she faced another nasty confrontation. She knew he had spoken to a local lawyer, one who was developing tracts of low cost housing.

One thing about living in a town the size of Chapin, everyone knows your business. Probably, I was the last to get wind of it.

He had mentioned selling the place to her, a casual suggestion at first. "Mom, I'm a banker," he said. "Investing is my business."

"We're land poor." He went on. "The money in our equity should be put to work, Mom." He put his arm protectively around her shoulder. "You've worked so hard all your life," here came the squeeze, "cut back and let the money work for you. If you want me to help out here, then let me do what I know best. I'm an investment banker. Let me put the money to work."

He argued that water was short. It was a problem that would not improve as they allocated more and more water to the first priority, the needs of the growing population along this side of the river.

"We have to short change the cotton crop to water the citrus. It hardly matters because cotton prices are so low it barely pays to water it anyway."

"Squatters are moving in all around our property and controlling the cotton insects is now a liability." Personal injury lawsuits had been filed, and worse, won against large cotton farmers down by the river.

High property taxes would go higher, eating away at the paper-thin profit margins.

In the beginning she and Allen had frank and sincere discussions.

Later it became nagging criticism, and now the talk around the coffee pot at Glen Wade's said that he was planning to develop the property, all of it.

She could hardly remember the feeling of optimism she had had when Allen came back home. Not only had he disappointed her with his rejection of all she valued, but also lately he had become secretive. Now she knew it was even more than that. Her mind had just brushed over deceitful, until her farm manager had come in to tell her of his concern about Allen.

When she made attempts at conversation with Allen, he turned ugly and spiteful. "Did you have a good day?" could elicit a response of, "Do you mean did I do anything useful today?"

He didn't come home until after midnight. He stayed in his room until noon, and left. She had learned not to ask where he was going; his response was always mean and sarcastic.

"Mother," he might say, "I'm all grown up. I'm a big boy. I don't need your permission to go out any more."

For a while, she thought that was all there had been to it. She didn't think he had any friends. No one ever came around, and she had no idea where he went when he left. Now she knew the bitter truth.

My God! She thought. I tried to get him to stay and run the farm. There is no way he could ever run this farm. I could never turn this operation over to him. What was I thinking of anyway?

I was afraid he wouldn't stay, and now I can see he's in no mood to leave. I'm angry with him when he doesn't come home until all hours, and it's even worse when he's here.

The mean words were not what was on Lilah's mind tonight. Her hands gripped the wheel tightly, her jaw clenched as she considered the events of the last two days.

It had started out well. She had arisen to another beautiful summer day; a day that began with a tap on the kitchen door from her farm manager, Rolando.

"Rolando, come in and have a cup of coffee," she had said, expecting him to refuse. This time he stepped inside and joined her at the kitchen table.

Born on the property, Rolando had lived on her farm all his life. When Dick had grown too ill to work with the cancer that eventually took him down, this man had been her lifesaver. He had worked at Dick's direction for many years, and Lilah regarded him as a trusted friend as well as an experienced manager.

He made small comments about the operation, and she could tell he was hedging for time. He was talking all around what he had come to say.

"Lilah, are you going to sell the place?" he had asked.

"I have no intention of selling my farm." She stated emphatically. She didn't want him to have any doubts.

"You're not thinking of leaving me are you?"

"I'll stay if you stay!" he smiled, "But I just wanted to hear it from you."

Rolando stood, placed his cup on the counter, and moved to the door.

"And how about Allen? Will he be staying too?"

"I don't know. Would it make a difference to you if he left? He's not much help around here anyway."

"Allen is not well," he ventured cautiously.

"You mean he isn't happy here. Have you been talking to the men at Glen Wade's?"

"No, I mean he isn't well, and it isn't something I heard from the men down at the hardware store." He didn't tell her he had heard it at Garcia's, under the big tree, after beers and cabrito had moved the men to tell him what they knew about his employer's son.

"I think Allen may need help," he said. Respectfully, he didn't say, 'Lilah, open your eyes,' but they had a close relationship, developed through the years, and she got the picture.

She made it her business to see Allen before he left, and she watched him when she could the next two days.

Rolando knew her. He knew she wasn't about to sell her farm. He had come to tell her something else, something about Allen. She had observed him closely, and now she knew. She had gone through his things. She knew what she was looking for, and she found the neatly folded papers of cocaine.

The big car turned into the long drive, and she allowed it to idle slowly forward. The light in the living room was on. The car crept forward. The light in Allen's bedroom was on. Allen was home.

She entered the house through the kitchen door. She laid her purse on the table and moved through the darkened room toward the light in the living room. She was prepared for a confrontation with Allen, but the blow, when it came was from behind. Lilah never saw it coming.

***

"I knew you would want to know. I didn't want you to hear it on the radio."

Lilah's farm manager Rolando turned his gaze across the yard and into the field beyond. The tall man had removed his hat and his arm came up to towel away his glistening forehead. He continued squinting through the bright sunshine and away from Connie who stood above him at the door

"Lilah is dead? No, I can't believe it. I saw her last night. We played bridge. She was fine. Are you sure?"

"Yes, I'm sure. I found her myself." He held on to the grille. He didn't turn to leave.

"You found her?" Connie slid the door back and pushed the iron grille open.

"Rolando, please, come inside."

He hesitated, and then stepped into the room. The ever-on television set rattled away against a long wall with two recliners facing it. With the exception of the recliners and a round glass-topped game table and chairs, the furniture lined the walls in the large family room. Connie put the TV on mute and sat down at the glass-topped table. She motioned for Rolando to sit with her, but he refused the chair and stood with his hat in his hands.

The his-and-hers recliners, which were never sat upon, gathered dust in the room. Connie sat at the table in a straight-backed chair. She hadn't sat in her recliner since the night of Hank's heart attack. He had died in his.

"You found her? Where was she?"

"I came up early, like always," he evaded. "I saw the door ajar. That didn't seem right, so I pushed it open. I saw her. She was in the kitchen. I called the sheriff."

"Did you call an ambulance?"

"Connie, she didn't need an ambulance. I could see she was, well, she didn't need an ambulance." He looked down at his hat and didn't mention the gruesome details of the scene in the kitchen.

"And Connie, there's more. You're going to hear she didn't die of natural causes."

"What do you mean? How did she die?"

Rolando hesitated, unsure how to continue, she didn't need to know how he had stepped over Lilah's scattered teeth. It was a brutal blow.

"The Medical Examiner, he called it a homicide." Rolando didn't need to be told.

"I waited with her until they came to take her away and until the homicide detectives left. Now, I should be getting back."

Connie sat bolt upright, listening and trying to comprehend.

"Where is she now?"

"She would be at the funeral home, I guess. I think that's where they took her."

He had waited for them, alone in the early morning light. He stood in the yard and watched the ambulance pull up to the back, and he waited as the blue light flashed. No one had bothered to turn it off as they worked inside. He saw it crawl across the white of the house and stutter across the hibiscus plants. It lit up his shirt. The light was cold and blue. They covered her face, and they took her away.

"Well," he said edging for the door, "I guess I had better get back."

Connie ignored him; her mind was fixed on Lilah. "Strong, brave Lilah! You know her, she's the most competent and self-sufficient person I know. I wouldn't have thought this could happen to her, of all people."

The tall Mexican man said nothing; he too struggled to deal with the morning's events.

"Rolando, you're young." He was a middle-aged man in his mid forties. "You didn't know Lilah when she was young, during the war years. Well, I did. Dick went off to war and left her to run that farm alone, and she ran it until he came back. And he didn't come back until the war was over."

"She does alright without him now, too."

"Things were so different then. The men all went off to war, and somebody had to do the work. Those of us left behind here in the Valley kept busy trying to do it."

She was suddenly conscious to whom she was speaking and was

prompted to add, "And you know, we couldn't have done it without the Mexican laborers."

"All during the war, in August, when they picked the cotton, Lilah would have as many as a hundred Mexican men camping in her back yard sleeping on canvas cotton bags and cooking on disc plates, over mesquite fires. Just her and the two little girls and a hundred men from another country."

If Connie had thought about it, she would have guessed that Rolando's father had been one of them. He took a step toward the door, but Connie didn't acknowledge his effort at retreat.

"They didn't kill people, they came here to work. What's happening in this country? We're not even safe in our own homes any more. This country's going to hell in a hand basket!"

Rolando waited politely and let her go on.

"This isn't the country I remember."

"Yeah, I know," he said, "well, I guess I had better be getting back. I just thought you would want to know, that's all."

"Rolando, thank you. Allen could have called."

Rolando looked down at his feet; the pause was strangely uncomfortable.

Finally, Connie stood, "I guess he has other more important things to do than call me." It was mumbled under her breath, and more to herself than to him.

"Allen's gone; we don't know where he is." Rolando looked at her now and changed his tone. "He's gone, and so is the Cadillac."

"Really."

"He's gone somewhere in Lilah's car. The sheriff's going to call the girls."

"Does he know how to reach them?"

"He knows; he's probably already done it. He's had plenty of time to do it anyway. The coroner didn't come right away. We had to wait."

Rolando stepped outside the door, but he turned, not ready to leave.

"Connie," he hesitated, struggling to phrase it carefully, "they're looking for Allen."

"Of course."

"They want to question him."

"Really?"

"That's what they're saying, but you can tell it's more than that. The place wasn't vandalized. We couldn't see anything was stolen. Connie, they think Allen did it."

"Allen would never have killed his mother! Never!"

"Yeah, well."

Connie bristled at Rolando's luke-warm response, and added defensively, "I have known Allen all his life. He would never have done anything like that!"

Rolando's face broke into a big smile, "Of course not," he said and pushed his hat into place low on his forehead, giving the brim a sharp tug, turned and walked down the drive to his pickup.

It's always the Mexicans who get the blame, he thought, but he didn't argue with her. He didn't tell her, either, how he had heard the hot arguments between Allen and his mother. And he didn't mention seeing the telltale signs of Allen's growing cocaine habit.

Who knows what Allen is capable of, he thought, the spoiled rich jerk.

***

The television droned on, but Connie lit a cigarette and ran over what Rolando had said. Allen didn't do it, that she knew. Quite the contrary, she thought, it wouldn't have happened if he had been there. If he had been in the house, Lilah wouldn't have come in alone.

The ashtray overflowed, and the afternoon had slipped into evening when Puppy barked, and Mark sprang into action with a long rill of howling yaps. Carl's shadow passed over the door.

"Connie, have you been listening to the radio?"

"No," she said, glancing over to the television set he couldn't see. "But I know what you're going to say. Rolando came over to tell me about Lilah."

"Well, have you heard they found her car?"

"They found her car? What do you mean? What about Allen?"

"I don't know anything about Allen, I just know they found the car not far from here. I saw them tow it away. They found it on the bank of the drainage ditch where it crosses Sioux Road. It was pulled off the ditch road into the field and abandoned.

"I'm so sorry," his face registered concern. "What can I do to help? Anything?"

He ran his broken hand over his forehead and held it up to shade his eyes. She let him stand outside in the afternoon heat.

Only then the tears welled up. Of course, there was nothing they could do. She needed to be alone, and she rudely ushered him away.

***

Rolando rolled the window down and sat in the pickup. He had a man irrigating a field of young corn, and he parked in the field road to check on him. He watched as the Mexican in black rubber knee-high boots directed the water down as many as six rows at a time. When the water filled each row to the end, the man moved the tarpaulin dam farther down the dirt-banked canal. He then submerged the siphon tubes under the water before expertly flipping them over, one at a time, to start the water in six new rows.

The scene in the field took a back seat in Rolando's mind as he replayed the grizzly scene in the kitchen. He was awakend abruptly by the jolt of the truck as it idled into the ditch and started climbing the canal bank. He jerked the wheel savagely and threw the truck into reverse.

"What the hell does this matter anyway!" he cursed into the air as he backed recklessly down the dirt track to the road and turned onto the pavement.

Lilah's girls will sell the farm to developers now for sure, and I guess I'm out of a job. And Ramona, what will she do? Where will she go?

The irksome ache at the thought of her, and the very idea that he would think of Ramona now, well, it galled him, and he leaned on the accelerator. He crooked his arm out of the window and allowed the wind to rush in. He ignored the flapping shirtsleeve and pushed the pickup down the road at reckless speed.

It's not my problem, where she goes! Stubborn woman, she's always looking over my head for a suit.

Now his hopes were further dashed. He wasn't a white-collar kind of guy, and Ramona couldn't see him for nothing, and she sure as hell needed looking after; now he was going to be out of a job altogether. His whole life seemed to be going up in smoke.

He steered the truck into a space at Garcia's, bought a cold beer, and plopped himself down into a white plastic chair out back. He was on his third beer when Raul showed up.

Raul managed a thousand acres of melons west of Encino and way the hell out there almost to Rio Grande City for a large packer in Edinburg. It was out there in the scrub brush and sandy soil where they had to use drip irrigation to keep them alive. Good looking and popular, Raul walked with a swagger and flashed a ready smile. When he came into town he had plenty of time to slap all the backs and entertain everybody with his tales of snakes and wetbacks and encounters with the border patrol.

Comfortable, and at home in his western cut clothes, Raul cut a colorful figure. They all enjoyed seeing him when he came. He sat down by Rolando on the patio, and three men appeared out of nowhere to join them. Raul was well aware of his own popularity, loved the attention, and he never let them down.

He laid a booted leg across a chair and said, "You know, them snakes travel in pairs. Yeah, they mate fer life, no kiddin! When you kill one of 'em, you better look out, 'cause there'll be another one around there somewhere, and he'll get you if you ain't payin' attention."

Now, when you're talking about snakes in south Texas, everyone stops to listen. The more experienced your audience, the more interested they are. They have all had an encounter, and they each have a tale of their own.

"You know, when we work the fields, we stir 'em up. Last week, I come up on one stretched across the road. He was so big that his head was on one side and his tail was on the other." He paused a minute to let them think about how big that was before he continued.

"He was a *grandote,* and I was gonna' get 'em! So I speeded up, and just before I hit him, I threw on the brakes, and skidded across that sucker right in the middle, and I heard him knock against the bottom of the bed."

"When I looked back, I could see he wasn't dead, but he was hurt, so I threw her in reverse and backed over him. I still didn't kill him, so I ran over him again. This time when I looked back, I could see him flippin' and twistin'. I knew the roadbed was too sandy and I wasn't never gonna' kill him that way."

"So I got out of the truck and got my sharp shooter. I was gonna' cut the head off that big bastard when I heard buzzin', and rattlin' right under my feet and there was his *señorita*."

Raul took this moment to swig at his beer and looked around the men. Every eye fastened on him. No one said, "What happened!" but the question hung in the air, and Raul let it hang there before he grinned and continued.

"Man, I bet you didn't know I could fly! Now, didya? Well, you'd a thought so if you'd a been there. I put one hand on the sideboard and vaulted up into the back of that pick-up truck so fast you would 'a thought I was flyin'.'"

Raul chuckled and added, "I looked like a Walenda!"

They howled with laughter, and he wound it up with, "I'm tellin' you man, they pair up fer life."

Rolando watched all this, and he thought about Raul's swaggering walk in his high-topped boots with the Levis tucked in. Those boots covered the calves of his legs and came up to just under his knees.

Raul is having a good time with us, but he works out there where if it doesn't stick ya, it'll bite ya. He fights the sand and wind and he wears snake boots. I guess he has to; he works knee deep in rattlers.

Rolando looked down at his canvas and rubber tennis shoes, and the reality of what a posh job he was about to lose rang in his head clear as all git out.

CHAPTER ELEVEN

Lilah's murder caused intense interest and speculation in the community until weeks passed without an arrest. Newspaper coverage dwindled and finally ceased. Allen disappeared and no one had seen him. Talk of it continued around the coffee pot at Glen Wade's, but with no new information, that too became pointless.

Carl had seen the sheriff's men tow the car away. They wouldn't tell him anything beyond that it didn't seem strange to them that Allen would have abandoned the car and fled the scene on foot.

It did, however, seem strange to Connie, so she made it her business to be home before dark. Connie carried her supper into the family room and ate at the game table. She watched television until bedtime, ten thirty, or so, after the news and weather. She gave up bridge, at least for a while, maybe forever.

She had become accustomed to riding with Lilah. The two of them had begun to find they had more in common than they could have guessed. The thirty minutes each week they spent in the car gave them a chance to discover these commonalities. They laughed and had fun. Connie missed that. Lilah had not shared with Connie the difficulties Allen caused her. Instead she mentioned mundane everyday incidents that reminded Connie of her own lonely existence.

When Allen had returned, Connie could see how happy Lilah was. Lilah just never mentioned the struggle that developed between them. Now, as Connie missed Lilah, she decided to give up the weekly bridge game. It was too painful.

She didn't replace the headlamp. Who needs it? she thought. Actually, she preferred to evade dealing with the real reason she didn't leave at night anymore.

On rare occasions, she broke the rule and went out with family or friends and came in after dark. She was all right after she got in the house, and settled with the lights on, but there was always that moment when she unlocked the iron grille, and slid the door back, just before she stepped into the house, when Lilah came into her mind.

This isn't how I want to remember her, and anyway I have two dogs.

She glanced down affectionately at her old terrier and saw him standing at the door to the living room, the pathway to the staircase and bed.

"Mark," she said, "you're becoming a tyrant in your old age! I'm not ready to go to bed yet."

Mark held his head down and his eyes were at half-mast.

"Sleep on the floor," she said to him affectionately, "I'm not going until this movie is over. You'll just have to wait."

The aging dog didn't hear too well and continued to stand at the door. Finally, he waddled back across the room on stiff legs and lay down at her feet. She reached over and stroked his head absentmindedly as she continued to watch the movie that he had interrupted.

"Sorry, dear," she said when the movie ended. She gathered up the dishes and carried them into the kitchen before going up to bed. At the foot of the stairs she bent down and picked him up, holding him under one arm, clasped the rail as they climbed the stairs together.

Her family expressed concern at her living alone in the country, especially since Lilah's death.

"I'm not alone!" she would say, "I have a watchdog right here in the house."

It's none of their business, anyway.

"Mark's old, but he's a barker."

Where else would I live?

"Terriers are very intelligent you know."

They want me to sell my house and move into a condo like Dottie.

The old dog slept in the bed with her. He snored like an old man, and slept so soundly he wasn't much of a watchdog any more. His hearing was going, but not his bark. Mark was still a barker.

***

A pulsing beat welled up within her. Connie woke to the anxious feeling; she had lost count. Four, five, or six, no seven, eight, nine, and now her lips were forming the numbers, ten, eleven, and finally she called out loud, "TWELVE!"

Mark heard her and raised his head. Together they listened to the echo of the clock's chimes still hanging in the air until the house fell into a profound silence. Connie lay very still, but only the ticking of the great clock on the landing traveled up the stairs. Its familiar measured beat should have had a calming effect, but the feeling of anxiety persisted.

Years ago they installed a security light on a tall pole in the front yard. It came on at dusk and went off at dawn. Its eerie green light filtered into the bedroom. She lay in the dimly lit room and listened.

She had become so accustomed to the sound of the clock striking the hour in the night that she usually didn't hear it anymore. Tonight it intruded as in a dream.

She must have been awake when it began to strike. Something other than the big old clock had broken her sleep. What? Something. Something she couldn't remember. She held her breath and listened.

Puppy began barking out at the back, not necessarily anything to worry about. Puppy's barks became more urgent, and she heard voices, men's voices at the kitchen door. Mark sprang to his feet, and began a series of ferocious, howling barks.

She grabbed the dog, holding him close to her to keep him quiet so she could hear. She heard, there was no mistake, the kitchen door being opened roughly, with force, and men entering the kitchen. They were laughing and talking to each other in Spanish.

Their alien voices carried up the stairwell. Mark jerked himself free, bolted to the edge of the bed and barked shrilly. Connie desperately tried to hush him. She pushed him down and over on his side. She rolled him in the bedspread. The barking stopped, temporarily, but he continued to resist. Surprised at his strength, she struggled to hold him, to keep him quiet.

Maybe they'll think nobody's home.

Connie held her breath and listened as the talking continued unbroken downstairs. No reaction.

Maybe they didn't hear.

But she knew they did. Mark's shrill yaps couldn't have been missed.

Over her beating heart she heard several voices, at least three. Laughing, they moved into the foyer, then stopped at the foot of the stairs. She held her breath.

Oh, God!

They moved on into the living room.

Mark still struggled. She pressed her leg over him pinning him to the mattress, and reached for the telephone. The line was dead.

Fumbling with the telephone, and dealing with her terror, she allowed the dog to squirm away. He leaped down from the bed and ran across the room, barking all the way. Frantic, she chased him out of the bedroom and down the hall. Just before he began his descent onto the staircase, she caught him by a back leg.

She snatched him up, put her hand around his muzzle, and brutally held his mouth closed as she crushed his struggling body to hers. Connie leaned back, pressed her body against the wall and listened. It was a straight shot down the stairs. She was in plain view of anyone who stepped into the foyer and looked up.

She held her breath and waited. Not a sound came from downstairs. They had heard; they were listening, too. She had no idea what to expect next so she waited, frozen, not daring to move.

Mark quit struggling. He may even be dead, she thought. She kept her hand tightly closed around his muzzle, and waited. Her eyes were fixed on the arch leading into the living room. Then abruptly, the activity downstairs resumed.

They're not afraid of me. I'm helpless. They know it.

She heard a crash as they pulled a drawer out and dumped the contents on the floor.

They're not coming up, not now anyway.

She leaned forward and strained her eyes at the arch as she backed away to the bedroom, barefooted and walking on tiptoes, not breathing at all.

She looked around the room for a place to hide.

Under the bed, that's too easy!

Still carrying the dog, she pulled the bedspread into the closet, and closed the door behind them. In the darkness she tried to rearrange the hanging clothes to hide them best as she could before sitting down to await her fate.

She continued to hold Mark tightly to her, although he was quiet now. She knew he was alive; she felt his breathing. The clocks began to chime, half past something, probably midnight or one.

They moved back into the foyer and then on into the kitchen. She heard the refrigerator door opened and slammed shut, and the laughter carried up the stairs.

They roamed through the house opening drawers and dumping the contents of her bookshelves, pawing through her things.

They're so casual, she thought. They don't even try to be quiet. All I can do is sit here and hope they don't come up and kill me.

Oh God! Please God!

At last, she heard the patio door open; they came and went through it. Finally a car backed down the drive.

Are they gone?

She didn't dare hope, and there was no hurry anyway. Fatigue had at last dulled her panic. Exhausted, she spent what was left of the night clutching the dog on the floor in the closet. When morning finally came, she crawled out, cramped and stiff, grateful to be alive.

CHAPTER TWELVE

Connie stepped up on the small covered porch of Ignacio's white frame house. A large plate glass window opened the living room to a view of anything that happened on the road. Ignacio had been standing at the window drinking a cup of coffee when he saw her coming across the yard, and opened the door before she could knock.

"Hi Connie," he said, his face broken in a big smile. His wife moved into the room and stood at the kitchen door to watch. Connie rarely came to this door, especially so early in the morning.

"Come in," he said opening the door, and stepping back so she could enter.

"Ignacio, could I please use your phone? My line has been cut. I need someone to come out and fix it."

"Sure," he said. "It's cut? What happened?"

"Well, Ignacio, I've been robbed. They came in last night and cleaned me out. They even took my car. The place is a mess. They cut the phone line."

"Oh! Connie! Come in! Please! Sure, sure!"

"I don't have a car or a phone, and I need to call the sheriff, too."

"Were you there?"

"Mark and I were upstairs."

"Are you OK?"

"They didn't come up the stairs, thank God!"

"Come in, come in! Claudia, get Mrs. Rogers a cup of coffee."

She smiled ironically, "They took just about everything but the coffee pot. It took a while before I realized they didn't cut the electric lines. They simply turned the power off at the box when they left. I've been up since dawn, and if I'm going to talk to the sheriff, I guess I could use a cup of coffee. Thanks."

Ignacio walked back across the road with her, and she waited nervously at the door for the deputies. She saw them as they slowly approached the house.

The patrol car barely moved; the deputies gave the house a good looking over. The slowly moving car sent Puppy into a rage, and Connie stepped out onto the porch to restrain her so they could enter.

"I have left things as they were," she said, "I thought that would be the thing to do."

The older of the two deputies took charge, stiff and officious and properly businesslike as he took her statement. His uniform, stretched tightly to his barrel chest, was neatly pressed. He removed his big Stetson and held it in his hands as he stood in the doorway listening to her story without expression or comment.

Together they walked through the disheveled rooms. The cushions had been jerked off the sofa and she picked them up as they passed.

"I guess they thought I would hide something there," she said. "If I had any money, it wouldn't be hidden in the sofa! What were they looking for anyway?"

The second deputy went about the business of taking fingerprints. He dusted a black powdery substance on the glass top of the table, and lifted it up with a tape. He then placed the pieces of tape on a card. Ignacio stood silently against the wall like an intruder watching the deputies. His presence was noted by the friendly finger printer, "This is not so bad," he said, "Sometimes they vandalize the place. I've seen them cut the sofa up, and spray paint the walls and everything."

When they finished the tour, the man in charge told Connie, "I'll need a list of the things they took. You can bring it by the station when you've finished it. I'll put it in my report. You're gonna need it for the insurance company.

"Did you keep the serial numbers off the television set and VCR? If you don't have positive identification, you can't expect to get anything back."

"How about my husband's guns? He had a collection of hunting rifles and shotguns, also a German pistol from the war. Some of the things they took don't have serial numbers."

"They're gone now. Even if we should recover something you recognize, we have to have a positive ID. And anyway it'll belong to the insurance company by then.

"I have title to my car."

"Sure, that's good, but we may never recover it. It's probably in Mexico by now."

"It was after midnight, and I don't drive after dark," she said. "My car has only one headlight."

"Then they won't drive it very far. We may find it around here someplace. Do you have any idea who might have done this? Did you get a look at them?"

"No, they didn't come up the stairs, thank God. They were speaking Spanish."

The deputy was filling out the report as they spoke. Merely routine, he had heard it all before. Connie's anger rose at his detached attitude. She had after all, been personally violated. Her life had been threatened, and he just stood there filling out a silly form.

"They were men, probably young men," she added, and her voice betrayed her irritation with him.

He nodded, and didn't look up.

The deputy taking the prints remarked, "I think I got a good one here on this bottle."

He held up the two liter plastic Coke bottle he had been printing. He nodded toward the patio doors, "I took some off the glass doors, there, they may or may not be so good," and looking back, "but, this is a good one. I think they had a party here." An empty bag of potato chips lay amidst the clutter on the table, and greasy fingerprints proliferated.

Connie could see the prints on the glass tabletop and wondered, since they had not taken hers, how they would know which ones were which?

Well, they're the experts.

The experts looked pretty young to her.

With the report filled out, and the prints taken, the man in charge handed her a business card with his name on it.

"Keep this card. This, here," he pointed, "is your case number. If you need to speak to someone, you'll need it," he told her.

"It looks like the work of kids," he said, and then he warned, "They'll probably be back. They expect you to replace the things they took. They know you will. They'll give you a month or so, then they'll be back."

He looked about the room. "This is a high profile house. They've already cased it. You'd better make plans to leave. It wouldn't be safe for you to stay here any longer. They're sure to come back."

"Leave?" Connie gave him a hard look. "What do you mean leave? Leave my home? Leave my property? I'm not going to leave."

"Well," he said, "You'd better think about that before you decide for sure."

He saw her rising anger and turned to go, but she spoke sharply, "They are young men, not kids. You have their prints. Surely you can arrest them before a month."

"You may not have a month. They know you're old and alone. You're vulnerable. You can't stay here safely any longer. They'll come back, and we can't protect you."

She watched them collect their things. She watched them walk across the lawn and get into the county's patrol car with the rack of lights, and the sheriff's insignia painted on its side. And, finally she watched them back away and drive down Morningside Road.

"We can't protect you," he had said. What did he mean, "We can't protect you?"

He stood there with his badge and nickel-plated pistols, and the authority of the county behind him, and he said, "You are old and alone. You are vulnerable. It looks like the work of kids, and we can't protect you."

"Well, Lilah," Connie spoke aloud, "I guess you were right! I guess we'll just have to do it ourselves."

***

"Mother, where is the car?" Susan asked.

"The sheriff had it towed in. It's at a wrecking yard on the highway south of Edinburg. I owe them $125.00."

"Where did they find it?"

"You know it wasn't very far from here. They pulled it off by the drainage ditch and into a field off Sioux Road."

"Wasn't that where they found Lilah's car?" It wasn't a question. It was a statement of fact.

"I didn't see where they found Lilah's car, and I didn't see exactly where they found mine. It's at the yard on South 281."

"Mother, that's where they ditched Lilah's car. It's too much of a coincidence."

Connie began placing her things back in her purse. "Would you look at this! Here's my Visa. They only took my drivers license and my social security card! Why do you suppose they didn't take the Visa?"

The running argument was on again, this time in earnest. Connie's son John, and daughter Susan, sat at the table with her, and they had her two on one. This time they determined to prevail.

"Mother, maybe these same men killed Lilah. Now, Mom, you can't stay out here alone. It's too dangerous out here in the country. You need to come to town," Susan said, and John nodded in agreement.

Connie held her white head erect, and her blue eyes blazed at the affront. "How can I do that?" She said in a firm voice, "I can't afford to move to town."

"Mother, you have to. You have no choice, and you can afford it. For what you can get for this thirty acres and house, you can afford it. You can live with me until we can sell this place."

Connie rolled her eyes in exasperation and said, "How can I sell my home? I have responsibilities here. How about Puppy? She can't live in town. And what about my cats?"

"Mother! Get your priorities right. They are pets, animals. This is a crisis for you, and it is one for them as well."

"We don't know for sure that the same men did it."

"Well, we can find out! Give me the card the deputy left you, and I'll call to see if the fingerprints matched."

Susan called the sheriff's office, gave the receptionist the case number, and asked to speak to officer Martinez.

"You may speak to a detective. Martinez isn't here. Anyway, no one has been assigned to this case."

"What? No one is investigating?"

She said, "We don't assign an officer to a case unless we have a lead," and quickly transferred the call.

"Detective Trevino, this is Susan Sheppard, I am Mrs. Rogers' daughter. Would it be possible to see if the fingerprints in Mother's car match the one's from Lilah Byrd's car. They ditched her car in the same place; we think it's a strange coincidence. Could it have been the same men?"

"We didn't print the car."

"Are you kidding? It was a stolen car, why not?"

He replied, "We only take prints from stolen cars when there's a special request for them."

"Who makes the request? Was it up to us? We didn't know."

"It wasn't up to you."

"I'm requesting it now," she said.

"It isn't up to you, and it's too late anyway. The car is contaminated now. It had to be done at the site, before it was towed in. No one had been assigned to the case, so there could be no request for fingerprinting."

"Really! How are you ever going to catch them, and if you do, what then? How can we convict them without evidence such as this?"

"Fingerprints are useless, we can't check a person's fingerprints unless we have 'cause'. Even if we know he's the perpetrator, we can't check them. Moreover, if we find your mother's car keys in his pocket, and we know they're hers, we can't use them unless we can show 'cause'. If somehow we got past that, the charge would be possession of stolen property, not theft. We couldn't hold him."

He added, "It's the protection of the law afforded all citizens."

"Thank you," Susan said before hanging up the phone.

When she had repeated the conversation, she said, "Can you believe I thanked him! They can't protect you, Mother, but they sure look out for the crooks who robbed you."

They were back where they started. Susan's voice softened, "Mother, you can't stay here. You just can't."

"I've lived here more than forty years. I plan to die in this house. Hank and I lived here, and he died in this room," Connie gestured to the chair where he died, "right there in that chair! I'm not leaving."

"Mother, the deputies said they'll come back. They will come back, and next time they may not leave you alone." Susan's hand was on her arm, "Mother, this is dangerous, they might kill you!"

Susan knew her mother was a principled person. Of course she understood the danger. They negotiated over the price she was willing to pay for her principles.

"You very well may die in this room if you stay."

"This is my land, I've worked all my adult life to pay for it, and I will not be driven off by a pack of hoodlums and their willing allies in the sheriff's department. If I leave, they're sure to come back and vandalize the house. Then I'll have nothing. I'll put the house on the market, but I'm not leaving until it sells."

That sounded pretty final, but they had made some progress. They had gotten her to say they could put the house on the market. Reluctant to give it up, Susan said, "You're right, if you go, they may come back and vandalize your house. If you stay, they may come back and kill you, how about that?"

Connie paused only a minute, looked directly at her son and said, "John will buy a pistol for me." She added emphatically, "I'll protect myself!"

"There are more than one of them," the daughter pointed out, "You heard them. Three? You'll be outnumbered. Can you handle three men?"

"I'll stay upstairs."

"What if they come up the stairs? What then?"

She responded, "I'll wait at the top of the stairs and shoot them one at a time as they clear the landing."

It was a game now. She had already decided. "And if they set fire to the house?"

She smiled broadly and said, "I'll have a rope ladder made. I'll keep it under the bed with my pistol." It was hopeless.

"Will you come and stay with me until we get you a car?"

"Yes, I'll do that, and I'll need a TV. We should call the insurance agent. I guess the real estate agent, too. I need to get Ignacio to do something about the kitchen door, and, John, buy me a pistol today, before you leave."

John bought her the gun. They were afraid not to.

CHAPTER THIRTEEN

Allen turned up. A man irrigating a sugar cane field south of Runn, less than a mile from the river, found his body. He had two bullet wounds to his chest. No one was surprised except maybe the sheriff.

Inquiries led to his old high school friend, Frank Palma, a man with a history of arrests for small time drug dealing. Frank had never been convicted of anything as serious as murder. The primary focus of the sheriff's investigation, he began to tap dance his way out.

Frank told of going out to the Byrd house with two hired gunmen, Pablo Acosta and Raul Quirarte. He knew of five kilos of cocaine Allen Byrd had bought, and they thought he had stashed it in his house.

"I hung around while they cased the house," he told, "then I left Pablo and Raul to look for the drugs."

He swore his innocence, "Hey, I don't know nothing about no murder. Nobody was home when I was there. When Allen drove up I thought I better get lost, so I left. I don't know nothing about no murder."

"Who else was with you?" he was asked.

"Nobody! Hell, man, you think I'm crazy! We were just casing a house, we didn't need no help," he lied. The truth is that Carlos Medrano had threatened to kill him if he involved him in the investigation, and Frank had every reason to believe he would do it.

David Ocampo and Eddie Ruiz were sent out to serve warrants for the arrest of the *pistoleros*. They went in the early morning when it would be quiet. A lot of kids lived in this neighborhood in the south of Alamo. The small houses had tiny yards filled with used up appliances, broken lawn furniture, children's toys and old cars. Two-ton trucks and pickups with campers lined the street, nosed in to the chain link fences that circled many of the houses. Other old cars sat on blocks over a bed of weeds, or under the shade of a tree when there was one. It was a poor neighborhood. Mostly immigrants. Undocumented. Unsavory characters would go unnoticed in this squalor, and if they were, no one was likely to report them to the police.

When they found the white frame house, it had an abandoned look, but a new Cadillac was parked in the drive. Hip-high weeds grew in the yard, and paper shades were drawn down on the windows. Ruiz stepped up on the small porch and checked the windows flanking the door. Dead calm. He opened the screen and knocked on the door as Ocampo went around to the back.

His knuckles on the wood resounded loudly in the silent yard. No one came so he tried again, but the house remained quiet. He didn't wait for the answer he sensed wasn't coming; he kicked in the door and leaned against the frame with his pistol at the ready. He got no response so he stepped cautiously inside.

When Ocampo went to the back, he saw the door ajar. He waited until he heard the cracking sound of the door being dispatched. He gripped his pistol and moved quietly, cautiously through the house. He could smell their presence, but he knew the men had fled out the back before their arrival. They had missed them only by minutes.

They went back to the station, but Ocampo had an idea. It nagged away at him for about an hour before he acted on it. They're headin' for Mexico, Ocampo thought, and they've got a lead, but they're on foot. The car's in the yard. They could pick up another one, but I don't think so. They know we'll stop them at the bridge if they try to cross there. My guess is they'll cross on foot. If I guess right, I can cut 'em off at the river before they make it across. They won't be walking down the highway, so they'll head for the cover around the water district lake.

Ocampo knew the strip around the lake. The water district left it in brush. Tall grass grew in the breaks between the huisache and mesquite trees, and it was peppered all throughout with prickly pear cactus and assorted other thorny scrub. You had only to go a few feet past the shoreline before it got pretty dry, and the dryer the rougher.

The trail would stay pretty well intact through the brush, and he knew they would have to stay on it. It would cross out of the county property, and then they'd be in privately held farmland. The land south of the county property was planted in fields of maize, cantaloupe and sugar cane down to a green belt along the river. They'd have to cross the Military Highway, probably at Runn, before they could make the cover of the brush line that followed the river. Once they made the cover, they'd want to stay on the trail through the mesquite.

Ocampo picked up his Stetson, and walked out alone. In the patrol car, he cut over to Alamo Road and headed south, taking his time; he knew where he was going.

As was the custom in South Texas, the deputy drove wearing his big, white Stetson hat. Even in an unmarked car he could be identified as law enforcement.

Ocampo turned east on the Military Highway. It ran parallel to the river, more or less, all the way to Brownsville. The old river took some pretty good loops. There were places where you could cross and still be in the United States. He knew every loop and ford on the river. It was his territory.

He neared Runn, an old settlement south of Donna, now mostly just a school and a *colonia*. It was only a mile from the river, not far from where the track would cross over, and he slowed the car carefully scanning the fields. This area was river delta where the soil was heavy, not suitable for citrus, so it was all under cultivation.

On the south side of the highway two men were irrigating a field of sugar cane, and he gave them a good looking over as they leaned on their shovels in their knee-high rubber boots. They were interested in him, too, and their heads followed his car as he passed. This field was where, he supposed, they had found Byrd.

He turned south, and eased the car onto a dirt farm road that bordered a maize field. At the end of the field, the road narrowed to two tracks and continued into the brush. It ran down to a pump that the farm owner, McCormick, had on the river.

He bounced along the crude lane searching the mesquite as he drove. If the men had been in there, they'd have heard the car on the rough road, and then it would have been *adiós*. But if they were on foot as he suspected, there was no way they could have crossed the highway yet.

Before he got to the pump, he pulled the car off into the brush. The thorny limbs dug long scratches in its sides as he eased it deep into the thicket. He winced at the damage, but didn't stop until he was sure it was well hidden.

An experienced officer, Ocampo had learned not to take chances out in the brush alone with a killer. Now it would be two on one. Before he got out of the car, he reached into the glove compartment and removed his insurance policy, a little .38 special snub nose. He stood up and clipped the small holster onto his belt. The little Bianci holster had a thumb release on the guard strap; he tested the snap, and patted it into place. Out there alone, the situation could turn on you. He could keep this little handgun concealed and could draw and fire it in a single motion, if he needed to. His business weapon was a .357 magnum he wore in his holster. He kept it clean and oiled. It was an automatic; he could count on it.

Ocampo walked around the pump and gave the ground a good looking over. Set up on the bluff side, the high bank protected it from flood. They had carved a slot into the clay soil so they could run a ten-inch pipe down from it to the water thirty feet away.

They'd have an easy walk up the road to cross the river here, he thought. They might do that, but the river is deep here and they'll be looking for a ford and cover, More'n likely they'll stay on the trail through the brush and cross at the ebony. Ocampo left the pump and moved east into the thicket, walking carefully, holding the limbs back with his hands and elbows, watching for cactus and snakes.

Before the dams, the river meandered unrestricted and in time of flood often changed course. He followed an old dry riverbed. It led him in an easterly direction generally and looped back around to the south. Between the loop and the river, the land was rough and marshy, untillable. It never had been cleared; there was no point in it.

A black bean ebony tree, an old timer, grew on this *banco* and drew traffic from across the river. Probably three hundred years old, the big old tree towered over the mesquite brush around it. Its deep, dark green leaves contrasted sharply with the light green of the mesquite and the willows that grew along the riverbanks. The old landmark could be seen clearly from the Mexican side. A path led up to it from the river and continued through the brush belt to the cultivated land. The canopy of the great ebony was ninety feet across. Its fine, dense leaves created a large shady area, which had become a refuge. Ocampo stepped in under the tree and looked up at its gnarled and weathered trunk.

South Texas natives, ebony trees are tough and hardy, but also woody and brittle. Usually broken branches litter the ground under them along with the big, hard black beans they produce. He saw relatively little of that under this tree. Those familiar with the area called it 'the bedroom'. Ocampo thought of this as his eyes traveled down to the clear area under the tree. He could see the sparkle of broken glass in the hard packed ground. Cigarette butts and other signs and smells of human activity lay about. Men had waited here. Wetbacks.

Ocampo looked for fresh footprints but didn't see any. He walked up the trail apiece and still didn't see any in the soft, sandy path. They hadn't been here yet. But he was sure they were on their way.

He moved on up the trail to where he found a dense growth of scrub and a place where he had a view of the trail and also cover for himself. He settled in to wait.

***

At dusk they finally came walking down the path. He hadn't counted on them stopping in at Runn for water and perhaps arranging for a pick-up on the other side. But here they were at last. He waited for them to make the tree before he stepped out onto the trail to confront them.

"Hey! *Pendejos!*" He said, "*¿Dónde vas?*"

The two men were much alike, short and stocky. At the sound of Ocampo's voice, they turned and waited for him to come forward.

Quirarte walked over and leaned against the tree, but Acosta stood and reached into his shirt pocket for a pack of cigarettes he carried there.

"We're crossing," he said. Ocampo allowed him to light his cigarette before he told them, "You're not going anywhere. The sheriff's looking for you."

"That's what we hear," Quirarte smirked, and the two men chuckled.

"He wants to ask you some questions."

"Yeah, that's his problem!" They snickered, but when they got no reaction from the scowling Ocampo, they changed tone, "Listen man, we're not gonna tell him nothing."

"You sure of that?"

"Hell, yes, we're not talking to nobody."

"That's right!"

"We're going to cross."

"No, you're not. You're not going anywhere."

The smug expression was gone from both faces, and they were

deadly earnest now. Acosta let the cigarette slip out of his hand, and it fell unnoticed at his feet. "We told you, we're not talking."

"You got that right."

They got the picture, and started to run. They didn't make it out to the brush before Ocampo took Quirarte down with a single shot. But Acosta stumbled and slid down the path's trough through the low bluff and made the river.

He slogged through the shallow water where the current was swift, and it dragged at him and slowed him enough so Ocampo caught him before he could get into the deep of the stream and away.

The struggle was short. Ocampo had trained for just this situation, and he was the larger and more fit of the two. He pinned the man's arm behind his back, forced him to his knees, then pushed his face down into the muddy, stirred up water. He held him struggling there in the shallows minutes after the last bubbles of air had broken the surface, longer than necessary. He had no love for this scum. He stood on the bank for a few minutes and watched the shallow water wash over and finally carry the body down stream.

Acosta's death would be called an accidental drowning while attempting to escape. Quirarte, the newspapers would report, was still at large. His body was never found.

CHAPTER FOURTEEN

J udge Tomas Uresti sat alone that evening and thought over the day's events, a day that had left him with mixed feelings. Old friends had called on him at his office. He'd expected them. Lilah's daughters, Helen and Ruth, were making a lot of fuss, and he knew they would come around.

Dick Byrd had been a community leader. He had been a deacon in the church. He had done his civic duty and served a term on the school board. A prominent family, they had money and while Dick lived he had connections with important political figures in the county. The investigation into the murders of their mother and brother was dragging, and they were out pulling all the strings.

Uresti had been informed they visited their congressional representative, and he could expect to hear from them, too. They mentioned Frank Palma everywhere they went.

When he got the call for an appointment, the judge wasn't surprised and he was glad to see them. The younger of the two, Helen, had been his classmate in high school. McAllen was a small town in those days. He expressed his heartfelt regrets over the murders, and assured them that although no one had been arrested, they could expect justice to prevail, eventually.

They complained to him that the 'proper legal channels' didn't seem to be making any progress and pressure from above might be needed. He knew it was coming and drew a breath when it did. They had no idea what a spot they put him in when they asked for his help.

A judge should avoid even the appearance of impropriety, he explained as diplomatically as he could. Any interference from him would be grossly unethical and read as meddling in the business of the district attorney.

Uresti's hands were clasped on the desk, and his erect posture didn't betray his feelings of the moment. Extenuating circumstances rendered his influence of little use. The district attorney had an iron in the fire, and any suggestion from him would go nowhere, he was sure.

Later, the meeting took on a social flavor. They reminisced about high school and friends they had in common, old times. Dick Byrd had been his sponsor. Uresti began his career as a young lawyer for the county's most prestigious law firm, largely due to Byrd's influence. He regretted that he couldn't return the favor, but under the circumstances, they could surely understand his restraint.

Upon Allen's marriage, Uresti had written their brother's will. The girls expressed their concern about Allen's son and his inheritance. This subject took up the greater part of the time he spent with the two of them as they filled him in on Allen's vitriolic divorce.

The marriage came late in Allen's short life, and it too, was short. It lasted long enough to produce a son, who at twelve years of age lived with his mother, her new husband, and their two children.

Since the divorce, or maybe because of it, Allen had descended into unexplainable irresponsibility and what they described as depression.

After the marriage went south, so did his job, and finally his shocking murder ended a life that had spiraled steadily downward. Allen's negligent behavior led them to wonder if he had amended his will after the rancorous divorce. Helen expressed her concern for her nephew's financial well-being.

They didn't limit their criticism to their brother. They described the boy's stepfather as a reckless dreamer who owed 'everybody in town'. He was a schemer, they said, and they wondered if the boy's inheritance would be gambled away on some crazy speculation.

Uresti listened to their complaints and decided to look into it when they had gone. Sure enough the will had not been updated.

Their visit brought back memories of times when things were simple. Back when he had a good grasp on what he needed to do, what he wanted to do, and how to do it.

Well, things change.

It was late in the evening, and the judge had doused all the lights except the ones over his paintings, resulting in a soft gallery-like atmosphere. He sat in his big leather wingback chair and leaned across to the arm-side table. He lifted the lid of a heavily carved walnut humidor and selected an Arturo Fuente cigar, one of the indulgences he enjoyed as a benefit of being single. He could smoke a cigar in the house or anywhere else he damned well pleased.

His thoughts drifted with the aromatic smoke, and he looked across to the least valuable of all his collection of Spanish colonial paintings, his favorite. The painting of Saint Jerome was small and usually overlooked by visitors to his home.

Visitors, mostly his political cronies, had uneducated tastes and they mistook the primitive quality of the paintings as inferior draftsmanship. They dismissed them as restaurant level decoration. Tomas got a sense of satisfaction from this exposure of their ignorance. The paintings were genuine, mostly done in the sixteenth century and represented an investment that would have astonished even the most astute of the bunch.

Tomas lived in a townhouse in the La Resaca development, a gated Spanish colonial revival along a man-made resaca in McAllen. The rooms were lofted and the developer had imported doors, beams and tiles from old buildings and churches in Mexico. Tomas filled his house with the Spanish and Peruvian paintings as he acquired them. Because the subject matter of the paintings was religious, the house took on the ambiance of a church. It was an atmosphere appropriate for a man who held the power of life and death in his hands, as do all district judges in Texas.

At first, Tomas was attracted to the paintings because of their direct connection to his Spanish heritage. They also presented an opportunity to invest discreetly monies he couldn't otherwise account for. It was a beautiful arrangement.

The art had arrived in the new world with the conquerors and was a singular artistic blend of the foreign and the native, a stunning cross-cultural influence. The artists were mestizos, commissioned by the church, unsigned and not likely to be recognized by the general public. As his knowledge of the genre grew, Tomas developed an authentic passion for the paintings.

When he acquired the painting of Saint Jerome, the art dealer explained its subject was a hermit in the Syrian Desert. From these humble beginnings he rose to prominence by his translation of the Old and New Testaments.

This lesson Tomas understood well. He had understood it early in life. He, too, had suffered the humiliation of poverty, and education had been the way out for him. His ambitions had driven him to outstanding academic accomplishment in high school and a coveted minority scholarship to Harvard where, along with his law degree, he acquired an education in art and other accoutrements of an aristocratic lifestyle.

The scene in the small painting is of Saint Jerome impoverished, bare-chested and clad only in a loincloth and red sheath. His eyes are cast upward, and his hand rests reverently over his heart as he removes the thorn from a lion's paw with the other. An open Bible is at his knee, and the golden aura of his halo shimmers against a dark and somber background.

Tomas felt pride in his achievements. Easing the pain of the powerful, represented by the lion, was his key to helping his struggling and victimized people. He had no regrets for things he had done in the past to accomplish this goal. His altruistic efforts had not come cheap. It had been necessary to remove many thorns from the powerful in the years he struggled to gain and maintain his judgeship.

In Texas, district judges stand for election every four years. The elections are hard fought political events. In the beginning, the writers of the Texas constitution thought partisan elections were a sure way to regularly review the performance of judges. They had learned this lesson during reconstruction of the South after the Civil War. But times are complex now, not simple as before. The general population of voters has precious little knowledge of the men who run for the judgeships. But the trial lawyers are the big-money contributors, they know, and these contributions don't come without strings. Tomas regretted that these facts of life interfered with his independence, but what could he do? He didn't make the rules, he just tried the best he could to achieve justice even if they got in his way at times.

The hour had drawn late and Tomas rose heavily from his chair and began turning out the lights. One by one he snapped the switches and his paintings vanished into darkness. He stood a moment before the huge painting of Saint Michael Archangel. Four feet tall, it hung in the entry foyer opposite the front door and was framed in gold-leafed, heavily carved wood. Resplendent in reds and golds, it was a striking painting of Saint Michael descending from the Heavens holding lightning in one hand and the scales of justice in the other. Patron saint of the sick as well as the police, Saint Michael savagely defeated the powers of hell. Tomas saw this painting as an admonition, and for some reason he couldn't put his finger on, he felt it was a rebuke as well, and he turned his eyes away as he snapped out the light and plunged it into darkness.

He decided that although he couldn't help with the investigation, he could help Allen's boy. He would call Helen and advise her to hire a lawyer to contest the grossly outdated and therefore unfair will.

The boy's endangered inheritance needed protection. Once the litigation began, the county would provide guardianship for the boy. The judge would be able to appoint a guardian ad litum, and they could protect his inheritance. That he could do.

As Tomas climbed the stairs to bed, he was already deciding to buy the very small, and precious painting of the Virgin Mary his agent had located.

CHAPTER FIFTEEN

Lilah's daughters, or their lawyer camped at the sheriff's doorstep. They pressured the grand jury to continue to examine Frank Palma, who with the hit men gone, was the lone focus of the investigation. When they came around, the deputies would drag Frank in and question him again. They made threats, some of them believable. Frank believed them anyway, so he decided to make a call on Carlos Medrano at his ranch house.

Frank drove west out of Mission. The valley, with the alluvial soil narrowed, became hilly, rougher, and arid. He passed through terrain where the ground was chalky and dry. Mesquite still grew there, but it was stunted and small. Cactus moved into all the spaces between the thorny, scrubby cover.

The people living along the road were Mexicans who had crossed the river and built houses similar to the ones they had left behind in Mexico. Most of them were newcomers, but some were refugees from the Mexican Revolution and had been here for generations.

You could still see old buildings the Mexicans called *jacals,* constructed from materials that could be found on the spot. They built huts of zigzagged cedar posts stacked with mesquite or cedar branches and plastered, inside and out. The roofs were covered with palm frond thatching.

The older ones had thatching made from bundles of tall grass tied with a sort of string they made from the Spanish dagger plant. A material that looks fragile, but weathers hard and waterproof.

Despite the bright blues and pinks some of the houses had been painted, they were a dismal expression of the poverty they housed. Here the topsoil was thin, and eroded gullies marred the small plots where the owners had allowed their cattle to overgraze, and the goats they kept had plucked the ground of all grassy cover. Chickens could be seen scratching in all the swept dirt yards.

Frank turned his tan Mercedes turned into a gated entrance. The simple gate opened electronically from a call box. No problem, Carlos expected him. He bumped across the cattle guard and began the two-mile drive up to the ranch house. A narrow one-lane caliche road circled into the thickly brushed land.

As he moved farther away from the river, the flat land changed to rolling hills that in the spring bloomed in resplendent shades of yellows of the prickly pear cactus, cat claw, the huisache, the mesquite and the retama trees.

On the rises he caught glimpses of the red tile roof of the ranch house that sat atop a knoll higher than the surrounding land. Sufficiently high, that on a clear day, the mountains of Monterrey, Mexico could be seen like a blue cloud formation along the southern horizon from the porch.

Occasionally he saw cattle in the brush. The fencing was barbed wire and first rate; five strands of taut, silvery, new-looking wire. Not the dull rusty red of the neighbor's fencing. A break in the fence and another cattle guard led off to the left where a dirt track disappeared into the brush. As he drove along, through breaks, he could see an air sock, so he knew a cleared landing strip was out there beyond the scrub he was passing through.

Finally he came to an impressive gate. A stucco wall ran up to posts ten feet tall topped with black iron eagles. He bumped across another cattle guard and drove into the compound.

The house was new, stucco, a Spanish ranch house. He had seen houses like this on ranches outside of Guadalajara; he smiled to himself, supposing Carlos had seen them, too.

Frank had chosen to build his house in a modest neighborhood in town. His house rose above its neighbors like, they all said, a fairy castle. On a dead end street, Frank's eighteen-acre estate sat back behind an elaborate gate. The house was situated close to the street, and the short drive up to it circled a five-tiered fountain. The fountain towered ten feet tall, and its crystal waters splashed over pink cantera stone carvings of iguanas. His humble neighbors were dazzled in the evenings by the prisms of light sparkling through the beveled leaded glass of the giant mahogany doors under the soaring parapet entrance.

Frank circled past Carlos' house to the building that served as the ranch office. The simple unimposing building had a *portal* across the front that was supported with stripped cedar posts and paved, as was it's interior, with Saltillo tile. Carlos was standing on the porch, and he met Frank with a big smile and a warm *abrazos*. He led him inside a dark, cool, room that had a soft glow of casual elegance that had been carefully engineered by a high-tone interior design studio in San Antonio.

A black leather sofa faced the fireplace. Hand woven mohair rugs in an Indian pattern of blacks and reds softened the satiny shine of the Saltillo tiles of the floor. Silver trophies glowed softly in a lighted, glass-covered case. A hand-tooled saddle with silver conchos dominated one corner of the room. The saddle had the large Mexican horn and its stirrups had toe fenders, the mark of a brush country saddle. Pegs along the back wall held a collection of bridles with elaborate silver bits along with one pair of leather chaps, another brush country indicator.

The sofa back table displayed a large original bronze sculpture of a bucking bronco and rider by a famous western artist, and a stuffed javalina snarled over the mantel of the fireplace. Carlos led him into a side room where a dark mahogany, very heavy and elaborate desk dominated the space.

"The deputies collared me again today. I didn't tell them nothing they didn't already know." Frank began, "They still don't know you were in the car."

The two men were a contrast. Palma dressed as a businessman who frequented the courthouse in his dark suit and tie. He kept his wing-tip shoes polished to a high shine, the perfect example of a successful and powerful lobbyist, albeit on the county level. He appeared at the courthouse, and everyone knew him, although it wasn't clear to most why he was there. He looked like a lawyer or a banker, but was neither although he associated with bankers and lawyers. The clerks in the records office often saw him with a county commissioner as they left for coffee. He had business cards printed with his name; his business listed as an independent real estate agent. He didn't have an office. He had a mobile phone number printed on his card.

Carlos, in contrast, usually dressed in black, western, with touches of gold on his concho belt and boots. He, too, dressed as a businessman. Although he rarely appeared there, everyone at the courthouse knew his business. He could more likely be seen at local restaurants, dining with men of similar attire. They would be sitting, usually four at a table, or booth. They spoke softly to one another, with four cell phones at their plates within easy reach if a call came in. When one did, they excused themselves and quietly left the restaurant to take care of business.

"Those girls want to see an arrest. They want somebody to pay. They're leanin' on the judge, and he don't want no attention right now. He's headed for the Supreme Court, and no little fish like you and me is gonna stand in his way."

Carlos sat facing forward. His eyes focused in the distance, only turning to glance at Frank occasionally when he spoke. Frank was the small fish, and they both knew it. He waited to let Palma get to the point.

"The *pistoleros* are out of the picture, but they already said too much. The girls want an arrest. They're after me, and someone else they think was in the car that night. I ain't told them nothing, but they're after me, and my guess is that you're gonna be next."

Carlos examined Frank's face, and said softly, "You jackass, what makes you think I'd be next? I shouldn't have even been there that night. It was a job for the boys." He turned to look away from Frank and softly added, "Why'd you bring the *pistoleros?* What were you thinkin' bringin' them?

Frank didn't answer the direct question, but he had Carlos's attention now. "The *pistoleros,* now we know they're done talking. How about you, Frank? They're never gonna know I was there if you don't tell them."

Frank's mouth was tight, and he said, "You know I got a record. Hell, you served me yourself. The grand jury might just wonder how we got to be such good friends. I'd never tell them anything, of course, but you and I both know this ain't gonna be the end of it."

It was a signal, and it wasn't lost on Carlos. Frank didn't intend to go down alone.

"You know Frank," Carlos said, and his face broke into a wry smile, "maybe, just maybe, we aren't such good friends as you think!" His mind was working on what he had to do to solve this problem. He wasn't worried about the sheriff, and the district attorney was his uncle. Frank was the problem. Frank and what he might tell the grand jury.

"Don't you even think about turning rat," Carlos scowled. He didn't add, '*chatos* like you don't live to go to trial,' but the threat was in his voice and Frank didn't miss it.

"Hell, Carlos," Frank said, "you got pull with the sheriff. Get him off my tail and save your own ass, too. If you don't, we're both in it neck deep."

Carlos didn't respond. He looked out of the window at a row of paddocks newly built to house his horses. He had just bought an expensive new quarter horse with a famous bloodline. Men were building a wooden fence to enclose a lot for the horse.

Frank shifted his weight in the chair. "They're ridin' me pretty hard," he pressed, "I got a record."

Carlos' head swung back to glare at Frank, and he said, "Hell, Frank, I don't have to tell you what to do. Keep your damn mouth shut!"

"Yeah, well, they don't know anything for sure, or I'd already be indicted."

Carlos looked back out of the window and let Frank stew.

"Right!" Frank said, "You're right! We don't have to worry about the *pistolas*. Now it's just you and me that knows what went on."

He let Carlos think about it a minute before he added, "Except your cousin, Amado. How about Amado? He was standin' around in the yard, and he saw you leave with us."

Frank leaned back and watched Carlos. Carlos looked back at him, but he was thinking about Amado.

"We picked him up at Johnnie's Cantina," Frank said, "he'd been in there all afternoon, and there was plenty of guys who saw him leave with us. Hell! You know Amado," he joked, "he's a high profile kinda guy!" Carlos was paying attention now. "They all know him in there," he emphasized. "It's his regular hang out."

Amado enjoyed the boost his reputation took to be associated with a high-powered business type, the likes of Palma. The *pistoleros* were dark and dangerous, and Amado slapped their backs and bought them rounds. He saw the looks of admiration he drew from the men at the bar, and he made sure everyone saw him leave as part of what he thought was a glamorous group.

"The dumb shit!" Carlos whispered under his breath. And he turned on Frank, "What the hell were you thinking bringing that *vació* there with you?"

"Hell, Carlos, he's your cousin. You don't think he'd talk, do you?"

Amado was family. He would not betray them; he'd take the fall if necessary. Fear was a factor, too. Amado wasn't afraid of the sheriff's men. The sheriff would put him in the jailhouse, but the family, well; it wouldn't go down well with the family.

"The sheriff is looking for somebody," Frank said. "You know he don't want you, and I don't think he really wants me either." The eyebrows went up.

"You know what? I think they're looking for Amado, don't you think? Yeah! I think they're looking for Amado."

Carlos glared out of the window and didn't answer, so Frank knew it was a done deal. He would finally, reluctantly, have to confess to the grand jury that one of the Medrano boys was with the *pistoleros* when he cut out, but it was Amado, not Carlos. Amado Medrano left in the car with the *pistoleros*, and as far as Frank knew, he would testify, he was still with them when Allen's pickup truck pulled into the driveway, and he left. The sheriff would have his man, and the girls would relax the pressure.

Frank read the situation correctly, "Your boys had better keep a low profile," he advised, a new note of confidence in his voice.

His arm rested on the soft upholstery, and he turned his hand and examined his gold nugget ring. He let the light glint across it, and examined his manicured fingernails. He had the Medranos, he had them, and he knew it. He spoke with authority now. He was in charge.

"Carlos, I'd suggest you better be lily-white clean for awhile. Send them boys out of town. Clean up the trailer and send the kids off on a little vacation. Pack 'em off to the Island."

Frank felt a lot better. "Those *pachuchos* have earned a little R and R."

Carlos put his hands on the desk and pushed himself erect. He stood, walked over to the window, and looked out at the chestnut stallion in his cramped quarters; its head was up; its eyes showed white at the edges.

Frank couldn't see the horse, but he could see Carlos, and he felt real good now. He shook Carlos' hand, and drew his stiff body to himself in an *abrazo*, slapped him on the back and said, laughing, "You do that, and I'll be a character witness for you to the grand jury. I know I'll probably be seeing them again in a few days."

CHAPTER SIXTEEN

Connie placed her left hand on the frame, her right hand on the brass button, and carefully opened the beveled-paned glass door. She reached forward to pull the brass chain all the way down to wind the chimes on the grandfather clock. Then she repeated the motion twice more to wind the works and the striker then softly closed the door. She stood there a moment longer with her hand on the little button knob.

She looked up into the familiar face of the clock, she knew it well; it was an old friend. Her eyes traveled over the moon dial, and just under her breath, she whispered, "Oh, Hank!" She ran her hand up the clock's smooth mahogany wall, and stood there a minute longer with her hand resting on its surface, before she stepped back.

Connie walked through the house to the dining room to wind the smaller, maple grandmother clock. This one she wound with a key. She slid her hand across the top. She felt the key and picked it up, rising on her toes to do it. She opened the arched door that covered the clock's face and fitted the key into the first of three small holes. She wound it four rounds, counting aloud as she wound, ONE, TWO, THREE, FOUR. She repeated the process twice more, closed the door, and replaced the key on top.

Although the grandmother clock was smaller than the large clock on the landing, it was taller than Connie.

"The older I am the shorter I get!" she complained.

The station house clock in the kitchen she wound with a key, too. The clock hung low on the wall over the kitchen table that she had pushed up to the wall. A worktable now, she didn't eat at it any more. A new microwave oven and a new portable TV sat there, and she used these two appliances more than any other in the kitchen.

Of the three clocks, the station clock was the least impressive. It was the smallest, but it was the only real antique she had in the house. It wasn't her favorite. Among the clocks, she had no favorite. They each were special, appreciated for themselves, and loved for what they represented. Her husband, Hank, had made the cabinet of the grandfather clock. A mechanic and pipe fitter who worked with metal, he loved working with wood as a hobby.

The mahogany clock stood tall and solid. It dominated the landing. Its heavy brass weights commanded resounding chimes that filled the house with its presence, and his.

The grandmother clock was hers, a gift from Hank on their twenty-fifth wedding anniversary. It was special, and it had always been hers. It stood smaller than the other. It was placed less prominently. Its chimes were softer than the large mahogany clock. But it had come first, and it was hers, and it was special.

The station clock was special because it had belonged to her father, and it was a working clock. It had worked in a railroad station just as her father had, for the Santa Fe Railroad. Just like her father, it wasn't ornate; it was dependable, and steady, and not too proud. Its solid oak cabinet had very little decoration. It struck the hour, but didn't get all fancy with the chimes.

Deep rich mahogany, warm maple finish, and sturdy oak, the house echoed with their chimes on the quarter hour. On the hour they struck a discordant chorus of resounding bongs, each with its own individual voice, and Connie didn't feel alone.

***

"Connie, things are changing in the county, and I want you to understand something before I leave."

They stood at the front door. Angie Cantu had come to put the sign in the yard. "FOR SALE" it read, and Connie averted her eyes from it.

"Angie, when you've finished, come on in, and I'll make us some tea."

Connie watched her friend, who was also her real estate agent, walk across the grass. She stood with her hand over her heart as Angie pounded the stakes into the soft lawn.

Prior to going into real estate, Angie had worked alongside Connie in an office. Although a large gap in their ages separated them, they were good friends.

Connie left the door standing open and went in to brew the tea. As she filled the glasses with ice, Angie joined her in the kitchen, leaning against the doorframe to wait.

"Is that your new TV?"

It sat exactly where the old one had on the table under the station clock beside the shiny new microwave oven.

"Yes, nothing much has changed," Connie said, as she poured the tea. "Except maybe that."

She nodded toward the kitchen door, and they both laughed at what they saw.

"They came in this door," she said, still smiling. "Ignacio fixed it for me, do you think it'll do the job?"

He had put a common hasp on the door, a large steel one that would have been at home on a barn door.

"I don't think a mule could kick this one out."

"Connie, did you have any problems with the insurance company?" Angie asked.

"No, I've been with them for years. They were kind and helpful." Connie hesitated a moment and added, "But you know the strangest thing, they don't seem to be interested in my serial numbers."

She set the sugar bowl out and continued, "I kept the manuals and had the numbers recorded on some of the things. I apologized for not having them all, and they said, 'Oh, don't worry, those things belong to us now.'

"This seemed a very casual attitude to me, and I said, 'If they're recovered, the deputy says you won't be able to claim them without positive identification. You'll need the serial numbers.'

"You know, I think she thought it was funny. I think I heard a smile in her voice."

Angie smiled sadly as well. She slipped her arm around Connie's waist, giving her a gentle hug.

"Come on, let's sit down. I need to go, but I have to explain something to you first."

They walked together through the house to the family room with Connie pointing out features she hoped would help it to sell.

"This is the powder room, I have added a shower and it's a full bath now. I bought new carpet and drapes. I had the living room done when I added the shower."

"This room will show well. I like the tile you added around the fireplace, and the carpet and drapes look really nice. This is a big room."

Connie responded with an impish smile, "Yes, it is! A twenty-one foot cabin cruiser can fit in this room."

Angie didn't know for sure how to take the strange comment, and she smiled saying, "Well, I guess it could."

"No guessing, I know, we had one in here once." Connie giggled youthfully. "We really did!"

"No, Connie! You're joking! You don't expect me to believe that!"

"You can believe it or not, but we really did. You know Hank, always full of surprises!"

Angie laughed, "Yes, I remember Hank, so I can believe it, but how did you get it in here? Or, how did you get it out?"

"You know, Angie, we didn't have much money," Connie said, her voice taking on a more sober tone, "If not having much money means you're poor, I guess we were. We worked all the time, just to stay afloat, but we didn't think of ourselves as poor.

"We had everything we wanted. If we needed something, Hank would manage to get it. We cut something else out, or he made it himself, and he made a lot of things. That's why I have that garage full of tools. Hank grew up on a ranch south of Ft. Worth. Ranchers in those days didn't just go buy things. If something broke, they fixed it. If they needed something, they usually made it in their shop on the ranch."

They moved on into the family room and sat at the glass-topped table to drink their tea. She continued her story, "Hank said many times, 'I'd rather make things myself. I can buy the tools for what someone else's labor would cost me. While doing the work, I learn more about something I'm interested in, and when I'm finished, I have the tools as a bonus.'

"Hank was interested in everything. He had a youthful curious mind. The thirteenth of fourteen children, his father was a sick old man when it was his turn to go to college. His older brothers all went to Texas Christian University, but they couldn't send him. A shame though, he would have made a wonderful engineer or architect.

"We went to the yacht basin in Port Isabel often, and to Corpus Christi. Hank yearned for a boat. He found a *Mechanics Illustrated* magazine with the plans for a twenty-one foot cabin cruiser, and drew them up to scale on butcher paper. They were spread out here in the living room. I stepped over them while he tried to find the marine quality plywood and brass screws and all the things on the spec list. Fiberglass had just come out and he taught himself how to work with it.

"Hank had lists and figures all over the place. He would come home from his job and stay up half the night working on this project. I don't know where he found the energy. He figured all the details. Each screw had to be solid brass. They cost thirty-five cents apiece, and he knew exactly how many he would need to buy. He figured every expense. He finished planning the project, even after he knew he couldn't afford to buy the materials."

"So he didn't make the boat?"

Connie said, "He didn't make that one. He made one he could afford. He made a sixteen-foot outboard motor ski boat, and he did it in the same way. He drew up the plans from the *Mechanics Illustrated*."

"Well, Connie, don't tell me he made it in the living room!"

"No, of course not! He made it in the garage like everything else. That's why he built that metal building. The old garage had been a barn with a dirt floor. He tore it down and built that nice metal building with the concrete floor."

"My goodness, Connie, was the boat he built seaworthy?"

Connie responded with an impish grin, "Yes, and I can say that from first hand experience, we took it out to sea one day."

"You actually took a sixteen foot homemade boat out to sea? How far out did you go?" Angie asked incredulously.

"Now, listen, just because Hank made it, don't say homemade as if it were inferior in some way. He made a very professional quality, good-looking boat. Only we knew he didn't buy it. It was constructed of marine grade plywood. He special ordered sheets sixteen feet long, and it had a beautiful fiberglass finish.

"I don't know how far out we went, but I remember passing the whistle buoy, which is seven miles. We didn't plan to go so far, but it turned into an adventure.

"Adventures aren't planned," she instructed with a twinkle in her eye, "adventures just happen. When we left that morning we were only going out in the bay to fish. Angie, have you ever seen the whistle buoy?"

"Heavens no, Connie, I don't even know what it is!"

"Well, I had never seen it either, and it's so interesting and strange. All alone out there you look across miles of nothing but water, and the misty sea spray smells salty and wonderful.

"And then, faintly, above the sound of the wind and the slapping of the waves, you hear a lonely, mournful whooping sound far in the distance, and it's the buoy. It rises up and down on the swells calling out and guiding ships into the channel.

"You hear it before you can see it, and the sound is mysterious and compelling. It draws you in, like, you know, the sirens in *The Odyssey*.

"When I heard it, I was enchanted. I was in its spell. I had to see it, and Hank took me out there."

"I remember the beautiful day, still and sunny, but not too hot. The water was calm and clear green, jewel-tone green, and we just kept going. It was an adventure. We fell under the spell of its power and magic.

"We went into the deeper and deeper water and further and further out. The gulf was like a living thing. It began to rise up in swells that became bigger and bigger. Before too long, they were so large, they were like hills, and we were gliding up, up, and then down, down, down.

"We rode on swells so big that when we were on top of one we were up very high, hilltop. We could look out over miles of water. We couldn't see land in any direction. The surface was smooth as glass, and we would slide down, down, into the trough.

"At the bottom, we looked up at walls of water, heavy and green, and solid looking towering above us. Time stopped, and we would pause there. Then the surface would be lifted, rising up as if alive, and we would be on the hilltop again. We weren't sliding on the surface; we were part of a pulsating, living, powerful thing. Oh! Angie, it was so exciting. You could just feel the power in the water. So awesome! I'll never forget it!"

"Connie! Amazing!"

"And, Angie, you know what was running through my mind? So silly, but do you remember Katherine Hepburn's line in the movie, *The African Queen*? Remember when they had made it through the rapids, and she put her hand to her throat and said, 'I never thought a mere physical experience could be so exhilarating.' Well, she expressed it so well. That's what it was. It was exhilarating!

"I had a beer bottle, and I held it out over the side and dropped it.

I watched it slowly sink, and I could see it for the longest time, gently slipping down through the green, green water. It wobbled slightly, spiraling down as it sank. I watched it until it was very small and finally disappeared."

"Connie! My God! Weren't you afraid?"

"Heavens no, why would I be afraid? Well, maybe a little, except that made it an adventure: the risk, the walking on the edge of our ability to control the situation, and the exhilaration, and the adventure."

"You went out to sea in a sixteen foot homemade boat, out to where you couldn't even see land. What if you had gotten turned around and instead of coming back in had gone on out into the Gulf?"

Connie said, "We weren't going to do that, as I said, Hank had control of the situation. He had a compass, and he knew how to use it. He even had a sextant, and he knew how to use that, too. Of course we didn't have the sextant with us, we left it at home."

She paused, "We had a good motor. I bought him a 75-H.P. Johnson outboard for his birthday, powerful enough to pull Johnny on water skis, just as fast as you would want to go.

"We experienced something together that, believe you me, I'll never forget." She laughed again and said, "I can tell you now it beats the heck out of sitting on the sofa with your hands folded!"

Then she added, "And we had so much fun! Hank always had something going in that garage, the boat, and the clocks. He made a lot of furniture out there you know. He made that table in my kitchen. He made our bed. He had an airplane out there for about six months, and I parked my car beside it."

"Connie, I've got to go now, but before I do, we need to talk about your house."

Carefully, kindly, Angie explained, "The colonia developments are becoming a problem for everyone except certain, well you know, greedy opportunists, and the county is taking steps to curb them.

"You may be a victim of unintended consequences. They have passed regulations making it against the law to sell property in less than five-acre blocks. This could make it difficult to sell your property."

"Oh, Angie, no, don't worry about that. It won't affect me because I don't want to break it up anyway. I want to sell the entire thirty acres and house all together."

"Connie, if you want to do that, we can put it on the market, and I can try to sell it. I need to caution you, we may have difficulty finding someone who can afford a house and thirty acres who would want to live this close to the Loma Linda colonia.

"I think your best chance to sell it is in five acre blocks, and you may have to do some owner financing as well."

Connie answered quickly, "Angie, this is a farm, not a development. I want to keep it together."

Angie reached across and patted Connie's hand, "We'll handle it any way you want to. We'll put it up for sale and test the market. We can always change later if we decide we need to." She stood to leave, but Connie's voice changed and she softly explained.

"Angie, I've just got to sell it all together. I can't take a chance on squalor like Loma Linda going up around my house. Then no one, for sure, would want to live here. Thirty acres of land would be a buffer to protect me and the property. Angie, if I sell off five-acre tracts, there's no telling who would move in. I might not be as safe as I am even now. And it boils down to this; I have to sell this house before I leave it. The deputies have already told me they don't intend to protect my property. Angie, my Social Security, this house and land are all I have. I own this property out right, and I can't afford to lose it."

Angie moved to the door, and Connie didn't see her sad smile as she walked across the lawn to her car. Connie watched her back the car down the driveway and turn toward town with Puppy in escort. She stood on the porch as the dog returned to join her, standing long minutes looking out across the lawn of the house, past the sign FOR SALE.

And she saw the young man open the door of the Rocket 88 two-door sedan, and fold the front seat down for his teen-age daughter, and she did the same for their eight-year-old boy. They drove across the rural countryside on a narrow strip of pavement lined with palm trees and fragrant with the smell of orange blossoms on a road called Morningside. And the young man was handsome, and he was self-confidant, and he entertained them with stories, and they laughed and enjoyed the ride. They slowed down as they neared a row of flowering oleanders bordering a long stretch of lawn that swept back to a white two-story house. The house had a high-pitched roof, and green trim

*and a porch in front with an arched roof, and tall pillars and the door
had an arch to match. It stood like a jewel in the orchard of oranges in
full bloom. The young man slowed the car down, and they all admired
it as they drove past, and the young man said, 'What a beautiful
house, now who do you suppose lives there?' And they all laughed with
satisfaction because they knew the house belonged to them.*

***

When she heard it the second time, Connie picked up the remote
control and pressed the mute button. It was dark outside, and the house
was quiet. The window unit air conditioner hummed away, and she could
hear the raspy breathing of the old dog at her feet, but nothing else. Not
satisfied, she held her breath and waited. Long seconds passed, but she
didn't hear it again.

"They'll come back," the deputy had said.

Connie checked the pistol. The clip was in place. Quietly, she placed
the remote control on the table and tiptoed to the door into the living
room.

"They are protected by the law," he had said that, too.

She kept the drapes closed at night. She knew she had locked the
front door, but she walked over and checked it anyway. Locked. The light
was off in the shuttered dining room. She walked across to the window
and looked out through the little slats to the front yard of the house.
Puppy was not barking, and the thin light cast from the security lamp
on the tall pole revealed nothing out of the ordinary.

She looked across to the Salinas' house and saw their light was still
on; it comforted her.

*Ignacio is just across the street, and Puppy wouldn't let me down.
God bless her,* she thought.

The telephone sat on the little wicker table in the corner. Connie
lifted the receiver and felt relief when she heard the dial tone. She didn't
replace it in the cradle. She sat in the dark room with the pistol in her
lap. She needed the reinforcement of a normal friendly voice, and she
dialed Lilah's number. She realized what she had done and quickly hung
up. The click of the receiver when she replaced it resounded in the dark,
silent room. She was even more acutely aware of the large, empty house.

"I'm losing my mind," she said aloud. "Where is Lilah when I really need her."

Her home of forty years, Connie could easily walk about it in the dark, and so she did. With the house in darkness, she could see the dimly lit yard, and no one could see in to where she walked, alone. She made the rounds, peeking out in each direction. With the pistol in her right hand, she gently parted the draperies with her left.

Lime green light cast from the pole at the front gave the lawn an unnerving strangeness Connie had never noticed before. It cast soft shadows that blurred the dark beneath the oleanders. She strained her eyes to focus them on shapes that seemed to swell and diminish as the breeze, or something, shifted the limber branches.

She turned her back to the windows, and her fingers traced the mahogany wood of the bookcase Hank had made for her. Expertly her fingers missed the framed photos of her grandchildren.

After she returned to her chair at the game table, she heard the noise again, a popping sound that she recognized as the settling of the old house in the night air. The realization did not put her at ease. She picked up the pistol, and held it in her lap, her eyes on the drape that covered the sliding glass door onto the patio.

The small black coach lamp at the door was motion activated. It remained dark, and the house was quiet. She took the set off mute and watched the end of the old movie, trying to ignore her nagging unease.

I'm not afraid. I live here, she thought, this is my house. I have lived here half my life, and this night is no different from any other.

Her eyes shifted to her husband's empty chair and quickly back to the set again. *I'm not going to think about this now. I'll think about it tomorrow, Scarlet.* She smiled to herself at the familiar quotation, strangely appropriate now.

The nights will be hard for a while, until I settle down.

Mark slept undisturbed at her feet, and Puppy slept outside. Her hand found the pistol still in her lap, and she placed it back on the table. The big old grandfather clock began to whir and then to chime.

"Mark, wake up, it's time for us to go up to bed."

She nudged the terrier with her foot and stood up. She snapped the set off, and Mark followed her out of the room.

When she came to the foot of the stairs, she bent down and picked him up. She carried the dog crooked in her arm, the pistol in that hand, and held on to the railing with the other. She slowly and carefully climbed the stairs.

She had trouble sleeping. She thought she slept, but she heard the clocks, which she had never done before. She heard the old house settling, and she strained to listen. The night passed uneventfully. The thin morning light finally brought sleep, and she slept soundly until it became too hot, around nine o'clock.

The days passed normally, but she dreaded the nights. She tried not to think of the men, but they lurked in the back of her mind. She still saw the reminders of their intrusion; there was the sign in the yard, FOR SALE, and an ugly bolt scarred the kitchen door, just as the incident had scarred her leaving her bitterly resentful toward the sheriff.

We can't protect you, they had said. When did the protection of the people in the county stop being the sheriff's responsibility? Is it optional? If he isn't there to protect us, I'd like to know why we even need him at all. I guess it didn't happen over night. I've been on my own a long time and didn't know it. Well, I know it now. Nothing has really changed, I guess.

He says they'll be back, and I believe it. He isn't going to do anything about it, so I guess they're free to come. If I know he isn't going to do anything, then I guess they know it, too. They probably know what's going on with the sheriff better than I do. It'll be different this time. This time I have protection, her hand tightened on the grip. This time they're in for a little surprise.

CHAPTER SEVENTEEN

onnie had two cats. She stood at the kitchen window and looked at them sitting on the roof of the wash house just a few feet away. They looked back across the span and watched her, too. They were wild, wild, wild.

"Wilder than anything," she liked to say. "Wilder than Comanche Indians!"

She tried to tame the gray one, but the cat tolerated being held with rolling eyes and tensed body, alert and ready to escape whenever Connie relaxed her grip.

"Jeanie, I know you love me. Why can't you calm down and let me hold you?"

They were mousers, so called, but Connie served them a can of carved fish every day. She opened the door and stepped outside to where the water faucet stood above a crazy arrangement of pans and bowls she had assembled to outsmart the ants.

"Ants aren't good swimmers."

She served the food on its own little island in a pan of water. She gathered the empty bowls and brought them back into the house. With her hand still on the door, she looked down at the ugly hasp, pushed the door shut firmly, and turned the thumb knob to secure it. The top half of the door had been glass. Ignacio replaced it with a tough Plexiglas when he installed the hasp.

The kitchen in the old farmhouse had two windows over the sink. They were big and beautiful and Connie left them uncovered. The light and cheery kitchen heated up on a summer afternoon, so she always carried her lunch into the family room to eat. The family room was more comfortable, and her favorite soap opera came on at noon. She didn't like sitting at the kitchen table alone.

She put her plate down on a cluttered table. She pushed the overflowing ashtray aside along with a game of solitaire she had dealt out and abandoned. Her *The Progressive Farmer* magazine lay on the table with its cover folded back. The television rattled away, as always. "It keeps me company," she would explain.

Connie was engrossed in her program when Puppy began barking out back, and a young man stepped up on the patio. The dog was giving him a hard time, and he stood with his back to the door waving a lug wrench to keep her at bay.

"Puppy, behave!" Connie shouted. "Leave that poor boy alone!" The dog continued to bark, and the young man could only half turn to speak to Connie. "Lady," he said, "does your dog bite?" Mark joined the fracas, and Connie stood at the door with dogs barking on either side of it.

The young man's head was shaved. Three old scars stood out prominently white against the dark stubble. Connie noted his complexion, pale and sallow, and thought, poor thing; he must be recovering from an automobile accident. His face lit up with a friendly smile when she opened the sliding glass door a crack and shouted through the grille, "Puppy, shut up!"

The dog backed off, but continued in her hostile attitude, growling and baring her teeth. "Puppy!" Connie ordered, and Puppy at last retreated, but continued to stand at alert just off the patio. Mark still barked ferociously. Connie picked the terrier up and tried to quiet him.

"I'm sorry about these animals!" she said.

"Lady, may I use your phone?" he asked.

Connie was contending with the squirming dog and before she could answer, the young man's almond eyes crinkled in a broad smile. "I bet the little one's the biter," he said.

"Yes, I'm afraid you're right. When you come in, he just might bite you!" she apologized. "Here, let me go put him up." And she left him to wait while she closed Mark in the bathroom.

When she returned, the young man's forehead was pressed against the grille, his hands cupped around his face, and he was boldly looking in. He dropped his hands and stepped back when she walked to the door.

"Is it a Chihuahua?" he said, in a conversational manner.

"No, he's a terrier."

"Those Chihuahuas, they'll bite you!" he said, smiling and continuing in a familiar vein.

She pushed the door open, and her hand went up to open the grille when she caught the smell of him. Sweet and musty, it was unpleasant, even offensive, and she hesitated just slightly. She saw his hand move, too, and when he looked up, and their eyes met, the smile had disappeared. But he flashed his white teeth again and said, "You sure have a nice place here."

Something was fishy, what was it? Did he seem a little too familiar, even brassy? She looked at the scars, healed over but raised up and shiny white. She saw the large, loose fitting white tee shirt and his baggy pants. He wore a cross on a long cord about his neck, a big one, at least four inches across. She had never seen a cross like it, so crude and ugly.

Who would wear a cross like that?

She noted his narrowed almond eyes, and changed her mind. She suggested, "Let me make the call for you, what's the number?"

"I need to make it myself," he said.

"I'd be happy to make the call for you," she said, "but I can't let you come in the house."

He didn't answer and he didn't leave. They just stood there looking at one another through the iron bars.

Now he affected a high whiny voice. "Lady, can't you help me? My car's broke down." The performance was farcical. It was broad comedy. "I need to call somebody."

"No, I'm sorry, I'll make the call, but I can't let you come in."

He put his hand on the grille, and his voice was calm and low again, "Look, Lady. It's just a phone call. I need to use the phone."

She noted the hand on the grille.

A short young man, he was taller than Connie. He sized her up, and his tone changed. "No, Lady," he ordered, "I gotta make it myself. I need to tell him where I am. Come on Lady! It'll only take a minute."

She didn't answer, but he pressed on, "Just use the phone. Just take me a minute."

"No, I can't help you. You'll have to go somewhere else."

His face registered exasperation with her, "If you won't let me use the phone, how about letting me use your jumper cables?"

She wanted him to leave, and she said firmly, "I don't have any. Now, please go away."

"I saw some," he turned, and his hand swept back to the garage, "back there in that garage."

125

He had been in her garage. Her eyes didn't follow his gesture, "I don't know what you think you saw, but I told you, I don't have jumper cables. I can't help you. So now you go on."

He stood quietly for a few seconds and then dramatically drew his arm across his brow, "It's hot. If I have to walk for help, how about a glass of water?"

She'd had enough of this clown. She answered firmly and with finality, "No. I can't help you in any way. Now go."

Then he changed. He was transformed. He bowed elaborately, and the ugly cross came swinging forward as he bent low. He clasped his hands as if in prayer, and she watched the cross dangling below them. He remained bending before her as he whined, "Please!" Slowly he lifted his face to look up at her, revealing an evil smile as his chin tilted up.

She felt an electric tickle of fear at this comical and frightening performance and she said, "Leave now." Firmly, "Leave right now."

"No!" he said, and his tone matched hers. "First, let me use the phone! Let me use the phone, and then I'll go."

She looked into his insolently smirking face, his attitude now openly threatening. His hands closed around the bars of the grille, and she saw him pull it toward himself, checking to see if it was locked, testing its strength.

"Get away from the door, and if you're not gone in the next two minutes, I'm calling the sheriff."

He released his grip on the grille; he stepped back from the door. Putting his hands defensively out front, palms forward and fingers open, he said, "OK, OK, lady." And he turned and walked away.

When he left, she stood a minute and watched for him. But it was quiet out side. She pulled the sliding door shut and felt a sense of relief that the iron grille had been there. She knew the kitchen door was locked and also the front door. She didn't have to check. She kept them locked lately.

What a weird creep, she said to herself. She felt a little shaken and nervous about the encounter. It seemed to be over though, so finally, she relaxed and went back to her lunch and her soap opera.

In a few minutes the set went dark, and the lamp.

Power failure? She didn't think so. She sat there a little longer, and they didn't come back on.

Well, I guess I can thank that insolent thug for this. He's probably still out there. This can't be a coincidence. Well, I can't just sit here and do nothing. I'd better go and check.

The breaker box was outside the kitchen door. She got up and made her way to the kitchen. When she passed the large windows in the living room, she looked cautiously out at the empty lawn. She didn't see a car, and she didn't see the young man. She passed through the dining room. She could look across it and through the kitchen to the kitchen door. She could see through the glass pane of the door, and she relaxed a little when she didn't see anyone.

When she stepped up to the door to open it and check the breaker box, she saw him working on the lock. She hadn't seen him because he had his head down examining the handle of the door. He didn't know about the hasp, and it no doubt puzzled him that he couldn't get it open.

Where is Puppy? She wondered.

"I told you to leave! Now I am calling the sheriff!"

He stood up and looked directly at her and smiled broadly. His smile unnerved her; she felt more than alarm now. She felt rising panic. He wouldn't leave, and he wasn't scared of her threat of the sheriff. She rushed into the dining room to the phone and picked it up. No dial tone. Her hand trembled as she replaced the receiver.

She was on her own, and this time she was downstairs. He knew she was there, and alone, and awake, and he meant to come in. She looked at the row of three large windows at either end of the living room and knew that he could come in whenever he wanted.

Quickly, she went back into the family room. She kept her pistol put away during the day, but she took it out and checked to see that the clip was in place and snapped the safety off. She hurried back to the kitchen.

Still there, his face close to the glass, he worked on the doorknob, bending down so he could look through and see what the obstruction was. She stepped up to the door and placed the barrel of the pistol within inches of his face on the other side of the window.

She said slowly, with as much authority as she could manage, "Leave, and do it now." And she tapped the glass with the barrel of the pistol.

This got his attention, and he stepped back. She pressed the barrel to the glass, and he got a good look at it. He turned to his two companions who she saw for the first time, and he said, "She has a gun!"

He stepped away from the door, and the three of them moved out of her line of sight.

They're not gone. I'm not fool enough to believe that! What am I going to do?

She leaned against the wall beside the door where they couldn't see her, the pistol gripped tightly in her wildly shaking hand. She lifted it and steadied it with both hands, and tried to calm down.

They want in.

I've got to think.

They want in, and they'll find a way.

They're having fun.

I don't have much time.

Do something! Do something!

She pulled herself away from the wall and took a cautious peek out the door. She didn't see anyone. She walked across the dining room and looked out of the shuttered windows to the quiet front yard.

She crossed into the foyer and looked up the stairs. *This time, hiding isn't good enough.*

An image of his smirking face flashed through her mind. She saw again his hand on the grille, moving, pulling at the grille.

This time they're after me. He wanted to have fun with me. I know it. I could see it in his eyes.

She found Mark and picked him up. She held him tightly in the crook of her arm and slid the glass door back and peeked out across the space between the house and the garage. The limbs of the bougainvillea stirred in the breeze and were the only thing that moved, however, the garage seemed farther away than ever before.

Connie leaned against the doorframe and took a deep breath, then she unlocked the iron grille, and with her arm extended, she fired the pistol into the empty yard. Then she pushed the grille open, stepped out, and ran the short distance to the garage, her hand held high above her head firing the pistol as she ran all the way to the car.

CHAPTER EIGHTEEN

When Connie had been robbed the first time, she had walked over to the Salinas' house and had called the sheriff. She hadn't needed to hurry. The danger had been over for hours.

That time, she *had* hid in a closet. She *had* lain there in the dark close quarters and pulled the bedspread up to her chin, tucking it under and forming a cocoon. She *had* held the dog close to her heart as he slept innocently. Connie's heart had pounded, her eyes squeezed tightly shut, and she had endured listening to the dirty hands groping through her personal things. She had felt the filthy fingers probing into places where they were not allowed and violating her beyond the loss of her physical possessions. When she heard them go, she was reluctant to leave the closet's close quarters. She waited. She waited for the dawn. Wrapped in the bedspread, she held herself; she held Mark and, she mustered her strength. She could do what had to be done. She could be strong but not yet. So she waited in the healing darkness for the morning.

When finally the light came filtering in, she was ready. She came stiffly down the stairs, holding on, taking them one at a time. She was a seventy-nine year old woman who had slept on the floor in a closet.

She had walked slowly through the destruction in her house, hardly in a hurry to report it to the world.

Barefoot, she passed from room to room stepping over her scattered possessions and the vestiges of their party.

Her silverware, handed down from her mother, was gone. She had left her wristwatch by her purse on the table, and it was missing, too. They took her VCR and pawed over a box of tapes. Some were missing. A new carton of cigarettes and a cheap little butane lighter were taken. Her radio was missing, her house key, and her car keys. The car was gone.

She put her hand on the bare tabletop where her television set and microwave oven had sat, and slid it across the surface. Her fingers left a slashing trail in the accumulated dust. She held her fingers up and examined the dust on her fingertips.

She looked up into the face of her father's clock, and watched the brass pendulum swinging on its regular beat. Steady, dependable, and moving on. She did the same. At eight o'clock, she had thought it not too early to bother her neighbors. With Puppy racing out ahead, she had walked across the lawn to the Salinas' house to call the authorities.

This time she didn't hide; this time she left the house running. She ran from the protection of the house and rushed into the open yard fearful and in a hurry. She didn't know if they would allow her to cross, but she knew she had to try.

When she reached the shelter of the garage, she turned back to see if they had followed. She didn't see them anywhere. With Mark in one arm and the pistol in the other hand, she fumbled awkwardly with the handle and couldn't get the door open.

Anxiously, she transferred the pistol to the hand hindered with the dog and finally opened the door. She tossed the dog into the back seat and quickly slid in behind the wheel. Frantically, she crawled over seats to lock the doors. She sat there a few seconds before she started the car.

With pounding heart, she turned to look back down the long narrow drive before accelerating out of the garage, weaving at full speed in reverse all the way to the road.

When she reached the road, random fate turned the wheel to the east. She barreled to Carl's house and turned into his drive. She still gripped the pistol tightly in her right hand when the car came to a squealing halt in his drive. With the sound still in her ears, and with trembling fingers, she placed the gun on safety to put it on the floor in front of the passenger seat.

She got out of the car and ran up on his porch. The metal door was closed and locked when she tried the knob, so she leaned against it and pounded until it was answered. When Carl came to the door, she pushed past him, moving toward the telephone, explaining as she dialed 911.

After she made the call, she started back to the car; Carl came running along after her. He ran holding onto the handle of the locked car door yelling, "Connie, open the door."

With the car still rolling back down his drive, she reached across and flipped the handle, and he got in.

When they reached the road, she sped away in as much a hurry as when she arrived. They flew back down the road, the tiny woman looking through the steering wheel clutching it with both hands, and the large man, his damaged hand on the dash and the other on the seat back, bracing himself, holding on for his life.

She turned the car into the drive and took it all the way to the back before stopping. She looked over to the rear of the house, and saw the drape flapping outside the living room window. The glass had been broken out. She bent forward and picked up the pistol and handed it to Carl.

She opened the door and shouted back to him," Hurry, hurry, they may still be in there!" She stepped out into the yard and began running to the patio door. When she realized Carl wasn't coming with her, she turned back.

"Come on! Hurry!"

"Connie, are you crazy? Get back here! You're right, they could still be in there!" Shocked, Carl sat in the car with one foot on the ground and his hand on the open car door looking at Connie. "Have you lost your mind?" he said, "Get back in the car. Wait for the sheriff."

Connie was furious. "Give me the gun," she said, "if you're not man enough, I'll do this myself."

"Connie, you can't go in that house alone!"

"Watch me!"

"You do as you please, but I'm not going in there until the sheriff gets here, which shouldn't be too long."

He gestured toward the road. "I saw a car parked in the road just a little past the Salinas' house. I'm going to check it out."

With that Carl handed Connie the gun, walked around the car, got in the driver's seat, and backed out of the driveway, leaving her standing in the yard with the pistol in her hand.

Connie unlocked the door, and entered the house alone to face down and shoot the man with the scars.

Fortunately for him, the man was gone and so were his friends. They had gotten in the car that Carl had gone to check, and sped away. Carl may have been in more danger of a confrontation with them than Connie.

That was the last time Connie ever spoke to Carl with any trace of civility in her voice. He had failed the test, the big one. The man with the scars had gotten away, and worse, he had gotten away with it. Connie knew this. She had sized up the sheriff's men, and of course she knew.

***

Ignacio had a keen interest in the activities across the street. He saw the three young men walk up and get into the old green Ford that was parked off to the side of the road. Not by a house or anything, just out there by the field.

He saw Carl driving Connie's car. That wasn't right! He saw Connie standing in the yard looking across the field. She was shading her eyes. She was looking for something. Now he was really curious.

"Connie," he yelled as he jumped the bar ditch and trotted across the rows to where she was standing, "what's going on? What are you looking for?"

"Well, Ignacio, I've been robbed again! Did you see the men? Carl said they had a car parked out here, but I don't see it."

"No, kiddin," he said. "You were robbed again? Connie, I saw them! They had an old green Ford. Three of them. One had a red bandana tied over his head! They looked like gang members."

Connie spoke with Ignacio as she scanned the field. She worked across the rows in the near distance and then worked her way back across farther out carefully moving across the bedded rows.

"Have you seen Puppy?" she asked and took a few steps into the dirt of the field. "It isn't right that we haven't seen Puppy." She called over her shoulder, "I know she would be right here if she were able."

She called and called but Puppy didn't come. "I'm afraid they have killed her."

"Do you want me to look in the field?" He turned to go, "I'll look in the field."

"Puppy may be out in the field, dead, but let's look under the house first."

The old farmhouse had a pier and beam foundation. Puppy had broken through the screening of a ventilation panel by the back door and spent hot days sleeping in the damp and cool under the house.

Connie got on her hands and knees and peered into the hole. It was early afternoon, but the sun's slanting rays didn't brighten the gloom under the house. She didn't see the black dog.

"Puppy!" she called into the darkness.

She heard a soft whine.

"Puppy, Puppy, come here Sweetie," she begged urgently, and Puppy answered with a whimper.

"Connie, do you want me to get her out?"

The two of them studied the hole. "It would be a pretty tight fit for you, and Heaven only knows what else is under there. First, let's see if she'll come out."

"I'll go."

Before he could crawl in, the black head came peeking out of the hole. She had been struck between her ears and had a cut matted with blood several inches long.

Puppy didn't stand up but inched toward them, pulling herself along.

"I think they kicked her, too," he said. "¡*Pobrecita, Pobrecita*!"

"How awful!" Connie said as she saw the bloody wound on Puppy's head. "I'm going to have to take her to the vet."

"I'll take her."

"No, Ignacio. I think I should do it."

The patrol car rolled slowly up the drive and came to a stop yards from where they stood.

"You talk to the police, Puppy needs to go to the doctor now. I'll take her. You can pick her up," he said. "I'll get my truck."

They watched the two deputies get out of the car, and Ignacio stated firmly, "You're going to be busy. You talk to the police; I'll bring her back here to her hole. She lives here. She's hurt, she needs to be here where she feels safe."

CHAPTER NINETEEN

Connie and two deputies stood at the living room window on a field of glistening shards of glass. The iron bar the thieves had used on the window lay at their feet.

"The blood on the bar is probably the dog's," the officer commented. "The blood on the drape would be that of the perpetrator. He must have cut his hand removing the larger pieces of glass, so he could crawl through the window." The new drape was smeared with blood. Muddy footprints on the carpet led toward the foyer. A clear bloody thumbprint marred the white painted newel post.

One of the deputies was cutting a blood sample from the drape, leaving a hole the size of his fist. Connie watched with disconnected attention. She saw the pleats, she saw the rod, but she avoided watching him working with his pocketknife on her new drapes.

"Mrs. Rogers, I'm going on up the stairs and take that thumbprint off the post up there. You don't need to come."

The spell was broken; she nodded in agreement.

The second officer said, "Let's go in the other room. I need to fill out a report."

Carl had called Susan, and she slipped in the door and stood silently watching her mother. She saw the deputy cut the hole in her mother's new drape with disbelief. How could she let him do it? Her mother's disconnected expression frightened her, and she touched Connie's arm as she passed into the family room. Her arm was rigid so she didn't interfere, but just followed and listened and watched.

Connie sat in her chair and motioned the deputy to take the seat across from her. The cluttered table bore her cold, abandoned lunch, along with her playing cards, an ashtray full of her half smoked cigarettes, and the gun.

The pistol lay where she put it down when the deputies came to the door. It lay there still, centered on the table with the clip in place.

When they were seated, they both looked down at the pistol. She put her hand on it, looked directly into the eyes of the deputy, challenging him to take it away, daring him to suggest she shouldn't have it. His eyes met her challenge, unwavering, and he didn't mention it. He let it pass.

"Mrs. Rogers, let's get some things straight. You keep saying, 'armed robbery'. We don't know if they were armed. A steel rod is not what they are referring to when they use the term 'armed'. They mean a gun when they say that."

"They were armed with that rod, and you don't know if they had a gun or not. You said they would come back. Well, if this is the same men, you know they had guns. They had my husband's guns."

"Well, it's irrelevant. That doesn't make it a robbery. It was a burglary. A burglary takes place when no one is at home, so there is no such thing as 'armed burglary'.

"I was here."

"Not when the burglary took place. And another thing, for my report, you do not live on Morningside Road, do you?"

"No."

"You live on Cesar Chavez. You know that, don't you? The name has been changed a long time now. Long enough for you to know there is no Morningside Road here."

"Yes. Thank you for correcting me. Get it right. It's changed now. It isn't Morningside Road anymore. It's Cesar Chavez, now."

"You can't tell me how old the person was or even if he was, did you say Asian?"

"Well, he had his head shaved and it's hard to tell how old a person is without a hairline. I think he was in his late teens. I think he was a Mexican, he had a Spanish accent, but his eyes were slanty like the eyes of a Chinese person. The other two were Mexicans, and one had a red bandana on his head. It could have been shaved, too, for all I know."

This burglary, just one of their everyday calls, was a life crisis to her, and she spoke carefully. She sat stiffly erect and began telling him what had happened. He sat across the table from her listening.

She kept putting her hand on the pistol as she spoke, and then lifting the hand, causing the pistol to spin slightly on the glass top of the table. She wasn't patting the pistol, just placing her hand on it and taking it away.

Clock-like, it gradually shifted on its pivot, inching its way toward pointing at the deputy. It was an unconscious gesture she made as she told him how the man had come back, just as they said, and threatened her before breaking in to her house again. He noted the slowly revolving pistol without ever looking directly at it. He didn't stop it, and he didn't move.

Connie spoke with controlled anger as she described the terrifying events. She had no respect for the deputy. She was tired, and they had been through this before. He pretended not to see the pistol, and his senseless show of bravado was lost on Connie.

The second deputy took the bloody thumbprint from the newel post, and they left another card. She had a new case number, but the warning was the same.

"Now, Mrs. Rogers, you are no longer safe in this house." They had said that before.

"They'll come back. You can count on it. The insurance replaced the stolen things. If you do this again, they'll be back. You're an elderly lady. You have a nice family. You don't have to live alone out here in the country."

This time the warning had to be taken seriously. The deputies were not going to be any help. They had no lead, so no one would be assigned to investigate. The crooks were still out there, 'at large.' There would be no investigation, no posse, no arrest, and no help. She was on her own. They had allowed her to keep the pistol, a clue that they thought she would probably need it. They were here to fill out the forms for the insurance company. A victimless crime, the insurance would pay.

But, who can put a price on the loss of one's independence?

And so she did what she had to do when the deputies left. Connie climbed the stairs and packed a little overnight bag, came back down and closed up her kitchen for the very last time. She would never again sleep in her house on Morningside Road.

CHAPTER TWENTY

The day's events had taken their toll on everyone. Carl was restless and sat on his porch into the late evening dusk. He looked across the field at the white house, and it looked different.

Connie's gone, well, things change, he thought. The house didn't change, but it didn't look the same. Before the lighted windows gave the house a warm, neighborly look. Now when he sat on his deck in the dusk, and the pole light snapped on, he saw a specter of a house, cold and oddly green, and he knew he had better be on his guard.

Ignacio was restless. About eleven o'clock puppy's barking drew him in a trot to the window. Puppy had backed deep into her hole under the house. The vet had stitched her head up like a football, but she was alert. When the pickup came driving up into the yard, she came out and began the series of howling barks that drew Ignacio to the window.

Ignacio saw the pickup truck as it drove across the grass in Connie's front yard, and disappeared around back. He walked out to the road to see what was going on. The truck was backed up to Connie's washhouse.

As it drove away, it passed under the tall pole with the light, and he saw Connie's washer and dryer in the back of the truck.

He dialed the sheriff.

"What's your name?"

"Ignacio Salinas."

"What's your problem?"

He tells them.

"Are they still there?"

"No."

"What's your address?"

"I'll tell you my address, but I'm talking about something that's happening across the street, at my neighbor's house. The house across the street from me."

"When you have a problem, call us. What happens to someone else isn't your problem. We can't respond to a call from you for someone else.

There's not much we could do about it tonight anyway if they're not there anymore."

***

At Susan's house they were taking the morning easy. They sat at the kitchen table with the remnants of sausage and scrambled eggs, and they were on their second cup of coffee when the call came from Ignacio.

"Connie," he said, "you need to come out here."

"Is Puppy alright?"

"Puppy's gonna be OK. She's fine. That's not why I'm calling."

He told her about the past night's events. "I'm watching your house for you, but the sheriff, he don't want me to call him. He said, 'It's not your house!'"

He had taken it as a personal insult. "So you have to call him yourself."

He explained, "I checked, the washer and dryer are gone. You have to report it," his voice was distressed, "yourself."

"Ignacio, you're a good neighbor, thank you so much for watching out for me. I'll call the sheriff, and I'll be right out."

Connie was wearing a print duster over her nightgown and she pulled it together with one hand as she returned to sit at the table.

"Ignacio said some people came last night and took my washer and dryer." She looked tired. She looked older.

"It wasn't the same men. This time it was someone with a pickup truck."

"How did they know you had left?" Susan asked, "Not from the newspaper, they didn't have time."

"Word of mouth, I guess." She spoke softly, with resignation. "I told you they would come if I left. They just came a little sooner than even I expected."

Susan flushed with anger. "Vultures! And the carcass is still warm!"

"Good old Ignacio! He's trying to help. He called the sheriff and they told him it was none of his business! They won't come out if he calls. They want me to call, so I guess I had better do it now." She lifted her cold cup of coffee and then set it down.

Susan stood to bring the pot over to refill the cups, and paused at the counter, a suspicious notion had come to her. She leaned against the cabinet with the pot of hot coffee in her hand and ventured, "You know, Mother, those men may have learned you were gone from the sheriff. How else could they have known so soon that you weren't there?"

Connie looked at her without much enthusiasm, and said, "Don't be so quick to make accusations! They may have come and taken my washer and dryer even if I had been at home. It doesn't seem to make a difference to them whether I'm there or not."

The hot coffee must have fortified her because her control returned and firmly now, she said, "Let's get dressed. I want you to take me out to my house. I want to look around and see if they took anything else."

She rose and added, "I'm going to call your brother and tell him we're going to need his pickup."

She carried her dishes to the sink and continued, "We'd better make plans to get what we can out of the house today, anything they would take. They may be coming back tonight."

She began to deal with the situation, "We'll need to rent a storage locker."

***

Ignacio had seen them. They stood in the sunshine of the summer morning with their backs to the washhouse door and waited for him. He walked in the tracks the loaded truck had left as it drove away across the lawn with her appliances the night before.

He waved and called out even before he reached them. "Connie, I saw the truck, it was a pickup. See, these are the tracks. I didn't get the number, but I saw it real good."

"Thanks, Ignacio. I called the sheriff. You don't have to worry; it's official now." She didn't mention that the deputies were not coming out again. They didn't want to fill out another form on the case. They said it would be better to just add the items to the list of stolen things. They had experience in handling these situations and suggested that the insurance company would regard it as a second offense and require a deduction that could be more than the cost of replacing the washer and dryer.

The cats looked down at them from the roof of the little house. Connie saw them, and then began walking back across the yard to the patio door.

"Connie, what are you going to do now?" Ignacio asked anxiously.

"Right now, I'm going to feed Puppy and the cats."

"They'll probably come back," he said, "maybe tonight. Connie, what are you going to do?" The urgency in his voice was contagious.

"Johnny's coming and we're going to take some things today, but we can't move anything large until tomorrow when we can rent a truck."

She unlocked the iron grille and slid the glass door open. The three of them stepped into the room and looked around inside the house. As they passed from room to room, they could see that nothing else had been disturbed, but somehow it all looked different today. Everything suddenly seemed to be at risk. The locked door no longer kept them out. The house and everything in it was vulnerable. *Up for grabs.*

"We have got to take everything we can today." Susan said, "Mother, I can put some things in my car. Is there anything special you want me to take first?" The question seemed simple at first, but now it had become necessary to put a priority on Connie's possessions of a lifetime.

"First? Well, first, where are you going to take them? I think you had better go to town and rent a storage locker before we take anything out of here."

"I have some room in my garage. Let me take a car load with me to town, and I'll rent a locker and come back for more."

Susan couldn't explain the anxiety she felt. She had been pushing her mother for some time to move because, rationally, she thought Connie was in danger here, but maybe she didn't really believe it. Susan had grown up in this house. She had been sheltered here growing up.

Well, she believed it now. She knew about the man, the one with the scars, and she knew he was still out there somewhere. She had seen the tracks across the grass. She had seen the cut hoses dangling over the empty spaces where her mother's washer and dryer had been.

Before, she had been concerned for her mother's safety, but now she felt responsible for her things, too.

"Everything I have is in that house," she could hear her mother say. "My life savings and everything Hank and I managed to accumulate over a lifetime."

Everything I have? She couldn't stand by and see her mother lose *everything.* We have to hurry! *What's the matter with me!*

"Go on to town, take a load if you want, but call a glazier and ask him to come out here. We need to get that window covered. Also, call the phone company and report the phone is cut again."

"Mother, is that necessary? Do you need a phone out here any more? Why not just cancel the service?"

"You're probably right about the phone. I guess I won't be needing it anymore, don't call them yet. Buy a lock for the storage unit. Get a combination lock so any of us can get in if we have to."

Connie turned to discuss something else with Ignacio, and they moved on into the kitchen leaving Susan alone in a room full of her threatened belongings.

As Susan crossed the patio with a box, Carl came walking up the drive. He motioned to her to wait. She watched the tall man as he approached. He didn't smile until he greeted her. They stood together in the yard, and he gave her his version of what had happened the day before. She listened with interest. He was, as always, so sincere and concerned.

"You're mother is losing her perspective. She did some things yesterday I think you should know about. Did you know she took that pistol and went back into the house after the men? She thought they were still in there, and they very well might have been."

"Really?" Susan said. "She didn't tell me that." She didn't add that she wasn't surprised to hear it. She, too, was concerned about her mother's determined attitude.

They were looking back at the house and the activity inside. "I'm really going to miss that sweet little lady. This neighborhood just won't be the same without her.

"I know she thinks this is a tragedy, but realistically, she's lucky to be alive. Those kids might have killed her. They just might have taken that pistol away from her and shot her with it."

"They were kids? Did you see them? Mother said they were young men."

"Salinas saw them, and he says they looked like gang members to him. That's what he called them, anyway. Just because they call them kids, don't be fooled. You know what they say, 'If a kid stabs you, try not to bleed.'" It wasn't funny, and they didn't laugh.

Carl continued, "I don't understand why we want to coddle them. They call them 'at risk boys', and pamper them and create programs for them, but they're old-fashioned thugs and when they get high on drugs you can't know what they might do. And, I might add, gang members aren't all kids any more."

Susan was disturbed at this new wrinkle.

"It's a good thing she's going to live in town with you," Carl said, "I know that's not what she wants, but she'll be a lot better off in the long run."

He assured her he'd try to watch Connie's house for her until it could sell, but cautioned, "That colonia up the road attracts transient riff-raff, illegals, and this neighborhood is going downhill fast. Crime is becoming a problem for all of us. You've got to keep your head up all the time."

He removed his hat and mopped his forehead with his disfigured right hand, and then said, "After what went on here yesterday, I was afraid they might come back and take the John Deere."

They turned together and looked at the empty stall in the garage. They hadn't thought to look in there yet and it was the first time Susan realized the lawnmower was gone.

"I took it to my place last night. It's in my garage. Just so you know where it is and that it's safe. You can come get it whenever you want to. In the meantime, I'll just keep it with me."

Susan was distracted and anxious to get to town. "Carl, thank you so much." She said, "And a good thing, too, you're so right, they might well have taken it last night along with the washer and dryer."

"What about the washer and dryer?"

He didn't know so she told him of the last evening's events.

"This isn't the end of it. They have her number, now. Is she going to leave any furniture in the house? I hear they like to vandalize what they don't take. Nothing's safe in there with her gone."

"We're taking all we can this afternoon, and we've got a truck coming tomorrow. We have to pack her dishes for storage. She's moving in with me and won't be needing anything but her clothes."

"What about the things in the garage? There are a few good tools left, but its mostly junk, now. She'll be needing someone to clean it out."

They turned back to look in the open door of the garage again and it all looked like junk to Susan.

"Maybe I can work a deal with Connie to clean it out for her in exchange for the mower. She won't be needing it anymore," he ventured. "I could sort out the good things for her to sell, and we could get the rest of it hauled off. You'll have to do it anyway if you sell the place."

"Sounds like a good idea to me," she said, and walked to her car.

***

As Susan worked that day, the feeling of pressure persisted. Carl had said, "They have her number now. They'll be back." So what else is new, she wondered. The deputies had said that, too, and they were right!

"They may not be kids. They may be on drugs," Carl had said.

I can't believe this is happening in America, she fumed. It's like what happens to people in third world countries. Like people fleeing the rabble in Algeria when the French pulled out, those people who have to run with only one suitcase and maybe an hour to do it. They are robbing Mother blind, right here, not in some foreign country. I can't believe it!

Mother can take a truckload, Susan thought, and we've got all day. So why am I so agitated? What's the hurry? She asked herself, and her mind slid back to the French refuges. They fled before an army, no, a rabble of looters and thugs. The thugs are here now. They're here! They're still out there waiting for Mother.

She had to talk about it. "Mother, if you could only take five things, what would they be?"

"I don't have to make that decision, thank goodness."

Connie's eyes stopped on the framed pictures of her great grandchildren.

"They probably won't want my photographs and books. What do you think, shall I take the lamps?"

She unplugged the telephone and said, "We can keep this in the car and I'll bring it back here if I need it, that is if I decide not to cancel the service."

The big clock began to chime, "They didn't take my clocks before, what do you think?"

"Mother, they'll have more time now." And sadly, "They'll take anything they want."

They put the clocks in the pickup.

As she worked, Susan picked away at the situation. We should have known this would happen. Mother knew it all along, Susan stewed. The sheriff said they'd be back in a month. It was almost a month to the day. We should have known. Mother knew the vandals would come. She told us so, but we were so dense, I just couldn't believe the sheriff would let them do it. Well, now we know.

The French were betrayed by their own government, and now it's happening right here in our own back yard! The sheriff has betrayed Mother in the same way! He knew they'd come, he warned us, and then he let it happen.

"Well, at least we weren't betrayed by the French government," she said, lamely, and laughed nervously at the joke.

When they finally left for the day, Susan looked at her mother sitting in the car seat next to her, a cut glass decanter in her lap, and her feet on a box.

So strong, she thought, to be so tiny and vulnerable.

"Mother, this situation reminds me of the French refuges from Algeria," she said.

Connie's voice was tired, "Yes, it does. Just like them, I'm a poor relative now, asking to be taken in."

"That's not true, and you know it! This is only temporary, just until we can sell your property!"

Connie didn't answer.

CHAPTER TWENTY-ONE

Connie was a smoker. She was old and set, and she had an old dog. She got up early, put the coffee on, and she and Mark and the cigarettes went out onto the patio where it was quiet, and where they could be alone. They sat out there and waited for the day to begin. They waited for the newspapers, and the breakfast, and later on, the truck, and the waiting was hard. She came back inside for breakfast.

"Sunday mornings are very quiet around here."

"Yes, but there'll be a lot of activity around the pool this afternoon. You're lucky to miss it." Susan lived in the La Resaca town house complex.

"I'm going to have to find a place to live," Connie said as she picked up the newspaper. Something on the front page caught her eye, and she gave it her close attention. "Would you look at this?" she said, pointing to a picture in the lower half of the first page. She passed it over to Susan with her finger still on the picture.

"It's an article on the inmates of the County Boot Camp. He looked like this. His hair was shaved just like that. He seemed to be about that age, late teens."

Susan and her husband Bob sat at the table with her, and they passed the paper around and discussed the possibilities.

"If his head was shaved because he had been at the boot camp," she went on, "then he hasn't been out too long because it hasn't grown out very much. Not at all."

Bob joined in, "The barber would remember shaving a head with scars like that, especially this recently."

"If that haircut is temporary, we have to find him before it grows out."

The excitement mounted, "Right! Right! Even better, they would have taken his fingerprints. They would have them on file there."

Susan announced, "Better than that even, it's a lead! They'll assign an officer to the case if there's a lead. Mother, this is too good to pass up.

I'm going to call the sheriff." She dialed the number. All eyes were on her as she waited for an answer.

She had the cards the deputies had left and gave the detective the case number and other relevant information when she got him on the line.

"Mother has seen the picture of the men from the County Boot Camp in today's paper. She says our man may be one of them. His head has been shaved like theirs, and he's about that age."

She was breathless from the excitement, "Could you check with the camp barber to see if he remembers cutting the hair of a man with three large old scars? Tell him it would have been recently, the hair hasn't grown out yet."

"It's Sunday," he said, "the barber wouldn't be there today."

"Well, could you do it tomorrow? If we could get his name, then you could cross reference the finger prints."

"Well, yes, the barber might remember him, but you know we can't check the prints."

"Why not?"

"These young men have rights. They're protected by the law, just the same as anyone else. We can't check his prints unless we can show 'cause'."

She turned to her mother and said, "Can you believe it? Can you believe it! You don't have any rights in this country until you break the law. And I said 'thank you' again, wasn't that silly of me? He certainly didn't do anything I should have thanked him for."

They prepared to go to finish moving the large things into storage. It was a sad day. It was a long day, and hard.

Moving from a place where she had lived more than forty years is not a simple thing. She had so much to go through and get rid of. The decisions over what is kept and what has to be discarded are not easy, and they came hard.

The activity had attracted the attention of the neighborhood. All day the neighbors stopped in to say goodbye.

"Why are you leaving? What happened?" they asked. And Connie knew, sadly, they were not protected either.

She had a bad confrontation with Carl when she asked him to return the John Deere. He brought it back, but was plainly miffed about it. He warned her, "You're going to lose everything in your garage. You need to get it taken care of right away."

"Carl, don't waste your time worrying about my garage. I know what has to be done, and I'm doing it." She didn't mention that she had arranged for Ignacio to clean out the garage in exchange for the mower. He promised to use it to keep the lawn mowed until the house could be sold as part of the deal.

Late in the day they walked through the empty house, passing through the echoing rooms for the last time that evening. Everyone became quiet. They stood together on the little patio, in the twilight, as she locked the door.

Tired, Connie braced herself with one hand on the iron grille, and her other hand shook as she turned the key in the lock. The key glided smoothly around, and no one else heard the clanging finality of the simple act except Connie.

Her purse sat on the bricks at her feet. As she stooped to pick it up, they heard a car in the driveway.

An old pickup rolled to a stop by the patio. Elaine, who had gone to high school with Connie's son John, sat behind the wheel, and her daughter Kathy was with her.

"Connie, are you moving?" Elaine spoke across the hood of the truck as she walked around it.

"That's right," Connie said, and put her arm around her young friend.

"Where are you going?"

"I'm staying with Susan until I can find a place."

"Did you sell the house? I've seen the sign." She gestured toward the front.

"No, not yet. I had really hoped to sell it before I moved out, but I've had a lot of trouble, and I have to go. I hate leaving the house vacant."

Kathy joined the group on the patio. "What trouble?"

"I've been robbed twice in the last month. They just come in and take what they want. They come even when I'm at home. It doesn't seem to matter to them, and everyone thinks it has gotten too dangerous for me to stay any longer."

"You were here? Did you see them?"

"Yes, I did. They hung around here harassing me for about an hour the last time."

Connie shook her head; "One of them kept trying to talk me into letting him in the house. I got a good look at him."

Connie's hand was on her cheek as she explained softly, "I see him in my sleep. He was baldheaded, but he was a young man. He had ugly white scars on his scalp. Someone must have beaten him up badly. I'll never forget his leering face."

"Connie, did you say his head was bald, do you mean shaved? And he had scars?" Elaine and Kathy, exchanged glances.

"Were they here, here, and here?" Her finger slashed across her own head, indicating the places graphically.

"Yes! Yes!" Connie said.

"Connie! We know this guy. Well, we don't know him, but we know who he is. He's been hanging around our park. A lot of creepy guys hang out in this old trailer in our park all the time."

"He doesn't actually live there?"

"No, I don't think any of them really live there. But they hang around an old trailer. A lot of girls keep coming and going, too. You don't want to know what they do in there. It goes on day and night."

"Do you know who owns the trailer?"

"No, but the guy with the scars doesn't own it."

Kathy said, "The one with the scars is kind of a leader of the creeps. He has a car. He's brassy in a disgusting way, and he used to come around and brag that he had a place on Padre Island. He's creepy, and I try to stay inside when I see them around. He's not there all the time. But I don't think he has a place on the Island or anywhere else, because he's here a lot. They peddle small electronics, VCRs and stereos and such, cheap! We know what they are. Everyone does!"

"Could you get his name for me?"

"Listen, these guys are bad news. I don't know what his real name is; the guy with the scars isn't dark like the rest, he's fair for a Mexican. They call him Güero, and it means "Whitey". They drive around in a scabby old Ford. They're so scary that we took down the license number. I'll call you when I get back and give it to you."

"Are they still there?" Connie asked.

"Probably, they have been. I'll check and let you know."

"Would you object to our passing it on to the sheriff?" she asked, cautiously.

She put her hand on Connie's arm, "Call them, call them! Connie, you know I'll help in any way I can. We'd be so happy to see them gone."

"Where does Elaine live?" Susan asked when the old pickup backed down the drive and pulled away.

"Elaine is divorced. She and her daughter live in a really poor trailer park just up Sioux road. Kathy is a horsewoman. She's into competitive western riding. They don't have much so they live in that old park because they're allowed to keep a horse there. Elaine calls the park East of Eden. I don't know if that's its name, or if that's just what she thinks of it."

As hard and as sad as the day had been, Connie had two good leads, and when she got back to Susan's they waited anxiously for Elaine's call. It was almost ten o'clock when it came; it was Kathy on the line.

"I'm sorry it took so long, but I couldn't find where I wrote the number. Finally, I walked over to the trailer, and the car was there. It's a Ford Galaxy, four door. It's a rusty burnt-out green color; the plate number is JYT36R."

Connie put her hand over the phone and announced, "She's got the number, and they're there now!"

"Kathy, I'm going to call the sheriff. I'm going to give him your name. He may call you."

"Sure, I'll be glad to talk to him. Tell him to call us."

They celebrated when she hung up. "Susan, I'm so excited, you call, please." Connie sat down at the table with a grin, and Susan made the call.

She spoke to a receptionist. "This is an emergency! We have found the man who robbed my mother's house. He's at a trailer park near here. We need you to send a deputy out there. We don't think that's where he lives, so he may not be there long. I have his license number."

"There isn't anyone here now that we could send out."

"What! Nobody's there?"

"David Ocampo is here. He's our Chief of Criminal Enforcement, and he may be able to help you. He's in charge of all criminal investigations. Would you like to speak to him?"

"Oh, yes, please."

When he came to the phone she said, "My mother's house on Cesar Chavez Road was robbed a couple of days ago. The case number is, just a minute, I'll get it."

"Don't bother," he said, "I know the house."

"Mother can identify the man. His head is shaved, and he has three large old scars on his scalp that show up very prominently in the black stubble. She described him to neighbors, and they know where he is. They have told us, and they have just called. He's there now!"

"Do you know his name?"

"They call him Güero."

"Güero is a nickname. It means Whitey. It probably isn't his real name."

She described the old green car and gave him the license number.

"He's at the first house in the third block when you turn in to the park, the East of Eden trailer park on Sioux road. He's there now! You need to go out there and hurry!"

"Let me explain something to you. It doesn't work like that. I can't just go out there and arrest this man." His voice was condescending.

"Tomorrow, you come down here and press charges. You're going to need his name."

"What! You can't go out there tonight?"

"When you get his name, come down here and press charges, and then we'll be able to go from there." It was late, and he sounded very tired.

"How am I going to get his name? Can't you get that for me? My friend can identify him. She says she'll be glad to talk to you. Could you go out and talk to her?"

She gave him Elaine's name and phone number. "She lives in that same park. You'll know her place. She has a horse.

"And another thing, the man who lives across the street from me saw the car the day of the robbery."

She gave him Ignacio's name and phone number.

"He saw the car parked in the road just past his house, and he saw the three men get in it and drive away. The deputies talked to him when they were here the day of the robbery."

"I'll check around. I know the park. I'll see what I can do."

"Oh, thanks. Thank you so much."

***

Carl, when asked, returned the mower. He didn't, however, expect Connie to give it to Ignacio, and so he was alarmed when sitting, as usual, on the deck for his morning tea break, to see Ignacio go into Connie's garage and drive away home on the John Deere mower.

"Those thieving Mexicans!" he said. "They're all alike! She's hardly out of the house, and he's already stealing her mower."

He left his tea to sweat on the redwood table while he went in to call Connie.

"Connie," he said, "the Mexican's stolen your mower."

"What Mexican?"

"Salinas, that thief. I just watched him drive it over to his house."

"Carl, I know he has the mower. I gave it to him. It belongs to him now. It's none of your business anyway."

"I thought you and I had a deal."

"I never made a deal with you about the mower, or anything else. I don't know what you're talking about."

"Well, Susan said she wanted me to clean out your garage in exchange for the mower."

"The mower isn't Susan's. It belongs to me, and I have made my own deal with Ignacio."

"Are you reneging on our deal?"

"Carl, we never had a deal. Don't call me again."

CHAPTER TWENTY-TWO

In the very early morning the phone rang, and it was Ignacio. He doesn't call the sheriff anymore.

"Connie! They came back last night! I heard Puppy. It was midnight, and she woke us up. She was barking like crazy, and I went out there to see what was going on."

Ignacio was excited and Connie said, "Slow down!"

"Connie, I seen it real good because I went on down to the bar ditch and lay down there, and I watched them.

"Connie, they was driving on your grass. They went right up to the windows, right in the flowerbeds. They was looking in the windows so they didn't have to get out of the car.

"I saw the car real good; it was a light colored car, not white. I could see it was a woman driving, it was two women."

"They just drove on the lawn? They didn't get out or bother anything?" Connie asked, puzzled.

"No, they didn't but after that, I couldn't sleep so good, and Puppy was barking again, so I went to the window. It was two o'clock, and there was a truck backing up to the front door. A man got out and kicked the door in. He kicked it in! He broke it! Then he carried out your air conditioners, all three of them. And Connie, guess what? The door's gone! The house is wide open. You have to come out here, and you have to call the sheriff."

The splintered door and frame required a carpenter. The air conditioners in the bedrooms upstairs were window units. The one in the family room was built into the wall, and she needed to close the hole where it had been. Connie, of course, had to pay a carpenter, and the air conditioners were gone.

CHAPTER TWENTY-THREE

The southeast breeze in the evenings stirred the rustling fronds of the tall palm trees, and their shadows danced upon the white stucco walls of the townhouse complex where Susan and Bob lived. The white buildings with their red tile roofs reflected in the resaca that bisected the complex. Fountains of sparkling water rose from the green pool sending cooling sounds to the surrounding houses. Flashes of red showed where goldfish begged at the arched bridge.

Migrating ducks raised their young in the bamboo ferns that lined the lake. Flocks of brilliant green Mexican parrots flew chattering overhead and landed to rest in the tall willow trees. They disturbed the jays that otherwise ruled over the smaller birds. Woodpeckers worked at spoiling the papayas as they ripened. An ornamental orchid tree bloomed purple at the pool by the waterfall. Hibiscus and oleander plantings flowered throughout the complex.

The Spanish style houses had windows adorned with elaborate iron grillwork. The grilles were functional as well as decorative. The common areas were gated, secure, and accessible only to those who knew the combination.

Connie was safe here, and she was unhappy. She brought Mark with her when she moved in with Susan, and Susan's two cats hissed and arched their backs when he came into the room. One of them, the gray one, defended her territory aggressively. The big gray cat took a few days to take measure of him and decided he could be removed. She stubbornly refused to run from his sharp barking. Finally she felt confident enough to inch toward him from a crouching position, hissing and growling low in her throat with her sharp teeth bared.

When he backed away, she became even more emboldened and swatted at his eyes with her claws. At last he retreated onto the sofa back for protection, so irritating Susan, he found himself banished for long hours to the patio.

Susan's patio was enclosed with high stucco walls. A mandevilla vine blossomed lavender in the warmth of late summer, and a fountain with a dolphin and cherub tinkled pleasantly at one end. A guava tree peeked across the wall from a neighbor's house. Its waxy, dark green leaves contrasted with the light green of the papaya tree that stood just outside the wrought iron gate. Brilliant red bougainvillea climbed the north wall. The heavy smell of gardenia blossoms overpowered the sweet potted petunias lined up along the east wall.

Connie spent a lot of time on the patio with the dog and her cigarettes. Her arguments with Susan continued. They just argued about something else now.

"Mother, please don't go out there any more."

"What!"

"Don't look at me like I'm from another planet!"

Connie made daily trips to her house on Cesar Chavez Road. Every day at four o'clock she put the pistol in her purse; she put Mark in the car and drove out there. She kept a sack of dry cat food in the kitchen and would pour some in dishes and place them in the back for the yard cats. She made sure they had water.

A working dog, Puppy got canned food in addition to her dry. Connie kept a can opener in the kitchen with a week's supply of pet food.

She left a white plastic chair and a little patio table in the family room. She would sit there, sometimes for hours in the room where Hank had died, and smoke while Mark exercised and played with Puppy. She slept in the town house, but her heart resided on Morningside Road.

Susan hoped she went to the house only to survey the new wounds and not to dwell on the old ones. A stone had been thrown through the dining room window, and they had not had it repaired. Glass still sparkled in the carpet. Connie didn't want the window repaired, and she left the stone where it had landed. She stepped over it when she went to the kitchen. It became a marker, a symbol of the open wound. Had a neighbor done it? She couldn't imagine who would want to hurt her further.

"Who would do this?" she wondered.

"You mustn't go out there any more. It's depressing for you, and I think it may even be dangerous," Susan nagged.

"What do you mean, don't go out there any more? I have to go. The animals depend upon me, and it's my responsibility. Puppy and the cats are still on the job."

"Mother, you face a life crisis, and it's a crisis in their lives, too. You need to do something permanent with your pets."

"What do you mean permanent?" Connie bristled.

"You know what I mean. You live in town now, and you won't be going back out there to live."

Connie was incensed, "Puppy will not be put down. I love her, and she trusts me. She was there for me when I needed her, and I'm going to take care of her now."

"Then, bring her to town."

"I need her to watch the house. Puppy's too big to live here. She's a yard dog." Connie's arm waved across the small space, "This patio's too small for her, and she can't live in the house."

Susan didn't answer, but of course she had to agree. Not only was it too small for Puppy; she didn't want the big dog on her patio.

Connie continued, "We can't even catch those wild cats. Are you suggesting I just abandon them to starve? I have to check on the house anyway. With Mark almost blind, he needs to exercise in a place that's familiar to him. He runs into things here."

Susan didn't glance over to her sofa back, but she resented the way Mark was tearing it up now that it was his sanctuary. She welcomed any time she could manage without the dog in the house.

"If you have to go out there, at least don't go there alone."

Bees worked over the potted Mexican lime tree and Connie sat watching them. Finally she retorted, "What do you mean, don't go out there alone?" her voice registered her irritation, "I can't wait for you. You're too busy. Anyway you have a life of your own. That's my house. Those are my pets, and they are my responsibility."

Susan didn't give up so easily. "I'm afraid for you to go out there by yourself. You know it isn't safe any more. The thug with the scars is still around there somewhere, probably watching to see what you're going to do. The deputies think he'll be back. He's probably on drugs. This time he may kill you."

"Nobody is safe. Anywhere! You live in a cage, yet you go out and get in that car. Do you think you're safe? This is my life. I'm still alive. I'm not going to just sit in here and be safe. I can protect myself," and she added firmly, "I still have my pistol."

"What's the point," Susan said, "of going some place that's so dangerous you have to carry a gun?"

CHAPTER TWENTY-FOUR

In the afternoon Carl called. "Susan, I know your dear little mother is upset and disturbed by what has happened to her, and it's perfectly natural that she should be, but there's something I think you need to know about the lawnmower."

Susan wasn't expecting this to come up so was not prepared for what he said next.

"That thieving Mexican has her lawnmower, and he says she gave it to him. He's a thief and a liar, and I know that can't be right."

His voice had an edge to it, and the hard words he spoke surprised Susan. Usually butter wouldn't melt in his mouth.

"Carl, she didn't give it to him. She traded it with him for his cleaning out the garage. He's helping her dispose of the rest of my father's tools, and he's going to haul off the junk. He's going to look after things in general over there for her until the house sells. He's going to keep the lawn mowed, and he'll work pretty hard to earn the mower."

"Well, I was prepared to clean out the garage and would have paid her something in addition to that."

The pause was long and awkward while Susan tried to think how to answer him.

"Now, I know you'll take care of this out of fairness to me because you told me," his voice trembled with anger, "that you wanted me to have the mower. I saved it the night she left. Those Mexicans would have taken it that night and you know it. You said so the next day, and you thanked me for taking it. I'm expecting you to speak to your mother about this."

Oh brother, she thought, and said, "Carl, I'll tell Mother about your call. You're right, she is upset about what happened, but she's still capable of making her own decisions.

"You misunderstood what I said the other day. That mower isn't mine, and I couldn't have told you that you could have it. It's Mother's and she'll dispose of it as she chooses. If she made a deal with Mr. Salinas, she's not likely to renege on it. Mother doesn't do that ever."

"Your Mother does renege on deals, she has reneged on her deal with me. I expect you to do the right thing about this. You have always been a fair and reasonable person, and you know I have looked out for her and helped her when I could throughout the time we've been neighbors."

"Carl, I'll tell her you called and explain to her how you feel. That's all I can do."

And she did. But that was only the beginning.

Carl didn't bother Connie any more. He bothered Susan. He called her, and he called her, and when he gave up on her he started calling her husband Bob. He called him at home, and then he started calling him at work. Bob told the secretaries not to put his calls through, so he began dropping by to harass him at the office in person. And he called Susan some more, but they were thankful he left Connie alone.

Now they were really sick of Carl. When he would call and interrupt whatever they were doing to whine and nag and finally threaten about the mower, they found it difficult to be civil with him. When the phone rang, and Susan heard his voice on the other end, her heart would sink and she knew she was in for about ten very unpleasant minutes. The thing was that Susan had absolutely no control over her mother. Carl had never bothered to try to understand Connie; if he had, he would have known that Susan couldn't make her do anything she didn't want to do.

No one could.

CHAPTER TWENTY-FIVE

The car came back, then the truck, and this time they took the dishwasher and the stove. In a couple of weeks they returned for the light fixtures. They stood on Connie's lawn chair and removed the small crystal chandelier that graced the table on Thanksgiving and Christmas leaving bare wires dangling where it had been. And they took the drapes. Not particular, they even took the one with the hole the deputy had cut out for the bloody fingerprint. They didn't take the sheer panels.

This time, Ignacio crossed the road, and hid behind the pomegranate tree. Two women drove a medium blue Nova across the lawn and up to the windows. Ignacio saw them and took down the license plate number.

He tried once more calling the sheriff, and Connie called. The sheriff took the number, but he didn't send anyone out, what could they do? The crooks had gone by now. Where was the proof they had come at all? They only had Ignacio's word. The sheriff needed something more substantial.

Ignacio rode his bicycle around talking to everyone. He talked a lot. He was still smarting about the disrespect the sheriff had shown him. He made his daily rounds on the bicycle, telling everyone, and he told it all.

CHAPTER TWENTY-SIX

Connie had the electricity turned off. The house was going to be dark now anyway. The appliances and the light fixtures were gone. The battle to keep the house repaired was lost. Now Angie called to tell her they needed to talk. They sat on the sofa at Susan's with coffee, and reluctantly Angie began explaining to Connie and Susan what she was up against.

"Connie, the house isn't showing very well. The longer it's vacant, the bleaker the prospects are going to be. I had some really bad news on it yesterday."

Connie sat forward in her seat anxiously, what next?

"I thought I had a good prospect, a man who was interested in the house and the land, all thirty acres. He called and told me he went by the Chapin City Hall to check on their restrictions for the place. You know you're in their extra-territorial jurisdiction, don't you?"

Connie said, "No, what does that mean? Are you saying that even though I'm not in the city limits I'm under their jurisdiction? How does that affect my property?"

Angie explained, "Even though you're not in the city limits, they have been extended to border on your property on the south and west. You are in their jurisdiction. That means you can't do things to your property they think will hurt the city."

Angie put her hand on Connie's knee, "This is so crazy, extraordinary really! Well, anyway, they showed him a map of their projected streets, streets they are planning for the future. It instantly killed his interest in the place. Of all things, one of the streets will one day directly bisect your house."

"What?" Connie asked dumbfounded. "I guess when it was a farm they didn't imagine a problem like this. It was natural for them to center the house on the original property."

Connie thought a minute and offered, "They'll have to move it, won't they, or tear it down? Well, if they tear my house down to put in a street, they'll have to buy it, won't they? Maybe that's good."

Angie shook her head; "It would be good if they planned to do it some time soon. He says they don't plan to annex that area for a long time; two years would be the soonest" Connie sat glumly and couldn't speak.

"They don't buy it until they condemn it for the street, and who knows when that'll be, maybe years." Angie sat back quietly and waited for Connie to digest what she had just said.

Stunned by the news, Connie said, "This means that I pay taxes on the property, but someone else decides what I can do with it?"

"It looks that way, doesn't it?"

"They have told me I can't live there, and now they say I can't sell it?"

Susan slipped out of the room to cut the cake. She thought they needed a sugar fix about then.

"Connie, we'll keep the property on the market. You know things could change without notice. We'll stay on top of the situation, and who knows what will happen."

"Angie, that's right, I don't know what's going to happen next. So far the news has all been bad. I spoke to my insurance agent yesterday, and she had bad news for me, too. She expressed her regrets, but because the house is vacant, they would need to go up on the premium. It would now be seventy-five dollars a month, and will only cover fire damage, one thousand dollar deductible!"

Connie shook her head, "It might just as well be a million. And, Angie, she said it was only a temporary tide over, just until we can sell the house. If we don't sell it within a year, they'll cancel my policy."

Connie leaned back against the cushions, "Angie, I've been with them for thirty years. I have never needed them before, and now that I do, they're going to cut me off."

CHAPTER TWENTY-SEVEN

Augst in the Rio Grande Valley is usually hot and dry. It's likely to be the hottest month of the year, and Ignacio rode in the full sunshine on a mission. His section eight rentals needed constant repair. This time it was the plumbing in a house he owned in Alamo. He stood and pumped faster when he reached Alamo road. He was in no special hurry. He saw a break in the traffic, and he wanted to move onto the pavement.

He recklessly rode his bike in the center. *Marano!* He said to himself with satisfaction. I'm a road hog, and he laughed out loud. Or snake! I'm a snake! His tires left snake-like marks in the soft tar expansion joints of the white concrete road.

Now early afternoon, around two, it had already been a good day. His spirits soared. He had just been notified by the regional hospital that he got the contract to handle their small hazardous waste.

A part time job, he could do it in a couple of hours, and he could hire his youngest son as helper. They would be collecting the bags of spent needles and swabs to deliver to the county for disposal. It would be a nice supplement to his income.

A paved farm road crossed Alamo Road, and a farmhouse on the corner had been converted into a business. A hackberry tree still stood in the front lawn, which now served as a parking lot. He stopped to rest awhile in the shade of the tree.

The business was a cactus farm. A stripped cedar post fence blocked the view of the cactus from the road, but standing up close he could look through the gaps at the neat rows of barrel cactus, and aloe, and the profusion of century plants, prickly pear, and other ornamentals grown there for sale to nurseries across the states.

Something was peculiar about this business. It was a real curiosity to Ignacio that they could make any money selling cactus. He felt a perverse pride that this invader, which evoked the romance of Mexico, thrived in the most savage of conditions, and which ranchers everywhere in south Texas fought at great expense, could be sold for profit.

Traffic picked up on the road. He pushed the bicycle back into the path that ran along beside it and continued on his way. The downtown plaza of Alamo had, in the early days, been the business center of Alamo, but now businesses strung out down Old Highway 83. The railroad followed along beside the highway, and so did Ignacio. The railroad tracks sent his basket to slapping up and down, so he put his hand out to steady it. The bar ditch that ran along next to the tracks had a beaten trail that he took. He would avoid the heavy traffic on the highway as long as possible.

He jaywalked his bike across at the building supply store, and pushed it up under the canopy to leave it while he went in. Something caught his eye. It was the blue Nova. He walked around to the rear of the car and checked the license tags. They matched the car he had seen driving on Connie's grass.

Ha! Ha! He said to himself, now we're going to find out who did it! And he crouched behind the car parked next to the Nova to wait.

A middle-aged woman came out of the store with a small bag and opened the car door. She put her bag in the back seat and as she was preparing to seat herself in the front, she paused and fixed her gaze on the hand painted, Kelly green bicycle with the girl's daisy-adorned basket. She examined the bicycle then got in the car and pulled away. He gave her time to thread her way into traffic. Ignacio walked the bike out to the highway and followed.

The traffic was heavy in the shopping area, so he had no trouble keeping up with her. She headed back into the center of town and turned south on the main street. After a few blocks, she turned to the west and entered a residential neighborhood. He had to be more careful here where the traffic was light, so he trailed along way behind.

The neighborhood had paved streets, but no curbs or sidewalks. He had to ride in the street and could be plainly seen tagging along behind her. Suddenly she speeded up. She drove much too fast for the residential limit. When he saw she turned back to the north, he cut through an alley and cruised in behind her.

She slowed, turned into a driveway, and he rode on past looking straight ahead. Then she did something unexpected. She backed out of the drive and now she followed him. He made a turn. She made a turn. He slowed so she would pass, and he could be following again, but she didn't pass, she pulled up beside him and drove abreast a few minutes. Her eyes drilled into him. When he gave her a nervous wave, she didn't smile and wave back.

He jumped the curb and cut across someone's lawn, pumping hard, bumping over flowerbeds and avoiding fences. She kept up with him seeming to anticipate where he would be crossing back into the street.

Finally he turned back and met her head-on. The car was slower to make the reversal, and he turned up a driveway, cut a path past the garage, and into a yard without a fence. He pedaled up the alley and pumped hard until he made the traffic of the highway where he jumped the ditch and followed the railroad tracks to Alamo Road.

Ignacio didn't waste any time riding home. The fixtures forgotten, he called the sheriff and pleaded for the name.

"I got the number, if you can't arrest her, then give me the name. She knows me; she knows where I live!"

"Mr. Salinas," the officer said, "you know, we have already told you, we can't do that."

Then he called Connie.

"Connie, I saw the blue Nova in Alamo. A woman was driving. I followed her. I thought I could see where she lives, but she saw me. Connie, these people will come and get you if you talk to the police. They got me once before."

"Ignacio, calm down. She has no way to know you talked to the police."

"She knows me. I think someone told her on me. I think it was the police. I think they told her. I'm never talking to the police again. They can't help anyway. They always make it worse. Do you know anyone who can get the name?"

He stood at the picture window, and he searched the road as he talked. He had placed his pistol on the telephone table, and his hand rested on it.

"They can get it," he said. "I know they have a way."

"Don't jump to conclusions, Ignacio, how could she possibly make the connection?"

"She gave me *el mal ojo*, the evil eye. She knows I told the police on her. I could tell. I think she may be coming after me because she knows."

"How can she come after you? You just saw her in town, she doesn't know where you live."

"Sure she does. She knows where you live, and she knows I live across the street from you!"

Connie caught the panic in his voice, so she hesitated before answering. What could she say? If this was the woman, then he was right, of course. She knew where they lived, both of them.

He went on, "They can check her name from her license number, I know they can, but they won't tell me. I called them, and they said no. I told you, I think they told her on me. Somebody did."

"Ignacio, don't be silly! The police wouldn't tell her." But Connie wasn't sure. She had given them his name several times. And he had called there, too. Whoever these people were, they might want to shut him up, or worse, he could be right, they might want to get even.

She called Detective Ocampo. "It's against the law," he said, "for me to give you a person's name. The law protects us, all of us, you too. I can't give out that information, it's for your own protection."

"You're right, Ignacio," she told him, "they wouldn't tell me either. They said it was for our protection. What do you think?"

CHAPTER TWENTY-EIGHT

At 1:00 AM the ringing phone awakened Bob. He rolled over and looked at the clock before answering.

"Who would be calling at this hour?" he mumbled, as he lifted the receiver, "Hello."

He heard nothing except heavy breathing into the mouthpiece on the other end.

"Hello!" Bob repeated, and again no response.

"Hello, hello!" Nothing.

He hung up, but he and Susan were both fully awake now. "I guess it was just a prank," he said. "Or, I hope so, anyway. Should I call Mother to see if she's OK? I'd hate to wake her up for nothing." Bob's elderly mother lived in another neighboring town.

"If it was your mother, she'll call back. It was probably a wrong number," Susan said. "Wait until morning."

In the morning when they checked, his mother reassured them she hadn't called. But who? A prank.

Thus began a series of mid-night calls from the prankster. The phone would ring at 1:00 AM or thereabouts, and the unresponsive caller would hang on the line and refuse to speak. This went on spasmodically, usually at night, but sometimes in the day, too.

They never learned who made the calls, but Susan believed the caller probably held the phone expertly gripped in spite of the missing fingers on his injured right hand.

CHAPTER TWENTY-NINE

Ignacio wasn't the only one talking. Susan grew more desperate as she watched her mother leave daily with the pistol to go back to the dangerous old house.

This can't go on. Something has to be done, but what?

The serenity of the water drew Susan; she loved the quiet, and it was a good place to mull over the tense situation they had found themselves in. She stood on the arched bridge that spanned the resaca and dropped breadcrumbs into the water attracting the ducks and schools of red fish.

She leaned against the railing and looked over to the house of Judge Uresti, one of the most beautiful in the complex. The front of his house had a splendid view of the resaca, and his patio gate opened onto the common area with the large swimming pool at the rear. The fountain in his patio was a work of art. Blue and white Mexican hand painted tiles adorned the back wall and a white, marble dolphin poised elegantly over the basin, water sparkling from his mouth.

When it was known, his name was on the president's short list as nominee for the Supreme Court, he moved to a more prestigious neighborhood. He didn't put his town house on the market for sale, much to the chagrin of the neighbors. It stood vacant; its patio in full view of the swimming pool, became an eyesore. Tall weeds obscured the beautiful fountain. Sprouts of mesquite trees from bird droppings squeezed up between the bricks, and the flowers withered and died.

By-laws regulated the abandoned property, but he ignored the letters the board sent him in an appeal to comply.

What can be done when even the judge disregards the law?

"You can put lipstick on a pig and it's still a pig." Susan said it aloud and it gave her a moment's relief, but she continued to stew about their problem. She had seen the deputies. She had been there and heard them say they didn't intend to do anything about the gangs threatening her mother.

The deputies are county law enforcement. Mother lives in McAllen now, and maybe the McAllen police can help us.

Susan knew a McAllen policeman socially, and he knew Connie. Susan went by to see him and told him how nothing was being done about her mother's case and how anxious she was for her safety.

"We practically solved the case ourselves. We gave them the name of the man, a description of his car, and his license number. We even told them where they could find him, and we have witnesses. Still, they do nothing. They need a murder, and I'm afraid if they don't act, they'll have one."

"Susan," he said, "I don't know what I can do, but I'll look into it. In the meantime, I have a friend in the sheriff's office that I think a lot of. I'm sure he's in a better position to know what's going on over there than I am. He's their public information officer. Why don't you give him a call? His name is Jim Neumann.

Susan called Jim Neumann and recited her story. He listened with interest and said he would see what he could do. He took special note of the fact that Connie's and Lilah's cars had been ditched in the same place on the canal bank.

Weeks passed and she didn't hear from either of them again. Her friend, the policeman, didn't ask her any questions about how things were going. When she saw him after that, he was very cool. He let her know with his manner not to ask, and she left him alone.

***

The neighborhood celebrated with a gala bridal shower. The young bride was a daughter of one of Susan's neighbors, and it was a lace tablecloth and silver service affair. Susan and Connie took the short walk across the courtyard and were among the first to arrive.

The elderly great-grandmother of the bride was in attendance. She knew Connie from years back when she played with the Tuesday afternoon domino club.

The bride was the star, but the old lady was also a center of attention. They sat her in a chair not far from the service table. Dressed in ecru lace, she wore a large pearl-crusted brooch, and sat erect like a dowager queen. Her hand rested on a silver headed cane, and she held it before her like a scepter. One could imagine a tiara would not have been out of place on the regal old head. Each guest made her way to pay homage as they filed through to the cake and tea service. Some stopped even before they spoke to the bride and her mother.

"Connie," she said, patting the armrest with her hand, "come and sit here by me. Someone bring Connie a chair!" It was an order and not ignored. When it had been arranged, she inquired, "Well, my dear, how have you been?"

"Fine," Connie said, "I'm doing fine."

The old woman pressed her head against the chair back; the steely blue eyes examined Connie's face, and there ensued an awkward pause.

"I'm still playing dominoes with the girls on Tuesdays."

Connie supposed it was going to be up to her to keep the conversation going. "We miss you," she said. "The group is dwindling. You may not even know some of the young women who play with us now."

Connie managed a plate of cake on her lap and avoided the woman's intense gaze. The bony old hand reached out and, in a consoling manner, patted Connie's arm. "I hear you've moved to town."

"More like the town has moved to me!" Connie smiled. "My house isn't in the country any more."

"My daughter tells me you're her neighbor now."

Connie hadn't expected this. She flushed with humiliation.

I guess I'm a charity case, and the focus of gossip these days.

She evaded, "Well, temporarily. My house is on the market, and I expect I'll be moving into a place of my own soon."

Others constantly interrupted their conversation, but to Connie's dismay, the old woman continued to pry into her circumstances as the ladies moved on and out of hearing.

"You know, Connie, it's a shame, but crime is something we've always had to deal with. There will always be folks who take advantage of others."

"Yes, I guess that's true, but it's a little different now. Now there's a new problem, drugs and gangs."

The old woman smiled, "There have always been gangs."

Connie found herself on the defensive. "Yes, but in the past, when someone broke the law, they were caught, and restrained. We had the protection of the law."

"Not as much as you might imagine," the old matron said, with a wry smile.

Susan had circulated the room and was collecting the dishes as the women finished their cake. She stopped to listen.

"When we came down here from Tennessee, this border was a frontier. Not long after we came, revolution broke out in Mexico. General Lucio Blanco's army was across the river and they were fighting in Matamoros and Reynosa. It was a lawless place at that time, they even sent the National Guard down here to protect us."

She remembered, "They sent those National Guard boys from New York down here in the middle of summer." The old woman's wrinkled face lighted up youthfully; she was laughing now, "We were in the throes of one of our worst droughts, and they sent those poor boys down here in wool uniforms! When they marched in they kicked up so much dust," she slapped her thigh and giggled, "they had them all out washing their clothes and those ignorant young men hung them out to dry on the prickly pear cactus!"

She had them all laughing now. "Some thought they were itching for a fight. We knew they were just itching!"

"That wasn't the worst of it. They put up thousands of pup tents and the weather turned on them. That was the summer of the hurricane of 1916. Those city boys didn't know what hit them when the storm blew in. The wind howled for twenty-four hours, and by the time it was over we weren't sure who was here to help whom! They were wet as drowned rats and suffering from exposure. We set up first aid stations and treated them as best we could.

"I remember it well. Those were good boys, the sons of New York's wealthy. Major Cornelius Vanderbilt was a charming young man, and I remember the day he came to tea at my mother's house."

It was Connie's turn to smile. She had heard the story, and she knew that wasn't exactly the way it went. In reality, the old lady's mother sold sandwiches to the men and gossip had it she did a pretty good business.

"Even if they hadn't been so green, they couldn't have done much to help us because they weren't allowed to do what had to be done. It was pretty much left to those of us who lived down here, and in the end it was the Rangers, the brush country cowboys, that put a stop to the marauding Mexican bandits."

Susan was listening and her mind raced, "The Texas Rangers?"

"Those boys were Indian fighters, and sharpshooters. They crossed the river when they had to, something the National Guard boys couldn't do, and anyway, they had to go. They had to go off to Europe to fight in the World War."

Why didn't I think of it before? I'll call the Rangers. I'll call them. Why didn't I think of it before!

***

She found a number in the phone book for the Texas Ranger's McAllen office and dialed with the intention of making an appointment. The receptionist said he was very busy and would only have time to speak to her on the telephone.

He listened to her story. She told him everything.

"I'm sorry," he said, "but this really isn't in my area of responsibility. I'm down here on a case, but if I can find the time, I'll try to look into the matter.

CHAPTER THIRTY

Ignacio called again. He had been excited when he called before, but this time he sounded hysterical. English was his second language, and Susan couldn't understand a word he said. She got the message though. Something awful was happening to him; he needed help. He wanted her to come, and bring Connie, and he needed her now! The deputies were at his house, but they said they'd wait if Connie came right away.

"Mom," Susan said, "Ignacio just called. He's scared; something's going on at his house. It's something about the sheriff."

"What in the world could it be?" Connie said as she prepared to leave.

"I don't know, but he said *hurry!* We had better leave now."

They turned onto Cesar Chavez Road in grim silence. Finally Connie said, "What in the world would the sheriff be doing over at Ignacio's place? You said he sounded scared?"

"He tried to tell me, but I just couldn't understand what he said. He was speaking English, I think, but he was so excited, talking so fast, I couldn't hear through his accent."

A black and white patrol car sat in Ignacio's driveway, and Puppy was there, too. She came out to meet them and followed as they drove to the back of the house where the car was parked. The two officers and Ignacio stood in front of the garage to wait. Susan and Connie got out and walked over to where they stood. They could see the lawnmower just inside.

"This is Mrs. Rogers, she's going to tell you the truth about the mower. She's going to tell you that I didn't steal it. She's going to tell you that she gave it to me, because I work for her. She's going to tell you that someone is lying and it isn't me."

He turned to Connie and said, "You're going to tell them I didn't steal this mower, OK?" His face was controlled but they could hear the desperation in his voice.

Connie spoke to the deputies, "What's going on here? Has someone accused this man of stealing my lawnmower? I gave it to him."

One of the officers said, "This is your lawnmower?"

Calmly and with a note of irritation in her voice, Connie said, "Yes, it is, or was, I gave it to this man, and I didn't report it stolen. What makes you think it was stolen?"

"We had a call from a neighbor. Is that your house?" He pointed with his pen across to Connie's house.

"Yes, that's my house. What did he tell you?"

"May I see your drivers license?"

"Why?"

"I need your identification," he said. He was stern and official. He recorded her drivers license number as he spoke, "There's been a lot of trouble at that house. Things have been stolen. We have been out here several times."

He turned his head to look across the road at the trailer, "Mr. Moore there, watches the house. He says he saw this man take the lawnmower," he pointed to the green mower with the pen, "from the garage over there."

Connie rolled her eyes heavenward, "Well, Mr. Carl Moore is mistaken, and it's none of his business anyway. I haven't reported my mower stolen, it hasn't been stolen, and Ignacio Salinas did not steal it."

He turned his attention to Ignacio, "We'll be watching you, and there had better not be any more trouble out here."

They all stood in stunned silence as the deputy scowled at Ignacio. "We aren't going to charge you with anything today," he said, "but this will be on record. If the man across the street, or anyone else for that matter, has a problem with you, we'll have to press charges, do you understand?"

He turned his attention to Connie, studied her a minute and without apology, he said, "When we get a report like this, we always try to follow up on it." Then he dismissed her, "I guess that's all we'll need for the present."

As they turned to go, she said, "Wait a minute, I thought you didn't 'follow up' on third party calls. Since when do you check out calls from someone about something that's happening to someone else's property?"

These men were not going to take any guff from a little white haired lady, and the officer gave her a stern look and didn't respond to her question at all for long seconds while the withering look took full effect, then he instructed, "It would be in your best interests to take care of your neighborhood squabbles yourselves. You and this man have taken too much of our time already."

Connie, Susan, and Ignacio were left standing in the drive to watch the departing patrol car and the men who were responsible for their security and their property slowly pull away.

They looked at each other and laughed, but the laughter rang hollow. Ignacio had just had the scare of his life, and this situation had become so twisted and so costly, they could hardly see the humor in it.

As they drove home, Susan said, "What do you think that was all about?"

"I'm not sure, but I don't think it was about the mower."

CHAPTER THIRTY-ONE

The calls from Ignacio in the mornings stopped.

"They got me on record now, Connie," he said. "I told you not to call the sheriff. I'm not calling him anymore, and you shouldn't call him either. I think it's dangerous. I know it is."

They couldn't glean much more from the house any way. Connie continued to go out with Mark every afternoon to feed Puppy but the cats had disappeared, eaten by coyotes or just moved on.

Connie searched for them every day. She stood at the edge of the field and called, but they didn't come back. She put fresh food out just in case they were still alive and desperate. She could see them in her imagination, gaunt and hungry, and living on what rats or birds they could find. She imagined them being chased with brooms or shot at by fed up neighbors. She grieved for them, and felt guilty that they had been abandoned for no fault of their own.

Connie sat in her plastic chair and thought about the situation. *This is becoming a pattern. Something has to change. I have to sell this property and find my own place to live, or the sheriff has to catch the crooks so I can come back here. They're taking it down a little at a time. Soon I won't have anything left to sell or a place to live either.*

She let her mind wander as she imagined elaborate scenarios where she caught the baldheaded thug and taught him a lesson. If I only had his name, I could press charges. They could get his name, but they can't give it to me. The law protects him. They protect the crooks now instead of us. Our property rights are just ignored as if they didn't exist. They haven't even assigned a detective to my case. What am I going to do? I can't be here to watch my house all the time, and the sheriff's not going to do it.

This is ridiculous, Connie thought. Someone has to be in charge here, and I guess I'm elected. I'm not a detective, and I'm not a policeman, but I know what has to be done. To come back here, I've got to get that baldheaded thug off the street. First, I have to press charges, and to do that, I'll have to get his name.

But how can I get it?

I'll just have to find a way.

***

"Can you tell me if there has been any progress on my case," she said to a detective when she got one on the line. "Did anyone ever go out to the trailer park on Sioux Road? Or do you know?"

"I didn't go out there," he said, "but I spoke to a man I know who lives there. He said he had never seen a baldheaded man with scars, or anyone who fit that description in the park."

"Elaine Sowers, I gave you her name, said you never talked to her. No one did."

"Well, Lady," he had work to do, "You know, we can't just go around the park asking questions."

"Why not?"

"Well, we have to be careful about asking questions," he said. "If he heard we were asking around, he'd be outta there!"

"I don't think Elaine would be likely to tell him you had spoken to her." Connie was getting tired of this run-around. "What if I just went up to the door and knocked and, well, just asked him his name. Maybe I could find out in a simple and straight forward way." And for the effect, she added, "I think I'll just go out there and do that."

Shocked by her boldness, he cautioned, "Lady, don't go out there, ever. Those men are dangerous."

So he knew someone who lived in the park.

No one had noticed a bald headed man with prominent scars?

The deputy thinks they're dangerous.

***

They know my car, she thought, or maybe not. They didn't see it in the daylight. Lots of people drive green Pontiacs. I'll be very careful.

She drove east on Sioux Road, passing fields of row crops and only a farmhouse before she neared the entrance to the park. The pistol lay on the seat beside her. She picked it up, took it off safety, and put it in her lap.

A cedar post and barbed wire fence set the park off from the cropland.

At the front, along the road, the bar ditch served as it's only boundary. One homeowner half-buried a row of tires between his trailer and the road. The black scar looped itself across the property line like the Loch Ness monster. Surely they did it to keep people from cutting across their property, she thought, they couldn't have thought it was attractive.

The park sat in what must have been a thirty-acre citrus grove at one time. A smattering of fruit trees remained scattered about. Hackberry trees had volunteered, probably brought in as seeds by birds, and were allowed to stand. They were all dry, and none of them looked very good.

Patches of Bermuda grass survived. No one mowed it any more; its lacy brown seed heads rose up and waved when the breeze ruffled across it. Sunflowers bloomed along the fencerow. No lawns or any attempt at landscaping could be seen in most of the lots, now. At one time, though, someone had high hopes for the park because there were still signs of the original attempt at grace.

The developers neglected to install curbs and gutters, but they did put in blacktop paving, and the entrance opened on a boulevard with a grassy median.

An old orange tree, the survivor of what had originally been a row down the median, still stood at the entrance. A piece of plywood leaned up against it. Someone had hand lettered, SLOW, 15 MPH, CHILDREN PLAYING, on the makeshift sign. It was badly weathered and although the wood had split and curled, you could still read it.

The park was planned for permanent residents, with large lots and plenty of space between the trailers for lawns and for children to play. The lawns and the children were gone now.

A few trailers had concrete pads and aprons, but most of the old trailers sat on blocks, and the driveways were gravel, or just ruts in the would-be lawns. Some of the residents had moved on, abandoning their trailers. They sat like rusted out hulks of ghost ships, windows broken out, the paint powdery dull. An abandoned car sat decaying in the drive of one of the vacant trailers. One abandoned trailer had been burned. Its black carcass was left like an insult to the others.

The place has a weird '50's' look, Connie thought, like maybe they all left at the same time, like they died of atomic radiation, or of an epidemic. Connie counted three blocks. The house would be on the corner. It had a concrete pad and drive. A small oak tree struggled for life by the driveway. Some concrete blocks pushed up to the door served as a porch. A barbeque cooker and a lawn chair sat abandoned a short distance from the front door.

The paint of the old mobile home had faded, and the grass of the yard was all beat down as if cars had been parking on it. The yard was clean. Neighboring trailers had old washing machines and assorted clutter in the yards. Not a scrap of paper, or cigarette butt, or tool of any kind marred the yard of this trailer. It looked vacant except for the lawn chair and a bare light bulb at the door burning softly in the glare of the afternoon sunshine.

Connie slowed her car to a crawl and rolled to a stop, snapped the door locks down, took a good look, then moved on. The place looks unnaturally clean, she thought, or cleaned up. She drove to the end of the boulevard and saw Elaine's mobile home. She had built a little shed for the horse, and a fenced lot was spread out across the rear of the park. The horse raised his head and walked over to the fence when Connie stopped to look at him. He shook his head and stretched it over the fence begging for a handout like a pet. She moved on.

She circled across the back, and drove to the front. The pavement was thin when it was new, now large patches of it were missing.

A few residents remained. One place had a beautiful yard, and she saw an old man with a garden hose watering beds of flowering annuals. He smiled and waved at her as she passed. He was very old and wrinkled and had an old Dodge sedan in his driveway. He had placed a row of gallon plastic milk cartons filled with water all along the front boundary of his lot to mark it off. The Loch Ness gardener must have inspired him, she thought. Or, more likely, he just wants to distinguish himself from his other trashy neighbors.

If she had seen the green Ford in the driveway, Connie didn't have a plan. She had called the sheriff before when the car was there, and he wouldn't come out. What would he have done this time if she had called him again? Probably the same thing, she thought.

I guess I struck out on this one. The trailer is empty and the guy with the scars is gone. I don't understand why the sheriff didn't send someone out here to talk to Elaine.

CHAPTER THIRTY-TWO

Connie," Angie said, "why don't you go down to the city hall and talk to them. There are some problems I can't explain well. You'd be able to better understand what we're up against."

"Is it because I didn't want to break it up?" Connie asked. "Things have changed. I don't live there anymore, and so I'm not so concerned about who might move in next door."

"Well, that's part of it," Angie offered, softly, wondering how she could gently tell Connie how bad the situation had become. "I had thought we could do better if we split it up into lots small enough that a prospective buyer into this neighborhood could afford. Now the county has placed restrictions intended to control the development of more colonias. They require you to sell at least five acres, no less. This narrows our prospects, and something else has come up. There's a problem with the water system, too. That's why I want you to go down there and speak to the zoning officer yourself.

"What problem?"

"They require fire hydrants. Your property is in the North Alamo Water District. The city of Chapin contends that the water pressure is too low to support fire hydrants."

"Angie, that really makes me mad! You know why our water pressure is low, and you know what we did about it!

"They made us let the colonia hook up to our system even though it's a co-op, and we all had to put up our hard earned money to join. When the pressure dropped so low we couldn't flush the toilet upstairs, they taxed us again to put in ten inch pipes!"

***

Connie drove the two short blocks of Main Street. She had driven this street often, daily in the early years. She didn't have a reason to go here much any more. The town had changed. The transformation happened gradually, and she didn't think about it much. This time she paid attention, and really looked at Chapin's main street. She didn't know the town any more.

It had been a thriving little community in the 1920's, and '30's, and the buildings in these two blocks dated back to that era, mostly built in the 20's. Now, like Alamo, the newer buildings strung out along the highway.

It wasn't the buildings that were different. They looked much as they always had. The businesses, however, had either changed hands or had closed up, and the ones that were still open were significantly less prosperous.

Chapin's stores lined up along the two blocks of Main Street and then, unlike Alamo that had a plaza at its center, Chapin had a beautiful shaded park with picnic tables just beyond the stores.

The silver painted water tower rose above the trees with the town's name emblazoned across the front. A red brick building housed the water plant in the far rear corner.

The City Hall was centered on the west side of the park facing Main Street. The new building had been an attempt at keeping up with the times she supposed, but it was a discordant note in the little town frozen in the thirties.

The building was severely contemporary, white, and its heavy glass doors were propped open with wooden blocks, an indication that the air conditioner was not in service.

The receptionist was talking on the telephone. She wore her long black hair in a fashionable frizz, and Connie assumed the dress she wore was the same one she had worn the night before at some nightclub. She had removed her gold loop earring and held it in her free hand as she spoke. She looked up to see Connie standing before her, and put her hand over the mouthpiece. Her party waited while she directed Connie to the office of the city planner.

The young man was expecting her; he stood and extended his hand across the desk.

"Mr. Avila, thank you for seeing me."

"How can I help you," he inquired pleasantly.

The office was very small. There was a straight-backed chair in front of the desk, and with a wave he indicated that she should take a seat. Connie looked across at a very young and smiling face. He put her at ease right away, and she launched into an explanation of what she needed to know.

"I own a house and thirty acres of land that are not in the city limits of Chapin, but are in the extra-territorial jurisdiction of the city."

He nodded, and she continued. "I've had it on the market for some time and have not been able to sell it. My real estate agent says the problem is complicated. It would be helpful if you could explain it to me, so I can decide what I need to do."

He leaned forward, his hands clasped on the desktop, and she had his full attention. His face registered interest in her problem.

She began to feel better. This is not so bad, she thought.

"Being in the extra-territorial jurisdiction of the city shouldn't keep you from selling your property," he said. "What is the problem?" His voice registered sympathy, and she relaxed even more.

"Well, good. I understand I must sell at least five acres net, no less than that, because of the county's new regulations. It'll be hard for me to find someone who can afford to buy more than five acres and also would live in my neighborhood. The Loma Linda Colonia is just west of me.

"My agent says there's a problem about the water district. Something about a law suit, and until it's settled it's a encumbrance to the construction of new houses on the property."

"If selling your thirty acres is what you want to do, then the suit shouldn't have any effect on it at all." He reassured her, "The suit only affects developers. Did you intend to develop the property?" he asked.

"I bought it as a farm and intended to sell it as a farm," she said, but before she could go on he interrupted.

"The county would not oppose your selling the property for agricultural use."

"My place is on Cesar Chavez very close to Loma Linda, and a mobile home park is nearby. The two of them make my area undesirable for a farming operation.

"The farmer who rented my property for years isn't renting it anymore. With all the people moving in, he can't use pesticides or herbicides. He says it isn't safe to leave his equipment there overnight because the last time he left his tractor in my field, it was stolen. He thinks it was someone from the colonia.

"School taxes are out of sight, and I don't have the income I had from the farm rental. I need to sell the property. Frankly, I need the money.

"My agent thought I had a buyer, but you told him there was a proposed street in your long term plan which would bisect the house. Can you do that?"

"Oh, boy!" he said, "I remember that, but really, they're just proposed streets, plans for the future. Nothing's going to change for a while, at least two years, probably longer."

"Would you buy a house that was straddling a proposed street?" she asked, "Even if it might be two or more years before the street came through?"

He smiled broadly, "I don't think so. Let's take a look at the city map, and you can remind me where your property's located."

He rose, and she followed him back down the hall and past the gesturing receptionist, still on the phone, to the conference room. He pulled down a large map of the city from a collection rolled together on the wall.

She was surprised at what she saw. The city limits of the city of Chapin looked like a spider with holes here and there inside the boundaries. One long narrow band extended up Raul Longoria Road to the new high school that had been constructed miles to the north of Connie's property.

The young man pulled out a chair, "Sit down here with me, and let me explain about the requirements for selling less than five acres."

A large conference table, the site of the City Council meetings, was centered in the room. They sat at one end where they could see the map.

"If you market less than five acres, you'll be required to submit a development plan to the City Engineer. You'll have to have the property surveyed, and you'll need an engineer. Your plan must have lots platted, and you'll need streets, curbs, and gutters. You'll have to tie into the sewer lines, and you must furnish fire hydrants."

He continued in a negative tone. "Your property is in the North Alamo water district. Your request will be rejected by the city engineer."

"There is a ten-inch pipe in that area with more than enough pressure to comply. Plenty for fire hydrants."

"That's the issue. The city engineer disagrees. It's what the water suit is about." The young man wasn't smiling.

"How soon can we expect a settlement?" she asked.

"Who knows," he shrugged his shoulders. "Could be, it'll be in the court of appeals for years."

"Court of appeals?" her hopes rose. "If it's in the court of appeals, doesn't it mean that there's already a court decision?"

"Well, theoretically, yes."

"Couldn't I ask for a waiver?"

He searched her face and didn't answer, and then he smiled, an ironic smile at her innocence and said, "Well, you could try. You could get a survey done, hire an engineer, have him draw up the plats, submit it to the City Engineer, and ask for your waiver."

He paused for the effect, "You could try, maybe you could get a waiver," his eyebrows went up and his face broke into a big smile. "What do you think?"

She wasn't so innocent that she didn't catch his meaning.

He softened, "But look, the water isn't the only hurdle you have to get over. The county isn't allowing independent septic systems any more. Any new houses are required to tie into the city sewer system. Let's look at the map," he said, "and see how close it is to your property."

He walked over to the map and pointed, "See these black dots? They're manholes. They show where the sewer lines are. If you will note, they are very near your property on the south. Looks like about a quarter of a mile, possibly a little more. You'd have the expense of putting in pipes to connect, but you wouldn't have too far to go to reach them."

His face didn't register any hope, "The area has already surpassed the volume of sewage we are able to process without a new lift pump. This is very expensive and would be the responsibility of the developer." He paused for the effect, "In this case, well," he shrugged his shoulders, "I guess that would be you."

He looked directly at her with his head tilted. His face didn't register any emotion, but she understood.

Connie wasn't ready to concede. She examined the map closely. "The city borders me on two sides. It should only be a matter of time until I'm taken in. How long do you think?"

He shook his head, "Not any time soon. The plan is to go farther north, not your way."

"That doesn't make sense. Here I am," she pointed to her property on the map, "right here, practically in the city limits now. Why would the city grow way out there into the countryside?"

He was tiring of the explanations. He couldn't help her anyway. "They are market driven, usually."

"Then, good! That's to my advantage!" she said. "With the mobile home park and the colonia, there are a lot of people living in my area. The area to the north is still farmland and sparsely populated. The way my neighborhood is growing the market will dictate in our favor rather than going farther north. When they take us in, the city would have to put in the streets, curbs and sewer lines. Wouldn't they?"

He rolled the map up to cue her that the meeting was drawing to an end. "I don't think you understand what is meant by 'market driven'," he said. "The developers put all that in and then they voluntarily cede the property to the city. It's a voluntary annexation. The city maintains the property. They do not develop it."

As dense as she had been, she finally understood. It was the cronies, the *acuñados,* the brothers-in-law. The insiders could develop. They could get waivers. They didn't need lift pumps. For them the pressure was always adequate. They had plenty of it. They were the *market.*

She left the building stripped of her innocence. The dreamy mist was lifted. Her eyes were wide open.

"This isn't the country I remember," she said. "I'm in another country."

CHAPTER THIRTY-THREE

As Connie left the City Hall, she drove back up Main Street where she saw a man she knew turning into Glen Wade's Hardware store. The tall slender, elderly man was a familiar figure in the town, not a personal friend, but someone she knew. Sam Saterwhite, before retiring, had been a constable in this precinct, and everyone knew him.

"I need a garden hose," she thought, but really, the sight of the trusted lawman prompted her to park her car and go in.

Glen Wade's Hardware had opened in the twenties with long rows of bins filled with bolts, nuts, and screws. Through the years the store had risen with the times. In early days there had been a screen door at the entrance and big doors at the rear accommodated deliveries and served to cause a cross breeze to cool the place. It smelled of oiled wooden floors, leather, and bins of metal fittings.

The building was air conditioned in the late forties, and white vinyl tile floors were installed. The bins had been replaced and the nuts and screws hung from pegs now, and were packaged in neat little bunches of six or eight.

The back wall of the hardware store in years past had tack and leather straps for harnesses and gear for mules and horses. Bits and saddles and paraphernalia associated with a technology long out of date were sold here. All that was gone now, too, and replaced with a circle of chairs and a coffee pot.

When she entered the store, the constable had made his way to the back and was pouring himself a cup of coffee. The tall silver-haired man was dressed in blue jeans and boots. His western cut shirt had mother of pearl snaps, and the yoke was double stitched with elaborate swirls. He was fitted out like a rancher now. In the past she had always seen him in his khaki uniform.

Two other men were seated in the coffee area. They were younger men she didn't know. They slouched comfortably and greeted Sam warmly. It was a very congenial group, they had been there awhile, and would, she guessed be there awhile longer.

"How about a cup of coffee?" Sam said, and reached for another cup for her."

"Thanks, I could use a cup of coffee, or something," she said, "I've just lost a battle with City Hall."

The man who was sitting in the barber's chair stood and gestured to the royal seat, "I'm just leaving," he said.

Connie smiled, "No thanks," and before he could argue, she took a seat in a rocker. "This is more my style!"

As she settled herself into the large oak rocker, Connie told them, "Things have changed so much around here, I feel like I'm in another country."

"Connie," the old constable climbed up into the chrome and red leather throne, "you're just a spring chick," and he laughed. They all did. "You haven't seen changes. You ain't seen nothing at all!"

She smiled, too. She was ten years his senior. But she just said, "I've been here since 1939, long enough to know change when I see it."

"That's nothin'. This place was already civilized when you got here. Now, me, I come ridin' in here on a pillow in 1922." Sam adjusted his long toed black boots into the footrest of the great chair. This coffee break looked so promising he might just settle in until suppertime.

"I was born in San Antone and my parents brought me down here when I was just six weeks old."

"Well, I was born down here, about six miles north of Donna," Glen said. The conversation caught the interest of Glen himself who was the only man in the room Sam's age. No customers were in the store, and he leaned with his arms crossed over the back of a chair.

"They said I was the only one that was comfortable. I came down here in a model T Ford on a pillow," Sam continued, ignoring his host's contribution.

"On a pillow!" Connie said.

"Yeah! At six weeks! In a model T Ford!"

"Tell you how things have changed, I took my first airplane ride between Donna and Alamo. We took off on highway 83." Glen injected. Highway 83 was now the traffic artery that ran the length of the Valley and was congested any time of day.

He chose a rocker and continued. "It was just a guy with a plane. He'd just fly you around for about ten minutes, not very long, and just for fun! I don't know what it cost, but we took off right down the middle of the highway!"

"They took me to my Granddad's house on the river down south of Donna," Sam continued, apparently undistracted by Glen's annoying interruptions. "We didn't live there, though. Mother and I stayed with them while my Dad found us a place to live in town.

"Mother grew up down there on the river. She was the youngest of ten children. And when it came time to go to bed, well, I remember Granny saying she had to call her because she was down there playing with those Gutierrez kids. My mother could speak Spanish and pat out tortillas as well as any Mexican you ever saw.

"My Aunt Mamie, Mother's older sister, taught school at Pharr. She rode home every weekend. She came down the old Military Highway, and that was during some of the old *bandito* trouble, too, you know. She carried a six-shooter. That woman could shoot a six-shooter like I can," he drew an imaginary pistol, "pshooo! Man, in fact 'til the day she died, which was just ten years ago, she could go out there with Granddad's old six-shooter and knock the eye out of a snake at fifty paces!

"She rode a horse. Get out of school on Friday, and ride home, and on Sunday afternoon she'd ride back at five o'clock!"

"Well, I guess I had better get on home," Connie said, "I've come to buy a garden hose. Since I had to leave my house, my yard is burning up!"

"Back in Granddad's day you didn't need a hose!" Sam continued totally ignoring Connie's statement that she was leaving.

"No sir! Grandma had a few roses and such, but they swept the yard! That's a fact! I mean it was dirt packed hard. No grass, they just swept it out to the brush line. They'd take a bucket of water, and throw it out there and sweep it!"

"Were they afraid down there on the river? Were there any problems with sleeping that far away from your neighbors? Being out there alone? I know by the twenties, the *bandito* business was finally over." Connie wanted to change the subject. She wanted to tell him about her battle with *banditos* of her own.

"Yeah, the Rangers came down here and took care of that." He paused thoughtfully, and added almost under his breath, "Eventually."

He recovered after a short pause, "Granddad was a crack shot!" he went on, with enthusiasm. "I mean he could handle a 30-30 like you would not believe! And he was pretty fair with a forty-five!

"Then, kids grew up from the time they were big enough to hold a gun, they learned to shoot, everybody on their own! Not that everybody went around wearing a gun or anything like that at the time. But we sure were there to protect our property!"

"That's still a problem," Connie said, "It's dangerous around here now, and I'd be especially afraid to sleep down there on the river," Connie said, "without a gun!"

"Well," the old man said softly, "I would, too.

"I had Granddad's gun for a long time. One of his sons, Uncle Nathan, finally got it. When he died, I don't know who wound up with it."

"My husband's guns were all stolen from our house," Connie said.

"It was a 30-30," Sam went on, undistracted.

"They just came in and took them all," Connie said. "He had deer rifles and shotguns for white wing and ducks, and he had some German guns from World War II, a Mauser and a Luger. They're gone now."

"A model 94," Sam went on, "you know it's a funny thing, I've got a model 94, 30-30 Winchester, same model, year model and everything as the gun my Granddad had, only mine cost a hundred and some odd dollars, and the one he had cost twelve when he bought it. And where mine has hollow roll pins in it, his had solid pins, and the workmanship was entirely different. They were better guns then. At least those were, I think revolvers have gotten less sophisticated now. Back in those days they didn't know what a double action was! You know the difference between a double action and a single?"

"I'm not sure, is a single action one that you have to cock it and then shoot?" Connie's pistol had a clip.

Glen took a .38 revolver from the case and handed it to Sam so he could show her.

"A single action is the one you have to cock. This one here is a double action. You put your finger on the trigger," Sam demonstrated, "the hammer comes back and then fires. You don't have to cock this." He pulled the trigger, Snap!

"See here?" He pulled it again. Snap, click! And again, snap, click! "You fire this like that!

"The other one, your single action, quick shots would fan the thing, they called it."

Sam extended a long leg and put his boot on the floor. He held the pistol next to his thigh and his hand came quickly up with the pistol. The palm of his left hand brushed over the hammer. "Cock it back like that," he said as his palm quickly forced the hammer open, and he pulled the trigger pretending to fire the pistol. Click! Snap!

"They'd shoot one time, then they'd have to cock it again. That's a single action. This one here is your double."

"After they broke in and took my husband's guns, my son bought me a pistol. I think you'd call it a 'Saturday night special'. It's a cheap little thing. It's a 22. I was like you, I grew up with guns in the house and I knew how to shoot. But when they came back, I shot into the air and they came in and robbed me again. I wish now I had shot him."

"Well, maybe you should have. A grand jury would never indict a woman your age for shooting someone in her house. Was it a kid? This gang thing is out of control. They've handcuffed the sheriff."

"That was the problem, I guess. He was outside. I showed him the gun. I fired into the air, and he let me run to the car. I guess, what I should have done is let him come on in and shot him dead on my kitchen floor. Now, if I had done that, I could go back home.

"Where do you live now?" he asked.

"I've moved in with my daughter and my house is vacant. The vandals are taking it down. The sheriff's no help. I'm not sure which side he's on.

"Can you believe it? He just says, '"move out and let 'em have it.'"

Sam shook his head, he knew what was going on and didn't approve of it either. "It's a good thing you didn't wing him with that little 22 caliber. You can't stop a man with a 22. Just wound him and he'll keep coming. If you ever draw a gun against a man don't hesitate, shoot him, or he'll have the upper hand. But," Sam advised, "drag him inside before you call the sheriff."

"You ought to let Glen sell you this revolver for your protection."

Connie took his advice and bought the pistol before she left.

CHAPTER THIRTY-FOUR

East of Eden?" Angie said, "Is that what you call it? Yes, I know that mobile home park. It's old and run down. It's been there on Sioux Road for years." She had come by for a report on Connie's visit to City Hall.

"The sheriff may not be able to tell you who owns that trailer, but I can get his name. It's a matter of public record. In those old parks the owner has title to the lot as well as the trailer."

"Oh, Angie, could you do that for me? Please!"

Angie had a dark thought, "Connie," she asked, "why do you want his name? What do you have in mind? You're not going to do something stupid, are you?"

"Of course not. I'm going to file charges against him. To do it, I have to have his name."

"But your man with the scars probably isn't the owner. He probably doesn't own anything, unless it's that old Ford he drives. The police are not going to give you his name, and I have no way of getting it for you."

"Then what can I do?" Connie asked. "It doesn't seem likely that I'll sell my house. I've given up the idea of selling it as a farm, but if I sell less than five acres I have to put in a fire hydrant and water lines. What if I didn't?"

"Connie, if they want to, they can fine you $10,000 and put you in jail for two years for non-compliance. You better believe it!"

"Well, it's a moot point. If I had the money to put in fire hydrants, they wouldn't approve my water pressure, anyway. Does that seem fair to you?"

Angie shook her head, "Connie, you are a case of what they call 'unintended consequences'. The new restrictions the county has imposed are to protect those poor newcomers from the unscrupulous developers who have been moving them onto property without the money to provide the septic and water connections for themselves. It's important and even necessary for your own protection as well as theirs."

Connie smiled, and her eyebrows went up, "How is it then, Angie, if they only want to protect me, their 'brothers-in-law' can get waivers and approval to develop large tracts of squalor, and I can't sell a little plot of my own land to someone who would live next door to me?

"If I managed, by a miracle, to sell off a lot of more than five acres, no one could build a house on it anyway until someone buys a new sewage lift pump. The zoning Tsar says that would be me! The water company isn't allowed to hook you up to water unless you can show them you have a sewage connection! I guess if they built next door I could run a garden hose over to them like they do over there at the colonia. Those crooks down at City Hall set this all up for their *acuñados* and you and I know they aren't going to give me a waiver. They pretty much as said so when I went down there. So, what do you think I should do?"

Minutes passed as they sat together in glum silence. Finally Connie offered, "The only possibility I have left is to get that baldheaded thug off the street. If I do that, maybe then I can go back home."

Angie sat back in her chair and thought about the prospects of Connie moving back in the now notorious house.

Connie was persistent, "So Angie, get the name for me, and then I'll know who I'm dealing with. Maybe I'll have an idea of what I need to do next."

CHAPTER THIRTY-FIVE

Things may be turning around, Connie thought, when she got a call from the Texas Ranger.

"May I come by to see you," he said. "I have some mug shots I'd like you to take a look at."

When he arrived, she was surprised to see he didn't look like the Rangers in the B-westerns. He was a small man, in his mid-forties, and dressed in business clothes. His name was Pawlik, and he got right to the point.

"Mrs. Rogers, I know it has been a long time, but you have been on my mind, and I finally got a chance to bring these over and let you take a look at some of the more troublesome young men we have on record."

Connie looked over the photos quickly for anyone with a shaved head.

"I'm not sure if I can identify him from these pictures," she said. "The man I saw had his head shaved, and I remember the scars on his scalp. He would look different with hair."

"Well, give it a try. Maybe there's something else about him that'll trigger your memory."

"These are head shots. I'll never forget the ugly cross he wore about his neck, and his clothes were baggy. Something was wrong with his pants."

Connie turned slowly through the pages of serious, full-face shots of young men, but either he wasn't there, or she couldn't see anyone who looked like the man she remembered.

***

Later that week, Angie dropped by.

"Connie," Angie said, "I have come with news."

"Great! Come on in!" Connie said, and she was hoping it was about her property. Maybe Angie had sold it at last!

"Let's go out to the patio. Mark needs to go outside a while," and Connie wanted a cigarette.

"I have some good news, and some bad news," Angie said when they had settled, "which do you want first?"

Connie smiled, her blue eyes twinkled, "Maybe, hmm, tell me the good first! I could use some good news. All the news has been bad lately."

"The sheriff has been indicted."

Connie already knew that. She had read the headlines in the morning paper, and she already knew how he had been accused of taking bribes to the tune of a hundred and fifty thousand. They accused him of laundering money, and charged him with racketeering.

"Dereliction of duty, I'd say, in my case," Connie leaned forward, "and, Angie, incompetence. That stupid sheriff let Amado Medrano go!"

"More likely, bribery, again!"

"Can you believe it? There's no justice any more. He's probably in Mexico right now having a Margarita and laughing his head off!"

"I guess that's the bad news. I've looked up who owns the trailer. I'm afraid to tell you who it is!"

Connie didn't laugh now, "Just a minute while I light a cigarette, and then you can tell me the bad news."

"I've known this for a week and wondered if I should tell you."

Connie leaned back in her chair, the cigarette held suspended, unlit, between her fingers. At last, this was what she had been waiting to hear.

"Now Medrano has been released, you have to know," Angie said. "It belongs to a man who has all kinds of connections at the sheriff's office. It belongs to Amado's cousin, Carlos Medrano."

"The name sounds familiar."

"Well it should," Angie smiled. "Remember the police dog scandal of a few years ago? Well, that was Carlos Medrano."

Connie sat up straight and her eyes widened. "You mean to tell me that the man who owns the trailer is a policeman?"

"Not any more. He was a deputy, assigned to security for the Chapin Elementary School. That was several years ago. They fired him!"

Angie explained, "They hired a new superintendent for the school district. He began trying to straighten out their finances. In going over the school's expenses he found they had paid $3,500 out of the district's discretionary funds to build a dog kennel for the drug dog, but they couldn't find it. Turns out it was built on private property. Not the school's."

"How could a dog kennel cost thirty five hundred dollars?" Connie said, amazed.

"It wasn't your ordinary kennel. It was ten feet by twenty-six feet and air conditioned." Then she added, "And of course, you can guess, it was a brother-in-law deal. They didn't take bids."

"Puppy sleeps under the house."

"King wasn't just an ordinary dog. King was special. He was a full-bred Labrador," Angie laughed now. "He was a working dog," she leaned forward and touched Connie's shoulder, "They put him out to stud, no kidding! They sold the pups and pocketed the money."

They were both laughing now, "Sounds like a bad joke," Connie said.

"No joke!" Angie held her sides, "This dog was really special!" She managed to get out between spasms of laughter, "He ate four hundred pounds of dog food every month! Does that make him special, or what?"

"Good grief! Four hundred pounds?"

"Anyway they billed that much to the school district."

"Surely the old superintendent could see the discrepancy."

"I guess he could have, but they sold what the dog didn't eat, and when they couldn't sell it, they traded it for booze and cigars!"

"Angie," Connie leaned forward in her chair and challenged, "you're pulling my leg. How do you know all these details?"

"Well, Connie, I guess everyone knows it. I read it in the *Wall Street Journal*, of all places."

"So what does all this have to do with Medrano?"

"The school records show him assigned as its custodian. Oh! He held up his hands and said he didn't know anything about it, but his name was on the line. If he didn't know, well, he should have.

"It gets worse!"

"No!"

"They had to call in a special prosecutor. The district attorney is Carlos' uncle."

"Oh, dear."

"There's more. Carlos' cousin is the county clerk, and his brother is a constable. He has all kinds of connections with law enforcement. And the final insult, he was no billed by the grand jury.

"The superintendent fired him anyway. Medrano then filed suit against the school district and the new superintendent for defamation."

"I'm not surprised the grand jury let him off." Connie was down on the sheriff. "I can't imagine they would be interested in anything so trivial as drug-dog misuse."

"It's not that they aren't interested in misuse of school funds. The grand jury didn't see the funds as misused. They do what they know and what they know is the patron system. They saw it as his concession, you know, his fiefdom. It's a top down power system. Around here, it's considered *pilón,* benefits of the job. The new superintendent and the special prosecutor didn't know the ropes. It cost them. Medrano won his defamation suit against the school district. He bought a ranch."

Connie listened, and thought to herself that the grand jury on Lilah's murder and Carlos on the dog incident had given the Medranos a pass. They couldn't be too enthusiastic if she should file another charge against him.

"Carlos isn't a deputy anymore. He found more lucrative work. The brother, uncle and cousin, however, still hold office.

"If you asked Carlos he'd say he was a rancher. Scuttlebutt is Carlos is a drug dealer.

"Everyone thinks Allen was buying drugs from these men, and they probably murdered him and Lilah, too."

"Well, here come the clowns," Connie said. "They let the crooks go free, and the rest of us can go to heck!" Then she added under her breath, "Which is where I think I am right now."

Angie leaned back in her chair and surveyed the lush tropical patio, and she smiled at the irony of Connie's statement.

"Hardly a bad place to be exiled," she said. "It could be a lot worse!"

Someone took a dive into the pool just yards away and Mark ran to the iron gate to check it out. Angie waited while Connie stalled for time with her cigarette.

"Connie," Angie said.

"What!"

"I have told you for your own protection. Promise me, now, promise me you'll drop this and not do anything stupid."

"Such as?"

Angie grasped Connie's arm, "This man is dangerous! You can't handle this! Accept it! You have no choice but to make do here until something changes."

Connie drew on her cigarette and didn't answer Angie's warning. She looked past Angie at the bees buzzing around the Mexican lime tree, some of them straying very close to the little dog as he barked at the swimmers just yards away.

"Would you just look at that silly tree?" Connie tried to hold Mark in her lap, but he jumped down and ran back to the gate.

"The stupid tree attracts bees all the time. It's a maverick, an attractive nuisance! Everyone knows citrus trees bloom in the spring. Everyone knows that!" Connie waved her hand toward the blooming tree, "This one just blooms away any time it feels like it. Any time of the year."

Connie didn't mention that the blooming tree troubled her because the smell of orange blossoms always brought back happy memories of Hank and their house in the grove on Morningside Road. The house was centered in an orange grove when they bought it. They lost the trees in the freeze of 1953, but the association of the happy time and the orange blossoms haunted her memory.

Angie sat forward and pulled Connie to her, "Wake up! Find a way to go on with your life. You have no other choice! Promise me! Promise me you'll drop it!"

"Come on Angie, don't ask me to curl up and die."

"You have no idea what a hornet's nest you're going to get into with these men. They might kill you, you know that!"

"But Angie, don't you see, you said it yourself. The news about the sheriff is good. You said I have to stay here until something changes. Well, something has changed. There's a new sheriff in town. Someone else is in charge there now, things might get a lot better."

***

Connie wasn't going to call on the phone. She was going in person, and she wasn't going to make an appointment either. She was just going to drop in and catch them off guard. With new people there they might, just might, finally help her.

The office of the Hidalgo County Sheriff was situated on the south side of the city of Edinburg, the county seat. Set back from the street, an intimidating drive led up to it. The narrow black top passed directly under the iron barred windows of the county jail.

A large parking area separated the jailhouse and the one-story office building of the sheriff. Several cars were parked in the lot, old and dirty, poor looking cars. Two marked patrol cars occupied the spaces directly before the walk up to the door.

Connie kept running over in her mind what she would say to the sheriff, or whoever was in charge in his absence. She sat in the car before entering the building and smoked a cigarette. She had been a little excited and angry. Now she was having a good case of the nerves.

The newspapers had been filled with the scandal of the sheriff's indictment. His office was being looked at with a microscope. There had to be a change for the better. Connie crossed her fingers and said a prayer. This could be her chance to get the bald thug off the streets and could, just maybe could, solve her problem.

Connie entered a busy and use worn room. Two chairs flanked the door she had just come through, and the receptionist desk was a counter in the wall opposite the entrance.

"May I speak with the sheriff?" Connie asked the young woman at the counter.

"The sheriff is in Austin."

Connie bristled. Here we go again, the usual run-around. She could feel it coming, and her voice was high pitched when she answered.

"Surely someone is in charge here in his absence. I need to speak to someone about the progress on my case. I have been robbed recently and I can't tell if anything has been done about it. I want to speak to whoever is in charge here!"

"If you don't mind waiting, you may speak to the Chief Deputy Sheriff, John Anderson."

Connie had not expected to see the sheriff, anyway. "Good," she answered without much thought, "I'll wait."

"He has someone with him now, but go through that door," she pointed to an open door, "And take a seat. I'll let him know you're here."

The waiting room was small. Three doors, two with black lettering on frosted glass panels opened off the room. Sheriff Montalvo was on one, and Chief Deputy Sheriff Anderson was on the other. Both of them were closed. The Montalvo door was dark, but there was a light behind the Anderson door.

Chairs lined up against the wall directly under a row of framed photographs of all the sheriffs of Hidalgo County, living and dead. Serious men looked directly into the camera, some wearing their white Stetsons, intimidating even in photographs.

She examined the picture of the current sheriff, now under indictment. In the months, more than a year, she had been dealing with his office she had never seen him in person. He had a round, youngish middle-aged face. Even in the photograph she could see he was a tall, big man.

She sat in a chair under the line of lawmen and turned her attention to the closed door of the sheriff's office. His trip to Austin is probably about the indictment, she speculated. She examined his door with fascination. This is THE DOOR, she thought. THE ONE.

A drug dealer in custody at the county jail told federal investigators he had received special privileges. He had conjugal visits with his wife and girlfriend behind that very door. He paid the sheriff $6,000 a month and $1,000 a visit. In addition to that, the sheriff was accused of taking kickbacks, referral fees, *mordida*. That's what got him, Connie thought, the Feds this time, and not a local grand jury like the one that no billed 'Deputy Dawg'.

She smiled to herself. Well, he did all right for a while, his *pilón* turned out to be a good deal more lucrative than the booze and cigars that Security Deputy Medrano settled for.

The other door, the one of the Chief Deputy Sheriff opened at last. The man leaving stood in the doorway with his hand on the knob and the conversation continued in a cordial vein. He waved a casual goodbye to what she could only guess, from his demeanor, had been a social visit.

Two large men stood as she entered, and the one behind the desk introduced himself, "John Anderson," he said, "and this is Jim Neumann. He's our public information officer."

She took a seat across the desk from a very relaxed and casual Chief Deputy Sheriff. The men were not in uniform, and the informal atmosphere in the room put her at ease. They gave every indication that the Chief Deputy's title could be temporary. The indictment of the sheriff had stirred the waters.

Connie turned to Neumann first, "You may remember me. I spoke to you several months ago on the phone about my robbery. That's why I'm here today."

Purposely, she used the word robbery. She had learned how to talk to these men. She had been robbed, and she wanted them to know it.

Her 'case' was in a manila folder on his desk. He picked it up, tapped it on the desk, and put it down again.

"Why don't you bring us up to date?" he said.

Once again she told her story. She told them every detail of the first robbery she had endured as the men ignored her presence and partied down below.

The two men listened without comment as she went over the terror of the confrontation with the bald man. She retrieved the cards they had left her and repeated the names of the officers she had spoken to, and their warnings, and their advice. "Move out."

And once more, she gave them the names and phone numbers of her witnesses.

"Now that I have moved out as you advised, they are systematically dismantling my house."

"Vacant houses are targets for vandals."

"This isn't casual vandalism. This is organized salvaging by a gang of people who know what they're doing. They have scouts and trucks. It's a business. One of my neighbors has had a confrontation with them, and now he's afraid for his life."

"If they are as you say, I wouldn't recommend confronting them. You should call here and let us do the confronting."

Connie rolled her eyes in frustration, "By the time I know about it, they're gone, and when my neighbor who is a witness calls, you have told him it's not his business. Your officers have accused him of being a nuisance and have warned him not to call them anymore."

"That doesn't sound right," Anderson said softly.

"As the destruction of my property is systematic and predictable, I should expect you to at least make an effort to stop it." She added with emphasis, "It is, after all, your duty!"

The two big men sat quietly and listened. Anderson rocked back in his chair, and Neumann slouched with his legs crossed. Finally, as her story wound down and came to an end, Anderson commented, "With that much information, you're right, this man probably could have been picked up. A lot of time has passed; it'll be harder now.

"The only explanation I can offer is that we're so short handed; we don't have the manpower to put an investigator on every burglary case. We have murder cases which go with too little investigation for the same reason, and they come first."

"The salvage of my home is predictable, not random vandalism. You could put a man out there, and he could catch them. As it is, I have to do it myself," she chastised them, "and it's your job."

Anderson, a young man, looked across his desk at the eighty-year-old white haired woman. She sat primly straight in her chair, about the size of his twelve-year-old daughter. "What exactly," he struggled to swallow a smile, "are you doing to protect your property?"

"Well, I just go out there and sit and wait, just as you would have to do."

The smile ceased to trouble him now. He leaned forward, "Oh, boy," he said under his breath, and he and Neumann exchanged glances. "Mrs. Rogers," he said, "you mustn't do that. You're putting your life on the line for a house. Don't go there. A house is not worth your life. It's not a good idea."

"I'm not afraid of them. I have a pistol, and it's not a 'Saturday night special' either. I know how to use it and believe me, after what I have been through I'd shoot them in a minute. What do you mean, 'just a house'? That house is my home, and furthermore, it's my fortune. It's the representation of a lifetime of work. It's all I have, or ever will have."

"When do you usually go out there? Not at night, I hope. Do you sleep in the house?"

"Well, no, but somebody should be there at night, that's when they're more likely to come. I go in the afternoon. I have to go out there anyway to feed my animals."

He interrupted, "Now, Mrs. Rogers, I know you're upset, but you know what? You're lucky to be alive! I know that neighborhood. You live out there just east of that colonia, Loma Linda. It's loaded with some really bad customers. Really bad!" the two men exchanged looks again,

"We can't control what goes on there; they actually shoot at our patrol cars, so we don't even drive through there anymore. It's a population of transient, undocumented, and lawless people. There's always something going on, murders and drug trafficking, and a gang that's constantly a problem. We just steer clear of that place. You live in an area that is being overrun with the crime that's coming directly from that colonia."

"What!" she interrupted, "Contending with crime and criminals is why we have a sheriff. We have policemen to deal with crime. It's your job. Does it occur to you that if you didn't ignore the crime in the colonia, it wouldn't spill over into my neighborhood?"

Neumann put his foot on the floor and adjusted his position on the chair, and the room grew quiet.

"Our hands are tied," Anderson said finally, and it was all he needed to say as all three of them could read.

The newspapers had been full of accounts of a man a deputy had followed into the colonia, chased on foot, and finally shot in a struggle for his pistol. The deputy was on administrative leave, and the militant minority organizers were after the sheriff on the issue of brutality to minorities. It had become a racial issue, a front-page event. The sheriff was a minority himself, an item the newspaper conveniently ignored.

"We can't afford to spare another officer."

"Are you telling me to learn to live with it? Ignore it! Is that what you're saying?"

"Mrs. Rogers, you were burglarized. I know you think we should do something about the burglaries, and we do what we can, but you really have no idea what's going on around here."

He sat forward in his chair, and his arm swept across, indicating the direction of the jail, "Just next door we have a jail that is full, *full*, of scum the likes of which, fortunately you know nothing about. And when I say it is full, I mean it. Thanks to Judge William Wayne Justice, we turn some loose almost every day. His rulings require us to control the conditions, and the number of them we keep, forcing us to release people who should not be turned out on the streets. We keep the murderers, the burglars are the ones we turn out."

Connie was frowning, not taking this explanation lying down. He noted her expression and said, "If you want to go with me, I would be glad to take you over there and show you what we keep. It's the very dregs of humanity. And our jail is full of them. They are men who were armed and dangerous and many of them were involved in international drug activities. They are killers." Then he added softly, almost to himself, "Some are sadistic killers." He had one in mind who had tied a man to a cross and burned him alive over a drug deal gone wrong. He shook his head sadly, "Lady, you have no idea! As the crime rate goes up, and becomes increasingly more vicious, our budget doesn't keep pace. We have too few cars and too little fuel for the cars we do have. They have actually cut back on our budget. Our officers are the lowest paid, lower than any of the area city police forces.

"Hidalgo is a big county, when we get a call sometimes it takes longer than it should to get there. We are spread too thin over this large territory."

"If you don't have the funds to give us police protection, what are you doing about it?"

"It's a political situation," another exchange of glances between the two men. "We can't do much about it."

"You're going to have to explain that to me. How in the world could it be political? Has crime control now become politically incorrect?"

"This is how it goes. You know who your county judge is. His name is Eduardo Pelayo. You voted for him. He holds an elective office. The sheriff is elected, too, but they're not equal. The county judge holds the purse strings. Old Eduardo, our county judge, has put the squeeze on us.

"Ask him yourself, he'd say, 'law enforcement is the sheriff's job. You elected him. If you don't like the job he's doing, well, elect someone else!' he'd say. 'Not my problem! I don't have anything to do with law enforcement.' But he does. We depend on the county judge and commissioners for our budget. We have appealed to them for more money. They know the situation," he was referring to the sheriff's indictment. "They use it. They have us by the, uh, throat. You might call it conflict of interest, but it's Hidalgo county politics as usual."

"Maybe," she interrupted, "the electorate needs to know about this. Have you gone to the press?"

"I tell you what I can do for you. I'll turn your case over to the chief of detectives, David Ocampo. Ask for him when you call, and he'll be familiar with all the details of your case.

"Jim, take her down to David's office and tell him to come in here for a minute."

***

"David," he said when they had gone, and the man came into his office, "here's a file on Mrs. Roger's case. Look it over and make sure a patrol car cruises by her house every afternoon about 4 o'clock. That old lady is hanging out there with a gun, and she's going to shoot somebody if they don't kill her first. Maybe a patrol car will discourage any mischief while she's out there."

The atmosphere in Ocampo's office was an abrupt change. When he returned, he didn't take a seat behind his desk, but sat ramrod straight on the desk, and spoke down to her.

He wasn't in uniform, and his dress shirt, although open at the collar, looked crisply starched. A sport coat and tie hung from a peg on the coat rack just inside the door.

"Mrs. Rogers," he was all business, "I'll be in charge of your case now, and if you need to speak to anyone about, it just ask for me. I'll look into it and see what I can do, but in the mean time," he instructed, "let me handle it. You don't need to be going out there by yourself."

She took immediate affront at his attitude. "I appreciate your concern. However, I'll go when I think I need to. It's my property and I still have responsibilities there. You have a responsibility, too. It's your responsibility to protect me in my home."

"Mrs. Rogers, your house stands out as more affluent than the others in the area. A house like that attracts attention. We have a lot of poverty. Where you have poverty, you have crime, and an elderly lady alone is an easy mark."

"Excuse me, Sir, but you are dead wrong, and you of all people should know it. Crime causes poverty, not the other way around. And Mr. Anderson is incorrect. These thugs are not from the colonia." She took a risk. "I have witnesses; you have their names in that folder who will tell you these young men come from the trailer park on Sioux road. They are members of a gang, the Medrano gang.

"If you'd go out there and talk to the people who live in that park, they'd tell you what goes on in the Medrano's trailer. Or did. I have called you about it before, remember? I spoke to you, and you said you'd look into it. I never heard from you again. It may be too late, now. You didn't go when I asked you, and now they may have moved on to another place. I have driven through the park myself, and their trailer seems to be vacant now. But the trailer belongs to a man named Carlos Medrano. He is Amado Medrano's cousin. The same one," she accused, "who escaped from your jail last week."

"He didn't escape," Ocampo leaned forward, she noted his reaction and smiled inwardly. "We released him on his own recognizance for lack of evidence."

"You should go out there and talk to my witness. If you had gone already, maybe you would have had that evidence you needed to hold him."

She had stepped over the line. He stood and showed her the door.

"Mrs. Rogers, I am familiar with that trailer park. I'll go out there and look around. I'll see what I can find out about a gang."

"Look in my folder," she said as she stood in the doorway.

"I have given you the names and numbers of witnesses who can describe the bald man. His name is in there, well, his nickname, and even a description of his car. I can't get his name, but you could get it from his license plate number. I know you could."

"Mrs. Rogers, you can go now. I know what to do." The meeting was over.

CHAPTER THIRTY-SIX

The whooping roar of the engine still rang in his ears, but the helicopter sat on the pad with its rotors drooping. Rolando opened the first of the two beers he had brought away with him. He leaned against the soft old wood of the tool shed and watched the heat waves off the engine blur the landscape and turn it all twisted and unfamiliar.

Well, things change, he thought. They sure do but there's one thing that doesn't change. I'm not going anywhere. They're gonna' need me and they know it. He looked out over the farm where he grew up and knew that he was the guy. His mother and father had lived on the place until they died, and now he was the man.

The corporation will send the Lear jet in with supervisors to work with the extension service. In the end, they'll still be furrow irrigating the carrots and onions. I'm the man, he thought. I'm the one who knows where the low spots in every field are. I know how far to run the irrigation water and where to put the canals.

They'll take soil samples, but I'll make the decision in the end which field is best for melons or onions. I'll decide which citrus groves need to be kept and which one's need to be pushed out. When they install the drip irrigation on the melon fields, my canals will furnish the water for the pressure pipes.

The sun sank low in the west and streaked the sky with brilliant orange. It reflected off the palm fronds and washed the buildings with color.

It's a carrot sky for the Carrot King. They call him the Carrot King, Rolando thought, wouldn't you know it! The glass of the helicopter cabin reflected back a dazzling orange.

He's put his stamp on everything. I guess, maybe even God is giving him his due!

He looked across to the disaster of a carrot field. They had come in and pushed out about a half acre of mid-season carrots, making way for the sheds that would house the big tractors they planned to bring in.

Well, they've come in here and messed everything up.

He saw the orange and green tangle of uprooted plants he had nurtured only the week before and grimaced in frustration. It pained him to see his hard work bladed away like nothing. Well, he said, 'No pain, no gain!' They could have waited a month or so, but they're in a hurry.

Things had gone fast, and the Byrd farm wasn't the only property the old millionaire oilman had bought. He bought an additional thousand acres. He bought the biggest and most aggressive shipping shed in the Valley, and when he bought the grain elevator, they threw a party. Carnival. Rolando grinned. They put up a big tent out there by the elevator and brought in a mariachi band, and barbeque, and kegs of beer. Throw a carnival and they'll all show up!

The arrival of the Lear jet caused a lot of hoop-la out at the airport. Not McAllen, but the little country airport at the town nearest the elevators. The airport in Weslaco couldn't host the jet set yet: the runway was narrow, too short, and the pilots grumbled about the tight landing.

To a generation of farmers accustomed to airplane dusters, seeing the helicopter all fitted out as a spray rig had been a novelty. They brought it in over the crowd at the elevator, and entertained them by dropping it in the middle of the festivities on the concrete pad. The pilot had brought along a young, scantily clad, and very blousy blonde, who blew kisses to the crowd and sent a roar of approval from the men.

The farmers were all there, and the suppliers picked up the tab. The farm chemical men, and the farm implement and tractor dealers were there. The seed men came, some with contracts and others who saw the potential and had come anyway with high hopes. And the bankers showed up. There was going to be a lot of money thrown around, and everyone could see the possibilities.

The old millionaire oilman turned Carrot Tsar got a lot of attention, but Rolando was surprised at the interest the farmers had given him.

He stood back out of the spotlight, out by the beer keg. They found him, and he got many warm abrazos and congratulations on his new position in the corporation. They all had one on him and the warm beer he was drinking wasn't the first beer he'd had today, and it sent his mind skipping over the day's events in a disjointed manner.

He glanced over to the maid's quarters and saw there was a light on.

I was always in the Byrd shadow, but in the end I made the decisions. Now this rich old bird's gonna lean on me, I'm the man.

I'm the man.

He saw a shadow pass across the lighted window, and disappear.

The rambling Byrd home was dark. It was a construction site. The corporation would headquarter here for the Valley farms and the operations in Mexico as well. Lilah's lawn was strewn with building materials and preparations had been made to pave a parking lot across the front, they were already taking the ornamentals down.

The plumbers and electricians had prepared the place for electronic communications that would be needed in an operation of this scale.

Accounting clerks were being hired to keep track of the government regulations. They would be required to keep records on the pesticides applied to the crops. They would track the DOT regulations and OSHA.

There'd be money transfers from Houston and secretaries would be hired to keep time cards, and checks would need to be written. There'd be a lot of bureaucratic paper work, and someone had to do it.

Ramona was cooking supper. He could smell chicken and tortillas and he crushed the aluminum beer can with one hand and dropped it at his feet.

She's still here, but things change. She's changed, and she'll be gone soon. They've asked her to vacate. She's lived in that apartment for ten years and it's overhead now.

He remembered the girl, the country girl, the *campesina*. Some things don't change. His heart still skipped a beat when he thought of her.

W.W. 'Bud' Clayton made an appearance at the festivities, but he didn't stay long. He got back in the jet and flew away to Houston. He left two men behind, and Rolando groaned because it was going to be on his back to tour them around, and he guessed they'd wind up in Reynosa.

When he opened the other beer, it was warm and shook up from the helicopter ride, and the tab came off crooked, and the damned thing shot beer all over him, and he stamped his feet and brushed his pants off before he leaned forward and let the foam run over as he took the first swig.

The sun was below the tree line now, and the security light in the yard came on, and he could hear her radio, and he put his hand on the wall and slunk down on his heels and his shirt was blue, not white and he didn't wear a tie, who needs it? He was the man, and it wasn't good enough for her.

Really, she was just an Indian. He wasn't usually attracted to the Indians, but something about Ramona was different. He saw it the first time, and he could still see it, and he could feel it, and soon she'd be gone, and the wall was dark old wood, and it soaked up the heat from the western sun, and he pressed the back of his head against it.

He'd take them down by the river where they had the celery seed farm, and they'd tour the green houses where they kept the flats of transplants all done up in little cones ready for the planters, and they might want to go on up to Los Ebanos and ride the hand hauled ferry across the Rio Grande and drive on down on the Mexican side to Reynosa.

They could do that. They'd see a lot of poverty on the Mexican side. He knew they'd want to. It made them feel all good and superior and they'd say things like, 'same land, same weather, same people, and look what difference government can make!' and then they'd feel really good and ready to eat some cabrito and drink a few margaritas before he took them back to McAllen to the big hotel.

She was lonely. He knew she was. She was always alone. Her family was all in Mexico. She had an old aunt in town that she never saw anymore.

They'll probably want to go to the island. That's another whole day. We'll need reservations at the Hyatt.

Her face had interested him from the first. Her smooth round olive face with its classic Indian features registered hopeful expectation and youthful innocence. She's young, very young, a beautiful Madonna, he thought. And he remembered thinking, she's surely a virgin, and the idea aroused a powerful attraction in him for her.

Well, she'd changed. When she came she wore her hair in a long plump braid. He had watched her walking casually going about her work, her long hair bouncing sensually against her back with each step, never suspecting he was watching. When he spoke to her, she answered with eyes cast down, modest and elegant in her innocence. When he came up to the house, he sensed her presence, and he watched for her light in the window in the evenings; it became a vigil he still practiced to this day.

She changed. Their relationship had developed to the point of marriage, but her attitude about marriage didn't change. She stubbornly refused to make that commitment. She cut her hair and gained confidence as her position at the Byrd household became permanent, but one thing never changed, he was the man, and she couldn't see it.

He liked the way they spoke to him with the proper respect and introduced him as 'Bud's' new farm manager. He was 'Bud's' new man, part of the team. They wouldn't hang around long at the Island, he knew that, he'd take them to the airport in Harlingen, and get back to his life, and his new responsibilities, and they had asked her to leave, her services no longer would be needed.

Maybe now, now that she had nowhere else to go, perhaps she would see him differently. Maybe she'd think he was good enough, now.

It was dark when he picked up his cans and took another look at the light in the window.

He was the man.

CHAPTER THIRTY-SEVEN

The green Ford Galaxy turned into the boulevard with the scraggly row of grapefruit trees and made the three blocks slowly. As it neared the old trailer, the car was hardly moving at all.

Four cars nosed in on the lawn. They were the cars of the big shots, the honchos. The boys in the sedan looked up into the trailer and saw men wearing big Stetsons silhouetted against the light. It was a conference. The *Ratas* were not welcome.

They crept on past, and when they got well on down the street, they began to laugh and talk of other things.

Güero didn't talk. He didn't laugh; he just drove the car and kept it to himself. "They can all go to hell!" he would have said if he had spoken. It was there, anyway, inside his head.

They had tired of the Island and wanted to cruise the old haunts. They especially missed the trailer-club-house.

"*Permanezca abajo,* stay down there, 'til the shit blows over," they were told.

Güero was informed the 'shit' was about him, and he better not be seen around, "*hasta que le decimos volver*". They'd tell him when to come back.

"The neighborhood has gone sour," Carlos explained. "You stepped in it," he told Güero, "That *abuela* is a friend of the horsewoman. The old lady's going to the police every day and stirring up a lotta' shit, and we don't need that kind of attention right now." Güero understood they didn't need that kind of attention, not now, or ever, meant he was to get lost from now on.

They made the turn at the back of the park and rolled past the horse in the lot. No one was at home in Elaine's trailer. She worked during the day and didn't get home until about six o'clock.

He let the car slip into idle when the horse came over. The boys rolled the window down and called out to it by name. She knew them, too, and was interested, but when they didn't give her any treats, the pet shook her head and walked away. They made the turn and drove back to the entrance and cut away to the east.

Remnants of the old citrus grove separated the park from a thirty-acre onion field. Now, late March, the onions were in the first stage of harvest. The tractor knifing the onions moved in a swirl of dust that drifted across the field with the prevailing wind. The driver raised the bar-shaped implement as he made the turn at the end of the row. The dust cleared momentarily, exposing the long row of pale yellow onions the tool had pushed up to the surface.

Güero nosed the car into the bar ditch in a place where the tractor had disced down the sharp angle to enter the field, and he turned the engine off.

Dust still hung in the air around them, and his passengers voiced loud protests. He ignored them and rolled and lit a smoke.

He took a long, dramatic draw on the cigarette. He held it out at full arms length so they could see it and made them wait while he savored the smoke. The car filled with the pungent aroma of marijuana, and the three in the back seat slapped him on the back and punched him, and he leaned forward and laughed before he passed it around. They laid their heads back and grew quiet as he rolled several more, one at a time, and handed them over his shoulder.

While they smoked, he watched the tractor move slowly up and down the rows. Güero knew the routine of the onion harvest. He knew that when they finished today, they weren't through. They'd be back in two or three days when the onions had time to dry.

***

Cars lined up along both sides of the road and Güero, alone now, parked the old Ford inconspicuously alongside the rest of the old cars. The onion field bustled with activity as a crew of about forty clipped the onions.

"*Pulgas!*" he called them. Fleas, he thought, crawling over the carcass of a dog! The men moved down the rows picking up handfuls of the bulbs, three or four at a time. They snipped off the roots and the shriveled tops and dropped them into burlap tow sacks.

'Las Ratas', they call us the little rats! We are the little rats, but these, they are the fleas.

It was nearly noon, and the clipping crews had been at work since nine. Already, the rows were lined with bulging brown bags of onions. The men worked quickly at the boring stoop labor. They were paid by the bag, not by the hour. Most of the laborers would be gone by three o'clock.

The fleas keep banker's hours, but they're not bankers. The jefes aren't bankers, either; they don't work in a bank. They do business there. They put their money in banks, a lot of money. They are businessmen.

The snippers would be finished sometime that day, and the field would be quiet again for two or probably three days, until the onions rattled in the sacks.

Güero sat and smoked, and he watched. Then he leaned his head back and looked at the smoke collecting on the soft head lining of the old sedan's roof. He felt a little sick, and he opened the window to let the smoke out and some breeze in while he plotted.

"They can all go to hell!" he said it out loud this time, and the sound of his voice gave some relief to the rage he felt inside.

***

The next couple of days Güero spent in a state of mounting anger. His mind focused on his rejection, and he occupied himself with schemes to regain his self-esteem. He returned to the onion field. Fewer cars were parked along the road now, but enough of them that his old sedan would not be noticed.

Today, three teams of tractors and two-ton trucks worked the field.

The tractor and truck teams moved together down the rows of bagged onions. A man on the ground followed the tractor and lifted the bags one at a time onto a belt. Güero watched the man standing in the truck bed. He was silhouetted against the sun as he dumped the onions into the truck and sent the used bags sailing into the air to land on the clotted rows.

To lift the bagged onions onto the conveyor belt the man on the ground had to straddle the bag and lift with both hands using the muscles in his strong legs to manage the heavy bag. The man in the truck hefted it into the bed with the others.

Even with the aid of a conveyer belt, the work was heavy, and hard. Güero watched and smiled contemptuously to himself. Their cars were old and worn out, like they would be, too, in only a few years. Frank

Palma drove a Mercedes and wore expensive suits. He was rich. These men would never be rich. Güero knew this.

And they were *gringo* onions, large yellow and sweet. No good for cooking like the white onions that suited the Mexican palate. They were the Texas version of Georgia's famous sweet, Vidalia onions. Here they were called 1015s, after the appropriate date for planting, October 15.

Güero left the car and cut across the field, walking along and over the rows, stepping across the bags.

The crews consisted of mostly men. Children didn't follow the women into the fields as they had in years past. The labor lawyers strictly enforced child labor laws. Children, even those who just came along with working mothers, were a liability for the packing sheds, so few women worked the onion harvest any more.

In contradiction, however, many of the crew bosses were middle-aged women. They were known to be the toughest and were preferred by the packing sheds. The crew boss leaned against the hood of a red pickup truck parked in the field road that ran between the onions and the scraggly grapefruit orchard. She was taking bites out of one of the onions, holding it like an apple. She had the other half of the onion and a pocket knife in her other hand. She wore a red bandana on her head in an effort to control her mass of dark hair, but tendrils escaped across her forehead and she kept brushing them away with her elbow.

Güero saw the boss leaning against the hood of the red truck and changed his course. She watched the young man moving across the rows of stooping laborers. He walked along with his head up and his eyes on her until he reached the truck and leaned against it.

He didn't speak; he just leaned back on the red truck and gazed out across the field. He wore his brown hair cut short, although he allowed it to grow longer above his ears and pulled it tight in a short pigtail in the back.

She asked him what he needed. He didn't answer or even acknowledge her question. He just looked across the field. He leaned back across the hood on his elbows, and his eyes focused in the distance. She let him dawdle there and said nothing more.

They stood together several minutes before he took her hand firmly by the wrist. He pulled her rudely toward him and helped himself to the onion half and the knife. He held her and took a big bite out of the onion. He smiled as he slowly chewed, then he spat it into the dirt at her feet. His almond eyes riveted on her face, he ground it into the dust with his shoe.

"Delicious," he said and raised his eyebrows and dramatically ogled her breasts, all the while smiling provocatively. She wasn't amused. He was hurting her arm, and she could feel his fingernails biting into her wrist.

She jerked at her arm, but he held on and tightened his grip. "Get out of here, punk!" she said, "Or go to work!"

"Why aren't you clipping?" he said insolently. "You're not clipping! Me neither! I'm like you."

"You're not like me, punk!" She knew what he was.

"Oh yes, we're alike. You and I don't sweat with the *pulgas*. We're independent businessmen," he said, and added, "I ain't no clipper. I'm on business."

He didn't relax his grip on her arm. The wind picked up her hair, and blew it in her face again. He saw her distress, and he smiled and let her struggle. He took another bite of the onion with his mouth close to hers, and hurt her again. Then he pushed her abruptly against the hood, still holding her by the wrist. He threw the onion down into the dirt, and leaned over her and held the knife up to her face a long minute. Then he closed it with one hand and slid it into his pocket, released her, and walked away into the trees across the farm road.

The sun shown brightly hot even for March, and the abandoned grove was in sad shape with curled leaves. Careless weeds, drooping from the heat, grew waist high, and the ground between the trees was powdery dry. The onion had left a strong taste in his mouth, and the encounter with the woman had left him worked up and sweating. He searched the grapefruit trees for an orange.

The trailer park just over the fence was familiar ground, and he bent low and crawled through the barbed wire to where he knew the orange trees were.

He found a late straggler and tried to score it with the woman's knife, but it was dull and he tossed it into the dirt. He pulled out his own that he kept honed and went along peeling the orange as he walked.

The cars were gone from the trailer, and the curtains were drawn. The only sign of life was the dimly burning porch light. Güero stepped up on the block-steps and tried the door. It was locked. He peered into the darkness through the tiny window and saw no one. He put the palm of his hand on the door panel and felt its warmth. He leaned his cheek against the metal and closed his eyes. He walked around to the back of the trailer, found the water hydrant, and turned it on. He filled his cupped hands and drank from them, splashing the cool water on his face, and kneeling beside the trailer with his hand on the faucet. The faucet was hard and cold, like the light at the front door, and the emptiness inside. He leaned forward to press his forehead against the wall of the trailer, but the shade had robbed it of warmth, and the metal was cold. He sank to the ground and sat with his back against the trailer. The ground was wet, and he rolled over and lay down in the narrow band of shade cast by the trailer.

He had known trust here, and comfort. He had been a part of things darkly sinful, exciting, and powerful. He had come to life here. Now his life was empty. He crossed his hands over himself. He had an urgent need for the satisfaction he had known in this place, but it was gone now and he was left with only impotence and frustration.

The trailer was dark and empty, and he was on the outside. He had been rejected and even blamed. He was sweating and cold in the wet grass. He raised himself up on his elbows, and a sense of desperation and rage swept over him.

Güero walked down the street and crossed over when he came to the old man's yard. He stood there a minute and studied the gallon milk jugs, white, clean and neatly lined up along the border of the old man's property.

He put the toe of his shoe against one and pushed. It resisted, so he pushed harder and it moved. He gave it a good kick and it bounced over, spilling its contents out into the petunias.

He picked it up and drop kicked it into the street where it bounced two or three times with a clackety rattle.

The old man watched from the door, and Güero smiled at him and waved, before going down the line pushing them over and stepping on them, one at a time, until they all were crushed and empty and he moved on down the street.

He picked another orange and began to pare it with the knife. He leaned against the wooden rail that ran along the top of the horse lot.

Kathy's horse came up and put her head over the fence, reaching over his shoulder for the orange.

He laughed and turned and held his hand out to let her take a section.

"You like oranges?" he began feeding the horse from his hand. The horse's soft muzzle tickled his hand as it groped for the small nuggets of sweet orange.

When he had fed the horse all the orange, he rubbed his sticky hands on her neck and finished it off by raking them across the seat of his pants while she backed away, nosing for his hand, still looking for a handout. He climbed through the fence and let the horse nudge him. He opened his hand to show her the orange was gone. He had to clean the slobbery hand on her neck again. The chestnut quarter horse was petted, and pampered and cared for morning and evening, and its brown coat glistened in the sunshine.

Güero ran his hand along the friendly horse's neck and over its withers and patted its back while it searched him for more treats. He let his hand move down to the horse's hindquarter and its head jerked up and she turned and quickly trotted away to the other side of the lot.

He walked after her, but she stayed just ahead of him moving along the perimeter of the fence line. He stood still, she watched, but when he called she raised her head and blew from her hose and kept her distance. He felt a growing anger with the *gringo* horse, but he wasn't getting anywhere. She liked oranges; maybe she wanted another. He found an orange and stood just inside the fence and began paring it.

Güero had watched the young blonde woman with the horse. He had seen her brushing and working with it early and late. The girls at the trailer were younger and sexy and easy. This one dressed like a boy, and she was arrogant, untouchable, and he came often and watched from the shadows.

Güero kept his eyes lowered on the orange and pretended to ignore the horse. He slowly pared a long spiral curl of rind and thrust his thumb deep into the juicy pulp to send sparkles of scent over to the animal. She was interested,and she lowered her head and moved a few steps closer. He could hear her teeth click and she began to lick her lips.

Güero took a few steps forward but stopped when the horse raised her head. They stood frozen for a few minutes before he ventured another step or two, cautiously. He held the orange in the palm of his outstretched hand and she let him walk up to her slowly and she took the orange.

While she was busy and distracted he began to rub her in front of the withers in a circular motion and he felt her take a deep breath and exhale.

She relaxed and let him rub her, and he put his cheek against her side and whispered softly to her in Spanish as he worked his hand down her leg.

He cupped her knee with his hand, and he pressured her to bend the knee until he held her hoof braced against his leg. Quickly he sliced with the knife through the flexor tendon below the fetlock joint.

CHAPTER THIRTY-EIGHT

The ringing phone in the night had an ominous feel, and Bob checked the clock before answering. Eleven, they had only been asleep a short while. What could it be this time?

This time it was the Chapin police.

"Does Mrs. Rogers live there with you?" a serious voice asked.

"Yes, she does," Bob said. He looked at his alarmed wife, and touched her arm to signal her to be quiet.

"Somebody needs to come out here," the policeman continued, "We've got the fire department out here. Her house is on fire."

"We'll be right there," Bob said, but to his wife, "My God! What next! That was the police. Connie's house is on fire. I'll go." He turned the lamp on and got out of bed. "You don't need to come," he said, pulling on his pants. Susan pushed the covers back and sat up. "Go back to sleep," he ordered. Susan wasn't having any of it.

"Don't wake your mother up this time of night. I can handle it."

"Are you kidding? I'm going and we better take Mother, too. Her house is on fire for God's sake! She'll kill us if we don't wake her up."

It was going to slow him down, but he knew she was right. Connie would want to go, no matter the time.

Only a couple of miles separated Susan's house and Connie's. The flat terrain and powerful spotlights of the volunteer fire department offered up an eerie sight. Long before they reached the scene, a column of white smoke shown with dramatic clarity against the deep blue night sky.

They turned at Garcia's store, and a man wearing a reflective vest stopped them. Bob rolled the window down, and the man leaned into it and said, "This area is blocked off. You can't come this way."

"We live over there," Bob said.

"We have a burning house ahead, and we can't allow traffic to enter the area. It won't be too long. Maybe an hour at the most."

"The police called us, it's our house," Bob said, and the man let them go.

There was a fire truck in the drive and another was pulled up on the lawn at the front of the house. Cars and another truck were parked along both sides of the road.

The floodlights were still trained on the house, but now only thin threads of smoke could be seen coming from the blackened hole where Connie's living room windows had been.

Firemen had shifted their hoses and were now directing water from the tank truck onto the roof. The brilliance of the lights directed on the house magnified the darkness beyond their reach, and Connie saw shadowy figures moving about behind them. Cars started up and pulled away into the night.

"It's almost over," the chief said to them. "You're very lucky. We managed to save the house because they started the fire at the front where it could be easily seen. Your neighbor saw it and called when the fire had been burning only minutes."

Bob looked at the heavily damaged and blackened wall by the living room windows. It would be expensive to repair, and he thought it would have been a blessing if the whole thing had gone up in smoke.

Connie stepped forward toward the house.

"Lady, stand back!" the fireman said.

"We can't let anyone go in there until we're sure we've taken care of any smoldering going on. The house could flare up and trap you in there. Stand back."

The chief, a young Hispanic, smiled broadly, and explained proudly, and with gestures how they had handled the fire.

"We think this is a gang job," he explained. "Probably some kids smoking marijuana."

"How could you know that?" His comment had their attention.

"We think they walked up from the field and broke a window out in the back. That's where they came in. They must have been sitting on the carpet, leaning back against the wall, and smoking.

"Wait to go in the house until tomorrow morning, but when you do, you'll see they sat under the sheer curtains and set them afire, probably with one of the cigarettes or a lighter.

"Those kinds of curtains burn fast and hot. As they burned upward, they separated from the rod and came falling down and set the carpeting ablaze. As the carpet burned it caught the wall on fire and the fire, moved up the wall. Now we want to be sure it isn't still burning in the attic space. Sparks can travel, and they always go up when they do."

"Are you saying you think some kids smoking accidentally set the fire?"

"I'd like to think that, but no, not really. The house was vacant. Vacant houses draw these kids like flies! I doubt it was an accident; they probably set it on purpose. Sometimes they hang around and throw rocks at us."

He didn't add they could make it really fast when they didn't have to wait for the police escort, like up the road at the colonia. What a problem! And the rocks weren't all, sometimes they threw bottles and the guys from Harlingen had their windshield broken to the tune of a thousand dollars. Sometimes they set the fire deliberately, and sometimes they called in a false alarm, but it definitely took more time when the call came from the colonia.

It was winding down quickly. The sounds of engines starting and cars pulling away punctuated the hissing roar of the water hoses. The fire truck parked in the drive left and took one of the spotlights with it. The blackness began closing in without anything for the remaining lights to reflect back upon as the crowd and the cars left. Finally the water was cut off, and they rolled up the remaining hoses and stashed them in the tank truck.

Bob shook the fire chief's hand and thanked him.

"Without your quick and excellent work here tonight, the house would be gone now."

The irony in Bob's statement was lost on the chief.

"Yeah, these boys do a good job," he grinned with pride. "We've been up to Texas A and M University for training. Just got back. They're volunteers, but these guys know what they're doing!"

A shiver gripped Connie, but not from the cold. "Where's Puppy?"

"Lady, I'm so sorry, but the black dog is in the back. I'm afraid he's dead, they must have killed him, I think they shot him."

As the crowd dispersed, Ignacio moved forward, and Connie saw him for the first time that evening.

"Connie, I saw it and called the fire department. They're good. They got here fast." He whispered to her, "I think we need a volunteer sheriff's department."

"Ignacio," Connie said, "they have killed Puppy."

"How do you know? Where is she?"

"She's around at the back," the fireman said. "We left her there."

"Ignacio, could you?"

"I'll go get her and take her to my house where the coyotes or anything can't get her."

"I'll come for her in the morning."

Ignacio brought her around, carrying her cradled in his arms. Her lifeless body, limp and the tail whip stilled at last.

Connie turned her head away to hide the tears, but it didn't matter because they all were crying now.

They stood in the yard and waited for the fire truck to go, and when it did, they left, too.

***

"It just kills me to see her sitting out there smoking and brooding like that. This has been going on too long," Susan said to Bob. "We need to do something to shake her out of this depression." It had been a tough week.

"Just leave it," Connie said when Bob offered to go out and put plywood panels up to cover the blackened wounds of her house. "At least for a few days," she said. And reluctantly, he left it.

"It's just for a few days," he said to Susan. "What difference does it make? Connie wants it that way and what could it hurt?"

The situation had gotten to everyone, and Susan was short with her answer. "You know what it could hurt! That house is an open invitation. 'Come on in,' it says. What about the liability? I think we need to worry about that now that we'll be losing the insurance."

"Not if we don't collect on it."

She let Bob think about it a while and added. "I'm worried about Mother." She motioned toward the patio doors where they could see Connie sitting in the shade, smoking.

"Her attitude has changed." She touched Bob's sleeve, "Look at her. She doesn't seem to care about the house any more. She hasn't been out there since the fire, and well, Puppy.

"She doesn't want you to close it up, Susan said. I think she wants to leave it like that until everyone has seen it!"

"Calm down," he said. "That's not nice. Be charitable."

Susan shook her head, "We'll never sell it now. It's famous, or infamous!"

Elaine had seen it. She had seen it, and she called to say she was moving into a condo in McAllen.

"Connie," she said, "I'll tell you where I am, but please don't give my whereabouts to anyone else at the sheriff's office. I'll give you a number where you can call me if you need me, you know, if you really need me, but I'd rather not be involved any more. I know the police can always find me, but I'd just feel better if I didn't attract their attention."

"Elaine, can't you get another horse?"

"Connie, Kathy's father bought the horse for her, and she trained it herself. She's spent three years training Star. A broken horse, trained to barrel would cost about ten thousand dollars. Her father doesn't have that kind of money, and you know I don't.

"It takes time and work to do it yourself, and anyway, Kathy doesn't want another horse. It broke her heart when we had to put Star down. We're moving to town."

"What training? Does a horse have to be trained to run around the barrels?"

"Yes, it does. The horse and rider are judged as a team. The arc they make rounding the barrels is important as well as their time. The horse performs just the same as the rider. And, Connie, the vet doesn't think it was an accident. He says the tendon was cut with a sharp instrument like a knife. Now your house has been burned. Does that seem like a strange coincidence to you?"

When Susan said, "Mother I think it would do us all some good to take a holiday. Let's go to South Padre and think about something else for a while."

Connie smiled, "The Island? I'd love to go to the island. Yes, let's go to the island."

CHAPTER THIRTY-NINE

A barrier island hugs the south Texas coastline from Corpus Christi Bay to the mouth of the Rio Grande River. It runs along one hundred and ten miles, and at one time consisted only of sand dunes and not much else.

Things change. A soaring causeway now spans the Laguna Madre that separates it from the mainland. Miles of beautiful hotels line its fine sandy beach and sparkling blue coastline. South Padre Island is a popular resort.

Her suggestion to go to the island and think about something else for a while had been received with a little more enthusiasm than Susan had expected. Now she knew why. Connie never intended to think about something else for a while. This wasn't going to be a vacation. Instead, her mother saw it as an opportunity to pursue her obsession.

"I'm going with you," Susan said, when she learned of her mother's plan. The island police station was located in a simple white stucco building set alone on a small lot. Soon after they were shown in to an office and seated before a uniformed detective, a man of about forty, another officer joined them, a pretty young woman.

Connie launched into her story; the words she had so often repeated tumbled out. She feared he would brush her off as had happened so many times before, but he listened with patience and interest. When she came to the part about Elaine and the license number, the woman asked if she had it with her.

Connie had come prepared. She fumbled in her purse and found the neatly folded paper upon which she had written the number. The woman took it and promptly left the room.

The officer allowed Connie to talk until she had finished her story. He listened attentively.

"This island has a pretty small permanent population," he said. "We have a group of men who live on the public beach, north up there past the hotels. They camp out and they come and go. We watch them carefully. I don't remember a man with shaved head and scars. I'm sure I'd remember if I had seen him. You say it happened last August?"

"Yes."

The officer frowned, "Hmm, more than a year ago. Of course, the shaved head may have been temporary, and his hair would be grown out by now. The hair would hide the scars. We can't count on that description any more. It'll complicate matters but not necessarily make it impossible. We'll have to rely on the license number now. I'll keep it and watch for his car. We'll stop him if we see it."

"I've been told you can't do that without, well they said 'cause', whatever that means."

The good-natured policeman smiled. "Well, there are ways and there are ways." He sat forward in his seat, "There's the letter of the law, and there's the spirit of the law."

He smiled broadly, "Let's just say this is in the spirit of the law. We can pull him over ostensibly on a traffic violation. It's a routine matter to check the plates. We could do a record check and if we see anything out of line, we could pick him up. At least, at the very least, we'd know who we're dealing with. We could get his name.

"The shaved hair is a good indication that this man has a record. You're right; they shave their heads at the boot camp correction facility. His age and activities are pretty good evidence he's been in that institution."

The policewoman returned and asked Connie, "Did you say it was a green Ford Galaxy?"

"Yes, an old car, kind of faded green, a sedan."

"I've run a check on the license plate number. The plates belong to a 1993 gray Taurus. The name it's registered to will do you no good. It can't be his."

The two officers exchanged looks. "If that's the case," the man said, "your man's green Ford Galaxy has stolen plates, and that's gonna' make it real easy. All they have to do is watch his house, pull him over, and simply take him in on the charge of driving a car with stolen plates."

"The sheriff," Connie hesitated, "well, he could have checked his number as easily as you have, but he didn't for some reason. Now, of course, it's too late, we don't know where he lives now. The trailer is vacant. That's why I'm here. He's bragged to his neighbors in the park that he lives here, but I know for sure he's been in my neighborhood as recently as last week. He set fire to my house."

"Oh brother, well, my advice to you is put some pressure on them at the sheriff's office. Have you been there in person?"

"I usually talk to them on the phone, but I have been there once, only I couldn't see the sheriff. I guess you know about our sheriff?"

He smiled, and ignoring her question, he said, "This case is important to you, not so much to them. You have to lean on them. Go down there in person, go often. There's a new man in charge."

"I know, John Anderson. I saw him. The sheriff was in Austin. On personal business," she smiled, "I imagine."

"Then you need to go for sure. John's not there anymore." He didn't mention that John was under investigation for problems of his own and was on departmental leave. "John's out," he said, "and David Ocampo's in charge now."

***

Connie had a long night. The drone of the hotel's air-conditioning unit was an irritating buzz, and she didn't think she slept at all. But she did, and during those lapses into sleep, disturbing feelings of helplessness, loss of control, and danger haunted her dreams.

She finally rose, quietly stepped out onto the balcony and leaned against the wrought iron rail. The sky was just beginning to turn from star-spangled black to a deep translucent blue. Silvery gray clouds banked low, just above the water line in the distance. A cluster of tiny bright dots on the horizon marked a drilling platform. They glowed faintly green and didn't move.

Out there, she thought, men have already gone to work. Connie watched the lights until they gradually disappeared with the rising sun before she went back inside and quietly got dressed. She heard Susan and Bob whispering in the adjoining room, and she slipped away to walk on the beach. She needed to be alone.

In other times, trips to the island offered views of the starry sky and pounding surf that worked an adjustment on her perspective. Not today. The nagging problem continued to eat away at her. A breeze rose with the sun and pushed ragged clouds inland, low over the island. She waded out into the gray water, out to where it swirled around her ankles and on out to where it came above her knees. She felt the undertow pull at her legs. She held her skirt, but it trailed in the water and tugged at her, too. Everything dragged at her, pulling and swirling.

It was easy. Just pull him over, she thought, it was that easy. 'May I see your license?' If they knew it on the island, they knew it in the county.

She walked back up out of the water and made her way in the wet sand beyond the waters edge stepping over the many scattered shells and the occasional blue jellyfish that washed up along the waterline. In the past she had searched for sand dollars, starfish, and shells she picked up just because they were beautiful. Today she walked without seeing them.

Her inner voice scolded her, hammering her with regrets.

I gave up so easily when if I had nagged and pestered they may have done something.

She fumed with anger at the deputies.

It would have been so easy. Just pull him over, and it would have been the end for him.

Connie knew she had been naïve.

I have been weak and trusting. I expected the sheriff to do the job, now I know I should have done it myself. If I had done it right, Puppy would be alive, Kathy would still be riding, and Ignacio wouldn't be afraid to go to town on his bicycle.

A lump rose up in her throat and tears welled in her eyes when she thought of Puppy.

Puppy knew her duty, and she did it, faithful to the end. She stood her post. She died for me.

Connie's guilty conscience gnawed at her.

I let everyone down. God only knows what happened to my cat. They depended on me. I had a responsibility. They were just innocent dumb animals, and I let them down.

And Hank, our house, I lost our house.

She felt a rush of anger at herself.

When they came back, I shouldn't have run. I could have stayed. It would have been different. If only I had another chance. This time I'd do it right.

She replayed it in her mind, and this time she stood beside the door out of his sight and waited. She didn't run to the car. This time she waited with grim determination for him to jimmy the door open and step into the room.

She saw the sun glance across the glass as the door swung open toward her. His back was turned. She let him take a few steps before she pushed the door with her foot, and he saw her leaning against the wall with the pistol firmly grasped and steady. She saw the surprise on his face as she raised the gun with both hands and aimed for the ugly cross that he wore as an irreverent insult to all Christians, and shot him without a moment's hesitation.

I wouldn't have to drag him in as Sam suggested. He would come in all by himself, and all I'd have to do is wait patiently. Not run as I did before.

She would only have to shoot one of them. She saw clearly in her mind's eye the other two watching in horror, their mouths open and their eyes popping, before beating a retreat to the car and never coming back. She smiled to herself when she imagined what they would be telling the others at the trailer.

"Don't ever go there, that old woman is crazy! She'll kill you!" she heard them say, and the smile broadened into a grin, and her spirits were briefly lifted.

The deputies said I was vulnerable because I was old and alone. If I had not run, maybe now they wouldn't see me as such an easy target.

The breeze blew up from the Gulf, steady and dependable. It picked up the scent of the salty spray where the breakers spent themselves on the first sand bar, only yards away, and it pulled at the wet hem of her skirt. She turned her back to the wind and stood looking at the row of hotels, modern and beautiful. Miles of them with sparkling blue swimming pools and elegant restaurants soon to be filled with vacationing diners. Early morning, but already people were on the beach. Later there would be crowds of them coming with their umbrellas and their children.

No wonder I trusted the sheriff. This isn't the country I remember. Everything has changed. Where have I been? I don't know this place. We came to the Island often in the old days, but this isn't the island I remember. The island I remember was very different.

Connie turned her back into the wind and felt it sweep against her hair, and she remembered the island as it had been, before the arching causeway with its stream of cars, like when they rode the launch across the Laguna Madre in the early morning to only a wind swept stretch of sand dunes.

The wind ruffled through the palm fronds, and Connie saw them as aliens, "Where'd they come from anyway?" she thought, "They've been brought in here from somewhere else. The island I remember had no trees. And where did the sand dunes go? Somewhere under the hotels, she imagined that the sand was beat down and conquered, not free and windblown, as it should be.

She remembered how they had laughed and clung to the crude seat backs as the World War I half-track carried them lunging and bumping over the dunes from the Laguna Madre to the beach. As the day wore on, the sun turned the dunes into a blazing hot barrier, and she remembered well the time they missed the truck and crossed on foot, stepping high, with their shoes in their hands at a run to catch the launch before it also left without them.

The island had a hotel then, only one. The old casino and bathhouse was wrecked by the hurricane of 1933, and abandoned. Only a skeleton was left, a ghost of a building, wooden and weathered silvery gray, soft to the touch. The wind moaned through the empty rooms, through paneless windows, carrying the distant squawks of the seagulls on the beach and the pounding of the surf. It was a cool haven from the savage heat of the noonday sun.

She walked slowly pressing the balls of her bare feet into the wet sand and the shallow surf, pushed ripples over them and drew it back sucking the sand away from under her.

The impressions she left behind were no more than empty holes. The waves washed up and filled them in, and she watched them disappear.

"Without a trace," she whispered. "Here and gone like those of us who came before, who lived and loved and laughed and now, like my tracks, are gone and who remembers?"

How can we remember? They've even changed the names, like the lighthouse on the point.

They call the town Port Isabel now. Hank called it Point Isabel until he died, even though he knew the name had been changed. He was right! I think they should stick with the real name, the first one. The one it had been given when the lighthouse had a purpose. I guess they don't need the lighthouse on the point anymore.

Hank was right about the lighthouse and just about everything else, too. He had his head on straight. He wouldn't have spent his time moping around and fiddling with the authorities we already know don't plan to do anything about the gangs.

Connie felt a wrench in her heart. She could see him young again, walking down the huge blocks of Texas red granite with his pants legs rolled up and in his leather shoes. Although the jetties were windy he never wore a hat. She remembered how the wind would lift his dark hair, and how his black Welsh eyes were always cracked in laughter. She couldn't remember ever seeing him wear sunglasses.

"How's your catch?" he'd say to the fishermen they passed on the way to an empty spot where he could set up. Connie loved to see the exotic fish the men showed them, fish like she'd never seen before, purple ribbonfish, and striped black and white sheepsheads. Occasionally someone would pull up a small hammerhead shark. Connie didn't remember too many fishermen, not like the crowds of men lining the jetties today.

Hank was never in a hurry. He would put a live shrimp on the line and cast it out, watching as the wind and the tide carried it quickly back onto the granite stones.

The faker, she laughed, Hank didn't really like to fish, and he didn't like to eat them either. It didn't take him too long to lay the rod down and watch the shrimp fleet parading out early, some not to return for weeks.

Ships with foreign registry coming up the channel to the port would distract him, and they would stand together and wave to the sailors lined up along the rails. They watched until their faces grew wet from the salty spray of the wake the ships created beating against the huge red granite stones.

Connie liked the end of the day the best, the finale, the trip to the jetty's end. Like all of life, they found the going easy at first, with cement between the granite blocks. Before long the concrete ended and the struggle began. Soon the blocks were farther apart, and it was necessary to do some climbing and jumping across spans where the frothy water churned and sucked back out to the gulf.

The deeper water became heavier, and the waves pounded into the blocks in a fine mist. The granite grew wet and slippery, and some days they had to time their progress to the rhythm of the waves crashing completely over the big stones.

I loved the delicious danger of it all. I was with Hank. I was invincible. The reward at the end made it worth the risk. Dolphins leaped into the air to celebrate our achievement, their fins glistening in a salute before they dove and disappeared. Hank and I made it all the way to the end every time and we stood in the shimmering spray watching the dolphins with the wind in our faces before we started back to the shore.

She had always dreaded the trip home. They were usually sunburned with sand in their ears and underwear, and it had been a misery.

Connie knew one thing hadn't changed. She had to take another uncomfortable trip home. She understood now she'd never sell her property. It had become clear to her the old sheriff could have picked the boys up, but never would have. She had believed they didn't want to fool with the complaints of an old woman against some 'kids', kids they couldn't by law do much about. Now she knew more about Carlos Medrano and his connections with the county administration, and she wondered if something more sinister kept them from taking action against him and his drug thugs.

Well, something's changed. We have a new sheriff.

"This case is important to you, not so much to them. You have to put pressure on them. Go down there in person," the Island policeman had said.

"Put pressure on them," Connie repeated, and she set her mind to do it.

CHAPTER FORTY

onnie didn't call for an appointment. A nuisance has to be assertive, she told herself. I'll push my way in, and she almost missed Ocampo. She caught him in the hallway and at her stubborn insistence, he returned to his office impatiently, although, he had, he said, an appointment at the courthouse.

This time he wore his coat and tie, and he now occupied the office behind the door, SHERIFF. She had never seen the inside of the famous room and looked about with interest as he seated himself behind the large sheriff's desk for the session.

"I only have a few minutes, Mrs. Rogers, how can I help you?"

The room belonged to him now. Photographs of a pretty woman and children sat on the desk along with expensive looking paperweights and a leather desk set.

The walls sported five black-framed photographs of little league baseball teams with a smiling Coach Ocampo. Two large silver colored trophies topped the bookcase and attested to his coaching skills.

"Sheriff, did you know they set fire to my house?" she began.

"Really, who would do this?" he asked pleasantly, as if it were no concern of his.

"I was hoping you could tell me. Surely the firemen reported it."

"No doubt, I'm sure they did. What did you expect me to do about it?"

"Well, let me see," Connie rolled her eyes in frustration. "You could have sent someone out to investigate, for starters. The firemen think someone set it deliberately. Arson is still a crime, isn't it?"

"And what could we have done?"

"The firemen think 'kids' smoking marijuana set the house on fire for fun. Or meanness. I think those same 'kids' robbed me. The fire chief said they were in the house fooling around and smoking a while before they set it on fire. He said there was a trail of footprints leading up to the back of the house where they climbed in the broken window. If you had come out, you might have taken fingerprints. We could cross check them with the ones you took before, and then we would be sure."

"Mrs. Rogers, fingerprints are no good." He smiled, shook his head and instructed patiently, "They're always smudged or incomplete, and if they were perfect, we couldn't use them anyway. They're inadmissible as evidence. It's a waste of time to even bother with them."

There it was again, he was patronizing. She knew the interview was going down the drain, and she couldn't conceal her rising anger and frustration. "I have practically investigated this case myself. I have given you so much information that you could have done something about this a year ago."

Her 'I told you so' sounded petty and childish. He grimaced as if she had told him a bad joke. She felt a rush of desperation. His demeanor rendered her weak and powerless, and worst of all, ineffective.

"If you had gone to the trailer park and talked to the people who live there, perhaps it would have helped us both. It would have helped me, and maybe with the information you would have gotten there, the grand jury could have indicted Amado and possibly Carlos Medrano."

He sat on the edge of his chair, cueing her he was impatient to go on to his more important appointment. This wasn't a business meeting. He twisted it into a casual visit to placate an old woman. She went there, no she had been sent to put pressure on him, and instead, he was condescending and brushing her off. He had 'real' business at the courthouse.

She had known it all along. They could have picked the guy up long ago. Surely they had checked the license number and had seen they didn't match the car. There was some reason they didn't want to do it. Were they protecting the Medranos?

"I'm giving up on you," she sputtered. "I've been talking to you for more than a year. A year ago, remember, you said, 'come up here and press charges,' well, I'm going to do just that! I don't know the name of the 'kid', but I've learned who owns the trailer where he and others like him hang out. I'm going to hire a lawyer and sue that Fagan who owns the trailer. He's responsible for these 'kids' who prey upon elderly, and vulnerable people.

"I have been to the park. I have talked to witnesses who will testify that this man is responsible for the gang that has done what amounts to felony crime against me and others who I will name. They are burglars; we know they're involved in car theft. I can think of a couple of murders they may have done. Everyone knows they deal in drugs. Now they have done arson. I have suffered the loss of my personal possessions, damage to my home amounting to many thousands of dollars, and resulting damage to my health and well-being.

"You could easily have learned the name of the young man, but you either didn't or won't tell me, so I'll name the leader of the gang responsible for him and thus for his crimes toward me.

"His name is Carlos Medrano, and I have many witnesses and much evidence to prove it. We will subpoena your records if we have to in addition to the testimony of my witnesses. This, along with the previous attention he has received from the grand jury, is surely bad news for him!"

She saw no reaction from the head of detectives turned sheriff, so she added, "I'll go to the press and make such a fuss that even his uncle, the district attorney, won't be able to ignore it!"

The sheriff leaned back in his seat and smiled.

"I'll picket the courthouse!" She was raving now, "I'll walk up and down in front of the courthouse with a sign, a sandwich board. I'm an old woman. The press will just love it!" His smile broke into a chuckle, and he laughed. He stood, walked around the desk and took her arm, showing her to the door.

"You do that!" He said grinning, "I can hardly wait to see it myself!" They left the room together, and he turned out the light before closing the door behind them.

***

She felt as heavy as the jetty's red granite stones. Maybe I have lived past my usefulness like the lighthouse, she thought. I didn't make any impression on him at all.

The threat of a lawsuit had just popped into her mind, and she blurted it out without thinking, but now, she began to consider the possibilities.

I'm an old woman, and he knows I really don't have enough evidence for a lawyer to take up a case against someone as well connected as Carlos Medrano. I'm no fool. If I hire a lawyer, he won't do the investigation. I could hire a detective, but I don't know how much that would cost, and I don't have the money anyway.

She got in her car and drove down the long narrow lane past the ominously barred windows of the jailhouse where they kept the men, too horrible to mention, according to John Anderson. She drove to the highway and turned south.

Connie thought seriously about talking to a lawyer. She ran it over in her mind. She wondered how she could come up with more witnesses and evidence to interest a lawyer in going after the nephew of the district attorney. Elaine and Ignacio were probably out of the picture now.

Elaine doesn't want to talk to anyone about them. Ignacio is afraid for his life. I need other witnesses, or more of them even if I can get Elaine and Ignacio to help me. If someone is going to the park to talk to the people who live there, even though it's risky, I guess it has to be me. Maybe it's time for me to take a risk.

***

The smile vanished from the sheriff's face as he walked across the parking lot to his car. He drove past the jailhouse to the junction where the lane met the highway and sat a few minutes with his hands firmly gripping the steering wheel.

Sheriff Ocampo had a drive of about a mile north to his appointment. There was a time when the jail and sheriff's office was a walk across the street to the courthouse. Through the years, the incidence of crime rose with the population, and the jail had to be moved away from the square.

Unlike European towns, where a church dominates the central plaza, the principal feature of the county seat's plaza in Texas is a courthouse where records are kept and justice is dispensed.

Hidalgo County's courthouse, built in 1908, was just such a building. As did most other Texas courthouses, the square building sat in a park in the center of the town and featured four doors, each one facing in a different direction, symbolizing accessibility to all.

Well, things change.

In the prosperous years following World War II, Hidalgo County razed the old courthouse and replaced it with a building, modern, cubical, and ugly. Main Street now slashes through where the plaza had been, and paving for parking covers the grounds where there had earlier been plantings of palm trees and carpet grass.

Ocampo pulled into the blacktop parking lot, nosed into the slot allocated for him, turned the engine off, and sat a few minutes before the building that no longer featured the symbolic doors. He was late for his meeting, and still he sat there several minutes. His meeting with Connie was on his mind and he sat gazing into space and mulled it over. It troubled him during his meeting as well, and when he returned to his car a couple of hours later, it was still needling away at him. He took off his tie and coat, folded them neatly and placed them in the seat behind him, started the engine, and backed out of the parking lot. He drove away from the courthouse and his appointment abruptly to the south. Connie's visit had made more of an impact on him than she could have imagined. He, too, had decided it had gone far enough.

***

Connie drove past the onion field without seeing the rusted out green Ford pulled up on the dirt lane that separated the onion patch and the trailer park. She paid no attention because men were working in the field. A man on a tractor was pulling a disc over the spent onions. She turned into the park at the 'children playing' sign, and drove slowly for two blocks. The park was quieter now. No one was on the street or in the yards she could see. It didn't seem so scary to her now; she had seen it before and nothing had happened. She found the faded yellow trailer and noted it still had the strange abandoned look. The yard was still the same, no cars and no people. The windows were dark, and the lonely bulb burned in its socket at the door. The lawn chair still sat by the bar-b-que pit. The grass grew up under them, and it looked to her as if no one had been there in a long time.

Elaine's trailer was dark, too. Careless weeds grew up along the horse lot fence. The park was almost deserted. The old man's flowers bloomed without the artistic bottle border. Several more forlorn looking trailers had signs of some activity, but if anyone lived there, they had to be at work.

The abandoned trailer still stood with its equally abandoned old car. The black hulk of the burned-out trailer seemed to be more in tune with the others now. She pulled up into Elaine's driveway and sat with the engine idling.

It's a matter of record that Carlos Medrano owns the trailer. I need witnesses who will corroborate Elaine's testimony against him, neighbors who have seen the shaved head, and will tell of the goings on in the trailer.

She studied the other old trailers for some evidence of activity. She left the car in Elaine's driveway and walked along looking into the windows for light or some indication someone was at home. One trailer appeared to be occupied. The yard was grown up, but someone had spread laundry on a bush out back to dry. Connie took a deep breath and knocked on the door. The metal door was soft, and she knocked as loudly as she could manage, several times. She was about to leave when the door opened, only a crack at first and then it came slowly open enough for Connie to see a Mexican woman with a child clinging to her skirt. The woman was very young, and she didn't say a word.

"Hello. May I speak with you?" Connie ventured. "I have a few questions." The door began slowly closing.

"Wait! Please," and then, "Do you speak English? *Habla Ingles?*"

The door closed, and Connie stood looking at it a minute or two, before she walked away. Some other ratty looking old trailers had cars in the drives, but the cars had Mexico license plates. As she had learned from her last encounter, they were not likely to want to help her. Anyway, she didn't speak Spanish well enough to ask questions and understand their answers. They probably wouldn't talk to the sheriff anyway, she surmised.

She walked back out to the road, and the trailer with the beautiful bedding flowers caught her eye. The old man came to the door. Thin and very wrinkled, he had wispy white hair, and bad teeth, and he had plenty to say.

"It's a sin what goes on over there," he said in his high crackly voice. "It's a crime, and the whole lot of them ought to be taken off the street!"

"The trailer looks vacant. Does anyone live there?"

"Hell, no! It's a business trailer, and I don't have to tell you what business they're in."

The two of them looked across the street at the trailer, and he ventured, "It's been quiet over there lately; sometimes I seen lights on at night, but you can't count on it."

"Is anyone there now?"

"Ain't no way to tell. Got one of them been hanging around there recently, but you never know when he's there. He walks up and mostly sleeps there. He's one of the gang, though. I've seen him when they're carrying on over there. They's cars parked all up the street and loud music and all kinds of ruckus for days, sometimes a week. Not lately, though."

"Did the person you saw have his head shaved?"

"I didn't see nothing like that."

"Could I count on you to talk to the sheriff and tell him what you just told me?"

The old man bent forward from the waist, his bony old knees pressed against his pants legs. He slapped his thigh, and cackled, "Gee-O-buck!"

When he recovered, he said, "No, Lady, no, I don't think so. Lady, those are mean boys. I'd rather kiss a snake! No, Ma'am. I don't think I could talk to the sheriff. No, Ma'am. I don't think so!"

"Have you seen anyone over there today?"

"No, Ma'am, not today."

She walked across to the yellow trailer, stepped up on the blocks and knocked on the door. She didn't expect an answer but if someone had come to the door, she planned to say she was looking for Elaine. The knock rang hollow, and just as she expected, no one answered.

She couldn't see in the high windows, so she walked around to the back. High windows. She dragged the lawn chair around there, took off her shoes, stood up on it, and looked into the trailer.

A tall Styrofoam glass stood on the table. A hamburger wrapper lay open beside it, and she could smell the onions. To her horror, there was a young man sitting at the table. He watched her a minute before he got up and walked to the door. She tottered on the plastic chair and stepped to the ground. She stooped to retrieve her shoes and would have run, but he spoke to her.

"What happened to your house old woman?" The young man with the soft brown hair knew her, and of course she understood when she saw the wicked cross he still wore on the leather thong.

"I think you know."

He grinned evilly. She had seen the expression on his face before. "It burned down, didn't it?"

"No, it did not!"

"Oh!" His mouth made a large, and exaggerated 'O'. Then he said, "It will."

"I'll shoot you in your tracks if you come near my house."

"You silly old flea. You're not going to shoot anybody. I'm going to burn your house, and you're going up in smoke if you're in there."

"The sheriff is watching my house. I spoke to him today, and he assured me that he'd arrest anyone who trespassed on my property."

He produced a genuine laugh at that, "You're a troublemaker, a *pulga*." He scratched his chin with his hand and said, "I know the sheriff, and you'll see, we are the same."

"I think not!"

"Oh, yeah," he said. "You'll see. He'd like to see you go up with the house!" He gestured with his hands and went on, "We want you dead. You'll see."

He laughed again. He was confident and smart. "Maybe I'll come tonight. Will you be there tonight?"

"If you come anywhere near my property again, I'll shoot you myself, don't think I won't!"

He enjoyed the exchange. His voice took on the sarcastic tone that she remembered from before. "Tonight," he said putting his finger to his chin and rolling his eyes, "or maybe tomorrow. Maybe you won't know when, but you know I'm coming." He leaned against the doorframe and from his behavior, she guessed he wasn't coming now, so she sat on the chair and put her shoes on.

That done, she stood and walked past him as slowly and with as much starch in her spine as she could muster to the road and heard him hiss as she passed, *"Bruja!"* A word she knew meant witch in Spanish.

CHAPTER FORTY-ONE

Shaken, Connie left the park and drove to Cesar Chavez. Unconsciously she looked for safe haven, and habit drew her back to her home. She let the car idle slowly up to the house.

Well, I guess this house is still good for something; it's still a tax liability and nothing more.

The white front was scarred with a black stain that ran from the ground up and across the second floor windows to the roof. With the living room windows broken out, and the frames charred beyond repair, Connie couldn't guess what structural damage might be under the burnt section of roof. The windows and some of the exterior clapboard could be replaced. A wire brush and some paint would cover a world of hurt, she thought.

She parked in the driveway under the ash trees and admired the lawn. Ignacio had mowed the grass and watered the fruit trees and ornamentals. The manicured yard looked better than it had in months. Maybe the house isn't a total loss, she thought. The fire insurance had a thousand dollar deductible. Maybe she could come up with a thousand dollars. The house could be repaired. Maybe it could be done.

She got out of the car and walked up to the kicked-in front door. It no longer required a key. She pushed it open and stepped inside. The damage to the inside was harder to estimate. With the carpet ruined and a section of the hardwood floor burned beyond repair: she questioned the condition of the joists under the floor. Drywall work and paint would be needed. She saw a lot of water damage. She'd need an electrician. If she couldn't dig the money up to fix it, there was no way she was going to sell the house now. Maybe she could sell the land and let the buyer repair the house, or push it off.

I'm old. I'm eighty years old, she thought; I may not live long enough to see that happen.

***

Connie sighed with relief when she entered the condo and found Susan gone. She wasn't up to "Mother, what happened?" and, "What did the sheriff say?" and, "What are you going to do now? Forget it I hope and accept the facts. It is what it is."

Well, yes, it is what it is. There is the sheriff, and there isn't going to be a posse. The Rangers won't come riding over the hill to rescue me and drive the criminals across the river. They're here and they're in charge now. It is what it is.

Connie walked through the house to the patio and sat with a cigarette in her hand and Mark on her lap. She had some thinking to do. Maybe she could save the house. She couldn't imagine spending the rest of the time she had left living with Susan.

You could hardly call me a guest.

She cupped Mark's head with her hand, so he looked up at her and she asked, "You hate it here, don't you?" She knew he did.

Maybe she could repair the house, but what if she did? The thug with the ugly cross would just come back.

He'd just come back. He said so.

He'd come back even if she didn't fix it up.

Even if I could sue the Medranos, and even if I won the case, he'd still come back. He's the problem. I just can't get around it. It's a moot point anyway, I think he plans to come and burn the house tonight.

She remembered the smirking face. He didn't even flinch at her threat to shoot him. He knew she had a pistol, he had seen it before.

He doesn't think I've got the nerve. Well, he'd better think again, I've learned some things since then.

Maybe she was about to get what she had prayed for. Maybe she was going to get that rare second chance to do it right. John Anderson had said not to stay in the house at night.

Well, John doesn't know everything. Where is he now?

David Ocampo had said, "Let me take care of this."

Where is Sheriff Ocampo now? I'm on my own. I guess I really always knew it. I knew it from the first day. Lilah told me so, and I guess she had it right. 'Well, Connie, I guess we'll just have to do it ourselves,' she told me.

Maybe I've lived too long. Things change, and I don't like the way it is now. I miss you Hank. I'm glad you aren't here to see things all gone to hell in a hand basket. I'm glad Lilah can't see what they've done to her house, either. Everyone risked a lot for me, and I've let them all down. Maybe it's time for me to take a risk. I'm old. I've had a good life. I have, after all, nothing left to lose.

And so she decided. Connie took a shower.

Mother always said to wear clean underwear. You never know. Those funny old notions made Connie laugh, and she had a rush of emotion when she thought of her mother.

She left Susan a note, "I'm not going to be here tonight. Take care of Mark for me and don't worry. I'm playing bridge and staying over with Dottie. She insists I not drive home after dark." Susan would love that.

Mark followed her to the door. She picked him up and held him crushed to her breast, stroking his face and ears in the fashion of a mother licking a newborn pup, and cooing to him before setting him down at her feet.

"Now, stay, and be a good dog!" she instructed Mark before she closed the door and walked to her car.

***

Connie drove to Garcia's, and bought a bottle of water and a bar-b-que sandwich.

"I'll take some potato chips. I like the one's flavored with sour cream," she said. She turned her back to the register and looked across the deserted store at the rows of candy and snacks.

"And I'll take a package of those chocolate cupcakes."

Loaded with sugar and cholesterol, who cares? The mini rebellion gave Connie a satisfaction she hadn't expected, and she smiled.

"Connie, I'm sorry about your house," Garcia said, making pleasantries as he rang her purchases up. "Somebody's going to have to do something about those kids."

Only a casual comment, but Connie perked up, "Would you like that?" she asked.

"Well, yes, it isn't right to let them get away with burning your house. They need to be stopped, but it isn't going to happen."

Connie asked him, "Why not?"

Garcia smiled ironically at her question.

Connie wasn't laughing; she gave him a stern look and asked again, "Why not?" The accusation was not lost on Garcia.

Garcia laughed again good naturedly and said, "Come on, Connie, I don't have to tell you why."

"Yes," Connie said thoughtfully, "of all people, I should know." She gathered up her purchases and walked over to the back door and looked across the patio under the mesquite. "Would it be all right if I sat out at the patio and ate?"

"Of course, Connie, of course," he said and held the door for her.

With just enough breeze to stir the lacy leaves of the big tree, she found it a pleasant place to sit and eat her sandwich. Connie smiled when Garcia turned the radio on to a station that played oldies. Garcia's house blocked out the view of the squalor of Loma Linda, and Connie allowed her mind to wander back to the days when this had been a carrot field.

***

Connie drove the short half-mile to her house, strangely calm. Things that had seemed complex and disturbing were simple now, and she felt a sense of serenity.

I only made it complicated myself because I didn't want to face the inevitable solution. There's only one thing I can do, and I really knew it from the very first.

She pulled the car around to the back and left it in the yard where Ignacio couldn't see it. He didn't miss much, and she didn't want him in on this.

Connie's staircase featured two steps up to a small landing that served as a pass-through to the back hallway before continuing on up to the second floor. The evening twilight faded into night. She sat on the landing watching the charred windows and listened to night sounds drift in with a moan she thought was darkly appropriate.

The oak stairs of the old house had borne the tread of many feet. They were soft, worn and familiar. Connie had waxed and buffed them countless times, and the knowledge gave her a sense of satisfaction. *My house.*

Life is so strange. Who would have ever imagined a scene like this? Here I am an old woman and on another adventure. I feel like a kid. I can hardly wait to tell Hank.

The unlikely scent of orange blossoms hung in the air.

***

Connie's mind wandered as she dozed fitfully. She was with Hank again. He held her hand, and the wind carried the shimmering spray to wet their faces as they watched the dolphins dive and play. They had made it all the way to the end, as she knew they would.

"*¡Bruja!* You old witch!"

Was someone on the stairs? That couldn't be right. She remembered seeing him climb through the window at the back.

"I know you're in there!"

He's in Hank's chair because that's where he must have fallen when I shot him. She remembered his head draped over the arm of the chair with his mouth gaped open and his eyes strangely fixed. The face morphed into a sneer, and it laughed as his hand thrust forward with the cross, jabbing it toward her.

"*¡Bruja!* You old witch! I know you're in there."

She was wide-awake now, and a rush of adrenalin drove out the sense of invincibility with which she had dispatched him in her dream. When she went to check, the room was empty. Behind her, Güero stood at the charred window and shouted. "I seen your car!"

This was no dream. It was dark outside, but the security light on the telephone pole had come on and she saw him clearly silhouetted in the window. His hands were on the charred sill, and he was leaning over into the room trying to see where she might be.

I should shoot him now, she thought, and raised the gun, holding it before her with both hands, and taking careful aim at the figure in the window. He needs to be inside the house, she thought, so she said, "Come in, the door's open."

"I have a better idea. Watch this!" He put a light to a roll of newspaper and threw it into the house. It burned brightly for a minute and died.

"You have to do better than that!" she shouted. "Come on in." She didn't see him anymore and he didn't answer. She stood a few minutes listening, but there was no sound of him either. She went back to the staircase and leaned against the wall, still holding the gun at ready.

She continued to listen for him with all her being. Dry leaves of the singed oleander rustled crisply and other night sounds carried in on the breeze, but it was quiet in the house.

Oh Lord, bless me and keep me.

"Don't hesitate," the constable had told her. "Don't think about it. If you raise a gun against a man you have to go through with it, or he'll have the upper hand."

He was upstairs; she could hear his footsteps coming down one at a time, clomp, clomp, and clomp. But it was only the wind in the leafless fiddle leaf fig tree knocking it against the house.

But where was he? She strained her eyes toward the window at the top, and if he had stepped onto the staircase, she could have seen him against the light. She split her attention between the windows in the living room and the one at the top of the stairs until she began to see soft shadows playing across the living room wall, and she knew.

He's not coming in. He's set fire to the house, and at the back this time. He said he'd burn it down. I should have shot him when I had the chance.

She smelled the gasoline before she stepped into the living room and saw flames licking up past the windows on the back wall.

The plan to lure him into the house and shoot him on her territory was going up in smoke. Now she'd have to see if the house would burn. She shivered at the realization that eventually, if it did, she would have to go out to where he waited in the dark.

The fire was between herself and the car at the back. If she had to run to the safety of the car, she would have to go out the front door and make her way around the house.

The options left to her were quickly narrowing down to one as the fire took hold. Connie saw the sheer curtains at the broken-out back window snatched away by the licking flames. A scatter of black flakes of ash drifted into the room as the filmy curtains vanished forever. Smoke curled in the window, and crackling flames rose up the inside wall and began to collect on the ceiling. Connie ran up the stairs and went from window to window, searching the yard for some trace of him. The fire was now lighting the yard at the back, and there were all sorts of moving shadows, but she couldn't make him out. The second floor rapidly filled with smoke. She went into the bathroom and wet her skirt to cover her face, but the heat drove her back down to sit on the landing as long as she could. The old wooden frame house was going up pretty fast.

Oh, Lord! Bless me and keep me and make your face to shine upon me. Give me, give me grace! Grace to do something I have to do!

It was time. She knew it was. She put her hand on the knob of the front door and leaned her face against the warm wood before pulling it open a crack. She didn't see him. She squared her shoulders and stepped out on the porch with the pistol clasped in both hands and at the ready. She stood there with her back to the door a few seconds.

The fire cast a flickering light on everything. It turned the ash trees a rusty orange and stained the drifting smoke, but the yard was quiet and empty.

She walked to the edge of the porch and looked from side to side, scanning the yard. Güero had flattened himself beside the door, and he watched her a moment, taking satisfaction at her unconscious vulnerability. Then he reached out from his post and grabbed her from behind. He jerked her off her feet, his grip cruelly wrenching her breath away. She sucked for breath as his strong arm crushed her to him, and his obscene cross dug cruelly into her back.

"Now! Now, who're you gonna shoot?" he sneered. She still gripped the pistol, but her arms were thrust outward and useless. "You gonna shoot me?" he laughed with his mouth in her ear, and Connie's stomach turned at the smell of marijuana, and sweat. She kicked backward with her heels, and the damage to his shins was enough to wipe the smile off his face.

"That does it!" he said. "Now you're gonna get your promise." He shook her violently, sending her dangling feet swinging.

"Remember? I promised you? Your house is gonna burn!" His arm was painfully crushing her ribs. He shook her again, and jerked her breath away. "Remember? You're going up in smoke!" She was lightheaded and struggling to remain conscious. He shook her again, and more violently, sending the pistol spiraling from her hand. He bent forward and picked up the gun, and when he did, she was able to reach his arm and drag her nails the full length of it.

"Damn!" he said, the smart talk ended. He readjusted his hold and began dragging her backward toward the flaming house.

In a blur Connie saw Ignacio, "Turn her loose," he said, walking up from under the trees. His voice was strong and commanding, and she struggled to focus. It was Ocampo!

"Hey man!" Güero said, and Connie felt him relax his grip and allow her to stand, but he continued to hold her about the waist.

"Where'd you come from?"

"Turn her loose!" Ocampo repeated.

"No, man," Güero tightened his grip and began backing toward the open door, "I got a job here. I made her a promise."

"Stop, right there!"

"Okay, okay, Man! But first she's going up in smoke!"

"Turn her loose!" The sheriff gestured with his revolver.

Güero reacted with surprise. His attitude changed when he saw Ocampo gesture with the gun. "You're not the boss here. This is my deal, see!" he shouted in a high-pitched voice, and Connie felt the barrel of her own pistol pressed against her temple. The hard metal transferred a frightening tremor. The smell, the shaking hand, the irrational behavior, drugs she thought.

"Drop the gun and let her go."

"No! You ain't God," he said. Connie felt his body stiffen with anger, "You know what?" he said. "I'll be back in a minute."

Güero twisted and elbowed the door open to push Connie before him into the intense heat of the fire that was rapidly filling the entrance. As he turned, the effort presented an opportunity and Ocampo's bullet found its mark. Güero's hand jerked suddenly, dropping the gun to the ground, and Connie managed to step away from him. He staggered back against the door, and she saw the expression on his face dissolve into one of surprise as the crumpling figure, no longer a threat, slid down the doorframe.

Ocampo stepped forward, put his arm around Connie, dragged her roughly away from the burning house, and didn't stop until she was safely under the ash trees.

"You okay?" Ocampo asked her.

Before she could answer, the porch roof collapsed upon Güero and the front of the house went up in a sheet of flames.

The volunteer fire department arrived on the scene a little too late. Ignacio had been watching, too. He had stood at the window with his hand on the receiver until he was sure the house was well gone. Then he had taken his time dialing the number.

***

The incident made the front page of the *Monitor,* below the fold, but it was a newsworthy event. Susan said, "Mom, you have a reputation, you're famous."

"Yes, you'd think so, I made the papers. It's a strange twist, isn't it? When I was a victim, I was on my own, and now I have the protection of the law. Jose Torres. I finally learned his name and I don't need it anymore. The threat is gone, but so is the house!"

Susan asked her, "Does that make you sad?"

Connie smiled, "No. My home and all the pleasant memories are gone. It's been slipping away a little at a time for quite a while now. By the time it burned, it was just a shell of a house. Morningside Road is gone for me now. Now it truly is Cesar Chavez Road.

"Realistically, I could never have repaired it. I have the insurance money. I'll buy another house. Maybe here in your neighborhood!"

"Mom, that would make me happy, but are you happy now?"

"Not happy, but satisfied. I like to think the sheriff was there to protect me, but I can't help thinking about Carlos Medrano. He's still in business. Lilah's murderer will probably never be punished, and that isn't right.

"I've heard it said, somewhere between what's right and what's wrong, you have to find what's possible. I guess I'll just have to be satisfied with that."

THE END

EPILOGUE

Years have passed, more than ten, and things change. Connie's property is still there. The old farmhouse is gone. The houses of Loma Linda, the pretty hill, have closed in and surrounded it now, like the river at flood, six miles across and shallow.

Connie, Carl, and Ignacio are gone now, to a higher ground. The trailer park on Sioux road is still there, but the scraggly fruit trees are gone as is the sign, SLOW, CHILDREN PLAYING.

There are no children in the park. Men, mostly young, populate it now. On a Sunday afternoon it is a beehive of activity. Every space between the trailers, where the abandoned lawns were, is crowded, elbow to elbow, with old trailers and old cars with Mexico license plates, and men standing around with heads that turn and eyes that watch carefully each car that passes down the potholed street.

There is a new sheriff, and if he slowed his patrol car and took a look at East of Eden, he would see a staging place for men, illegally here, and waiting for transportation *norte*.

The sheriff's eyes are closed. He doesn't turn in, and you might ask, "Does he have that option?"

ABOUT THE AUTHOR

A native Texan, Peggy Snodgrass grew up in the Rio Grande Valley and currently lives in the Texas Hill Country with her husband Joe. A graduate of Texas Tech University, she has had a career in fine art and taught at Baylor University. *In Another Country* is her first novel.

Made in the USA
Columbia, SC
19 July 2018